Read,

KIDNAPPED
BY THE CARTEL

Stay safe!

All the best,

Karen Scirscin

KIDNAPPED
BY THE CARTEL

A NOVEL INSPIRED BY A TRUE STORY

KAREN D. SCIOSCIA

TWO HARBORS PRESS

Two Harbors Press
212 3rd Avenue North, Suite 290
Minneapolis, MN 55401
612.455.2293
www.TwoHarborsPress.com

ISBN-13: 978-1-938690-44-0
LCCN: 2012950841

Distributed by Itasca Books

Cover Design by James Arneson
Typeset by Kristeen Ott

Printed in the United States of America

This book is dedicated to all abduction victims and their families.

May they receive the peace and resolution they so deserve.

AUTHOR'S NOTES

Kidnapped by the Cartel is a novel loosely based on my recollection, notes, photos, and interviews with various people and agencies involved during the time of the abduction of a family member. Names have been changed to protect the innocent, characters created and/or combined, and events or episodes compressed or recreated. Some of those episodes are not intended to portray actual events, and any similarities to actual persons, either living or dead, are merely coincidental.

K.D. SCIOSCIA

ACKNOWLEDGEMENTS

Special thanks to the San Diego Police Department, *la Policia de Tijuana,* Mgr. Judy Atkins at Mesa Vista Hospital in San Diego, and all unnamed others who were instrumental in my California and Mexico investigations and research. Atty. Mel Levine, Atty. David Tsach; Two Harbors Press; Roland Wilkerson of the *Charlotte Observer*; Tony "Tony Nap" Napoli; Israel Baron; Pessia Ebgi; Tony Rafael, author of *The Mexican Mafia*; writer Charles Messina; author Sonny Girard; Lyn Conger; author Diane Fanning; producer and director B.J. Davis; Atty. Hank Schuelke; Atty. Robert B. Barnett; author Connie Bruck; Vikas Swarup, author of *Q & A*, on which the movie *Slumdog Millionaire* is based; Craig Wilson of *USA Today*; Alan Davidson of RP Web Design; Atty. Paul Reichs; author, forensic anthropologist, and professor Kathy Reichs; Sabrina Liberatore, Tom Devereaux; Hannah Lee; Danielle Adelman; Rosey Cashman; Brenda Rathje; Mary Frankle; Kristin Dodrill; Tony Ignatz; and Jim Devereaux. All of the above were most instrumental in my being able to bring this novel to completion.

The love and support of many people kept me going when I wandered. To list them all would fill another book, so I'll do my best to keep it short. My husband, Tony, has been my rock and main source of support. The patience and encouragement of all my children, my father, and my wonderful family and terrific friends helped spur me on when I was ready to hang up my hat. My mother in heaven is the daily wind beneath my wings. Dominic, thank you for the love and unending joy you bring into my life. I am grateful to the *Charlotte Observer* for publishing my weekly columns and to the people who take the time to read them. Thank you to all who read my stories on Yahoo.com. If I have neglected to mention someone, I am truly sorry. Thank you for reading *Kidnapped by the Cartel,* my first novel!

Kidnapped by the Cartel is a suspenseful, action-charged thriller. Fear grips the heart and doesn't let go as you ride the horrifying train of drugs and torture along with the kidnap victim. Drug lords rule by terror, and Mexican drug cartels are experts at dishing out blood-chilling messages to all who stand in their way.

Kidnapped by the Cartel is also a cautionary tale. Anyone who has had a family member or friend caught in the addictive web of drug addiction should read this book. The road of addiction often ends at the doors of hell. Pass through those doors, and there's no turning back.

CHAPTER 1
SHE'S GONE

The sick feeling in his stomach worsened with each call, squeezing his gut like a vise.

"No, Mr. Tate, haven't seen her."

"Sorry, Steve, she hasn't been around in a while."

"You tell me where that girl is. She didn't show up for work. Again." Amanda's boss was clearly at the end of her rope.

"Like I know where she is." This from her bitch friend, Sara, who was always high.

Sweat formed on the back of Steve's neck, and bile burned its way up his throat. His daughter was gone for sure this time, he could feel it. Feel it in his fiery gut. He had to find her before it was too late.

I need help. I have to call Pam, he thought.

Steve and his sister were close. They'd been through a lot together over the years. Some of it they couldn't remember, which was probably a good thing. With cell phone in hand, Steve jumped in his truck and floored it. The phone slipped from his sweaty palm as he sped around a corner. He leaned over to pick it up and almost hit a cab.

"Fuck!"

Steve pressed Pam's speed-dial number as he jerked to a stop. *Fucking red lights.*

Across the country, a cell phone rang. Pam eyed the caller ID and answered. "What's up, Stone?" She often used her brother's nickname from another time and place.

"Amanda's missing, and I need help."

There was an awkward silence. Finally, Pam said, "I hate to say it, but I've heard this song before. She'll come back, Steve, she always does."

Steve knew Pam was right. "I know she's taken off for days at a time before. And I'm well aware of Amanda's problems with drugs, but I wouldn't be calling now if I didn't need help."

Another silence.

Finally, Pam said, "I hate that Amanda puts you through this."

"No, you don't understand. It's different this time." Steve was firm. "She's been gone a couple of days already, and we have no clue where she is."

Steve's mind raced with thoughts of where Amanda could be and what she might be doing. His shirt was wet with sweat.

Pam sighed. "What did Daniel say? Did you call her friends? What about her job at the mall?"

"Her boyfriend's no help," Steve snorted. "I'm on my way back to his place now. But shit, Pam, you've got to know I've gone down the fucking list, or I wouldn't be on the line with you now. I'm scared, and I need help. I mean it."

"I think . . ." Pam began, pausing before continuing, "I think maybe we should ask God for help."

"Fuck God. She's gone. She's gone, and I need you to help me find her."

Steve could hear the pounding of his heart like a tribal

drum, getting louder and louder. He didn't care if his entire chest exploded. The only thing that mattered to him now was finding Amanda. He'd never be able to live with himself if something happened to her.

Steve's words hit their mark.

"If you're sure this time is different . . ." Pam let the sentence hang in the air.

"I am, dammit. It happened on my watch, too." Steve's voice cracked.

Pam heard it and could feel his desperation through the phone. "Okay. I'm going to come out there. I'll ask Benny if he can help, too."

Steve's mind flashed a picture of Benny, Pam's husband. Benedetto Angelo was named after his father and grandfather. Born in the seaside town of Sorrento in Southern Italy, Benny had come to the United States with his family when he was just a kid. He was a former marine—still built like a brick shithouse—and the current president of an international construction company. Benny didn't take crap from anybody. He was someone you wanted on your side.

"Thanks, Pam," Steve answered as tears welled up.

Steve knew it was his fault Amanda was gone.

Where is she? The question whirled around in Steve's head like a dervish out of control. His fearful answers churned his insides. Soon, nausea joined the internal chaos, and he had to pull over to puke.

What would become Steve's first day of hell had begun like any other in Southern California. Coffee, work, just doing his thing. Steve liked his morning routine, it made him feel grounded and in control. He'd worked long and hard to get to that place.

After stretching against the kitchen wall, Steve called his number one foreman.

"Jose, you ready to rock? I went for an early run, and I'm itching to get this job done."

"Yeah, boss. The crew is geared up to push, too. Everyone has places to go and things to do," Jose answered.

"Great. I'll meet you at the site, and we can evaluate how much longer this job'll take." Steve chugged his coffee. "I'm thinking four, five days max."

"I agree. See you soon," Jose said.

Grabbing his briefcase, a six-pack of water, and an apple, Steve strode out to the truck to begin his workday. Life was good.

Then came the call from Amanda.

CHAPTER 2
SHE'S AT IT AGAIN

T he beginning of day one in hell for Amanda.

"I never know where you go or what you do anymore. It's fucked up," Daniel fumed.

"What are you talking about?" Amanda was angry, too. "I can have friends, you know."

Daniel glared at her. "What happened to the fun, sweet girl I used to know? The one I fell in love with? You need to stay away from your new so-called friends, because they are fucking you up."

"You can't tell me what to do!" Amanda shrieked.

"If you want to lead your own fucking life, then go join your stupid, fucked-up friends!" Daniel shouted as he stormed out. "I don't need this shit."

The door had barely slammed shut before Amanda went to the hiding place where she kept her stash of drugs. Mad at Daniel, she downed all the pills she had. But it wasn't enough. For an addict, there was never enough. Enraged, Amanda paced around the bedroom like a caged animal. Catching a glimpse of herself in the mirror above the dresser, Amanda saw wild eyes looking back at her, and she turned away. Afraid of coming down off her high, she wanted to score.

I need my car, Amanda thought as she wiped the sweat

off her brow with a tissue from the nightstand. *Gotta call Dad.*

Steve was driving to the job site when his cell phone rang.

"Dad, can you . . . can you come and get me? Daniel's a shit. He's just impossible to deal with. I left my car at your house yesterday, and I need it now. Just pick me up, okay?"

The words flew out of Amanda's mouth so quickly, they sounded jumbled, even to her. She hoped her dad couldn't tell she was high.

They're at it again, thought Steve. *Daniel's a nice enough guy, but Amanda's too much for him. She walks all over him, orders him around and does whatever the hell she wants.*

"I'll be right there," Steve said, shaking his head. "Is Daniel home?"

"No, I guess he went to work." Amanda's eyes darted around the room as she nervously twisted her hair through her fingers. "Is . . . anyone with you, Dad?"

"Nope. Sit tight. I'm not far."

Steve knew Amanda had taken drugs the moment he heard her voice. He had heard her mumble and slur like that before, on several occasions. It was so disappointing. Amanda had been to rehab at least four times already. Nothing seemed to work.

Steve picked up the phone again. Amanda's mother wouldn't be happy to hear this latest development, but she needed to know.

"Hello." Diane had a soft voice. Steve loved hearing it.

"Diane, it's me. I'm on my way to pick up Amanda. She called to tell me she and Daniel are having problems again. I don't know what's happened this time, but you know how demanding that girl can be."

"She's also very sweet, Steve," Diane countered. "You said you don't know what happened, so don't jump to conclusions. I hate when you do that."

Steve could tell Diane was exasperated. It was no secret they had problems of their own, and Steve often felt he had to walk on eggshells when talking to his wife.

"You're right, but their troubles are getting old. I don't like how Amanda sounded on the phone, either."

"Fine. Call me if there's anything I should know," Diane said flatly.

"Okay."

Although Amanda lived with Daniel, she still kept some of her things at her parents' house in Point Loma. She was fond of saying that she liked keeping her options open. Steve drove to Daniel's apartment in the trendy area of downtown San Diego. The Gaslamp Quarter had everything necessary for a good time: shops, upscale restaurants, and great bars and nightclubs with live music. There were also hotels, condos, and a few apartments. Most nights, it was party city. Daniel had been one of the lucky ones to score an apartment. Now there was a waiting list. He and Amanda liked being where the action was.

As Steve rounded the corner, he spied Amanda. Sitting limply on the curb outside the apartment building, she looked disheveled. A beautiful girl who normally took great pride in her appearance, Amanda seldom went anywhere without first having spent some time in front of a mirror. When Amanda looked her best, people took notice. It made Steve sick to see her looking this messed up.

He hurriedly parked the truck and shot out, practically tripping over his own feet as he sprinted to his slumping daughter. Amanda, too high to climb in the truck by herself, got a boost from Steve. Even with his help, she had a difficult time getting in the cab.

"My God, I can't stand to see you like this, Amanda," said Steve. "The drugs'll kill you if you don't stop." He shut the door, went around the truck, and climbed in.

Amanda looked at her father through glassy, bloodshot eyes, half covered by heavy lids. She leaned against the door, which Steve immediately locked.

"I'm hurting and I need something bad," Amanda muttered.

Even though she pissed him off with her lies and drug use, Steve had refused to give up on his daughter. *If I stop trying, who will help her?*

"We're going to Mar Vista right now," Steve said.

"No, Dad," Amanda wailed. "I just want to get my car."

Ignoring his daughter's protests, Steve drove straight to the detox center at Mar Vista.

"Might as well tell you," Amanda said, starting to cry. "They'll probably find heroin in my system."

Steve slammed his fist against the dash. Furious, he said, "Dammit, Amanda. I can't fucking believe it!"

His daughter just closed her eyes and let the tears stream. Steve seethed with barely controlled rage. Then, just as it felt like he might explode, he was overcome by a sensation of intense and utter sorrow, bordering on helplessness.

"I don't know why I'm surprised," Steve said sadly. "This has been going on for a long time, hasn't it, Mandy?"

She put her face in her hands and started sobbing.

The opiate use had begun a few years earlier, when Amanda fell and hurt her back. The doctors prescribed Vicodin to help ease her pain. She had used the prescription painkiller, and then abused it, developing an addiction.

"My head and body hurt unless I take Vicodin. I can't get by without it," Amanda had said at the time. That was when Steve and Diane had first begun looking into rehab facilities.

Amanda's loud crying jolted Steve back to the here and now just as his cell phone rang. It was Diane, wondering why he hadn't called.

"In a nutshell, she's messed up, Diane," he told her. "We're almost to Mar Vista now."

"Oh, not again! Let me know what happens," sighed Diane.

Steve saw the familiar sight of the detox center approaching on the right. He turned in, parked, and practically carried his daughter through the front door, where he was greeted with bad news.

"Can't take anyone now, sorry," said the intake officer, Ms. Marshall, as Steve and Amanda approached her desk. She scanned the charts and added, "We just don't have any available beds."

"What are we supposed to do?" Steve snapped, visibly incensed by this turn of events.

Amanda sobbed and screamed, "I need help!" Tears fell from her bloodshot eyes as Amanda gripped her stomach, overcome by cramps and pain.

Steve couldn't take it. "She's been here before—can't you help us?" Steve implored.

Ms. Marshall asked for Amanda's full name and then pulled up her information on the computer. Amanda Tate's drug history and previous visits to Mar Vista were well documented.

"I'll call for Dr. Owen," she informed Steve. "He's the

physician on duty today. Have a seat. It'll just be a few minutes." Ms. Marshall picked up the handset and placed the call, all the while keeping her eyes on Amanda.

About ten minutes later, which seemed like hours to both Steve and his crying daughter, a nurse came out of the back.

"Amanda Tate?"

"Yeah . . . that's me," Amanda said haltingly.

"Dr. Owen will see you now for an evaluation."

Amanda got up and slowly followed the nurse through the door to the examining room. Steve hoped Dr. Owen would be able to find a bed for her. He glanced around the room. It had a clinical look and feel. The pale gray walls were barren, save for framed official documents. He noticed a drinking fountain in the far corner. A paper cup dispenser was hanging next to it.

Fifteen minutes later, the nurse led a weeping Amanda back out to her anxious father. "Dr. Owen prescribed medication to get your daughter through the night," she told him. "He wrote a note with dispensing directions," the nurse added.

She handed Steve a couple of small packets containing clonidine (to help with withdrawal symptoms), Vistrail (to ease itching and aid breathing), and diazepam (for anxiety). Then she gave Amanda three tablets. "Take these for now. The water's over there," she said, pointing to the drinking fountain.

With shaking hands, Amanda accepted the pills from the nurse and made her way to the fountain. Steve held Amanda up while she swallowed the pills.

Out of the corner of his eye, Steve noticed a look of understanding mixed with pity briefly cross Ms. Marshall's face. *Maybe she had someone close to her hooked on drugs or alcohol,* he thought. *Perhaps she can understand how absolutely frustrating it is to deal with an addict. Or maybe she's a recov-*

ered addict herself.

Steve hoped for compassion.

"Are you sure you can't find a room for my daughter?" he pleaded. "You can see she's in bad shape."

Ms. Marshall shrugged. "I'm sorry. There's nothing I can do. You'll just have to come back in the morning. There's a good chance of being able to get a bed assignment then. Keep an eye on her tonight."

The officer saw this every day. Everyone who came through her door was in bad shape. Hands tied, she sent them on their way.

Waiting out the night won't be easy for Amanda. Or me. Or Diane, for that matter, thought Steve.

He put his arm firmly around Amanda's shoulders. "Let's go," he said, guiding her out of the uninviting office.

They didn't hear Ms. Marshall wish them good luck as the door shut behind them.

CHAPTER 3
AMANDA SLIPS OUT

Steve helped Amanda climb back in the truck; he then drove directly to the house in Point Loma. A furious Diane greeted them.

"What is wrong with you, Amanda?" demanded Diane when they got inside the house. "Why can't you quit this crap? I kicked marijuana years ago and haven't missed it."

Sweaty, shaking, and crying, Amanda said, "You're kidding, right, Mom? Don't you think I hate being like this? Just leave me alone."

Steve knew Amanda was barely holding on. He didn't say then that Amanda's drug dependencies were deep—and very different than Diane's former "marijuana habit" had ever been. He and Diane had argued this point too many times to count already.

"Come on, Mandy. I'll help you lie down on your bed. You can sleep tonight and tomorrow we'll go back to Mar Vista," said Steve.

"I don't want to lie down here, Dad. I want to go back to Daniel's and sleep. You can get me in the morning."

"I don't know what's wrong with your staying right here for the night," Diane intoned. "You know how nice and pretty your room is."

Diane always kept Amanda's bedroom looking immaculate in the hopes her daughter might want to move back and start over. She thought seeing the robin's egg-blue walls and white eyelet curtains with matching duvet might provide Amanda with a sense of comfort; maybe encourage her to get back on the right track.

Steve grasped his daughter's arm firmly and led her into her room.

"Just relax in your bed. Sleep it off. If you need something, we're here."

After helping her settle in bed, Steve hoped Amanda would be able to calm down and get some sleep, even if just for a few hours. He walked out and tried to reassure Diane.

"We're going to help Mandy, and she will get better. I truly believe that," Steve told Diane, praying that his words would ring true at some point.

As if on cue, Amanda came stumbling out of the bedroom. "I can't sleep. They didn't give me enough meds."

Steve knew that after several years of drug abuse, Amanda had developed a tremendous capacity for drugs. *The clinic probably gave Amanda only the minimum amount of medications when we were there, which is why the nurse gave me those extra pills,* he thought.

"Hold on, Amanda, you can have a couple of these pills. The nurse wouldn't have given them to me if she didn't think you'd need them," he said.

He got a glass of water and handed it to Amanda, along with the pills from Mar Vista. Amanda downed the pills quickly.

"Okay, I'm sure you can sleep now," said Steve. "Let's go back to your room." He again helped Amanda into bed.

"I don't know if they'll work, Dad," a forlorn Amanda said.

"Don't fight it, honey, let your body rest."

Diane was in the beginning stages of a panic attack when Steve rejoined her in the living room. Her body was shaking, she was crying and hiccupping, which is what usually happened to Diane whenever she got upset.

"I know this is upsetting, Diane. I don't like it any more than you do. But we have no choice except to work through it with Amanda," said Steve.

Diane wouldn't look at Steve.

"The counselors tell us Amanda is an adult now, responsible for her own actions. But I can't help feeling some guilt, you know?" she said through gasps and hiccups.

"I know," said he gently. If he was hoping for a little comfort himself, he didn't get it.

"You're the one who should feel guilty!" Diane suddenly stormed at him, finding her voice. "You had wild parties here when Amanda was little. Everybody was high on something."

"Including you," Steve said quietly. "My drugs of choice might have been stronger than yours, but we were both lax."

"Don't you dare lump me in with that crazy crowd. I don't even like to drink, and you know it."

The tension in the air was thick as pudding.

After a long minute, Steve attempted to diffuse the growing antagonism. "We need to look forward, not back," he said firmly. "I'm going to check on Amanda."

Diane sat on the sofa, whimpering. Her heart ached for her daughter, but she also was tired of going through Amanda's ups and downs with drug use.

I don't deserve this, Diane thought. *I've been through enough with my own life.*

Steve came back into the room and said, "Amanda looks like she's going to be out for a while. There are a lot of drugs in her system right now. I'm going to run over to Vons real quick and get some Tylenol PM for you. You know it helps you sleep when you're stressed."

While he felt pretty stressed, too, Steve knew he wouldn't be taking anything. He needed to maintain a clear head.

"I don't want to just sit here," Diane protested, still hiccupping. "It'll make me crazy."

Steve shrugged. "Do you want to go to Vons, then?"

"By myself? No. You said she's in a deep sleep anyway."

"Well, I guess we both can go. It'll only take about twenty minutes to run there and back. Amanda should sleep for a few hours at least."

"I agree. It can't hurt to be gone that short of time, and I sure could use some help getting to sleep."

"All right, let's go," said Steve, helping Diane up from the sofa.

They left the house quickly and quietly, driving the short distance to Vons. After making the purchase, Steve drove home as fast as he could, but it wasn't fast enough. The empty spot in front of the house where Amanda's Mustang had been parked told Steve and Diane their daughter was probably gone.

"Oh, no!" Diane gasped.

They parked and ran into the house. The place was a shambles. Amanda had thrown things all over, looking for the car keys. Steve's empty "change jar" validated Amanda's desperation. He looked in Amanda's bedroom. The bed was empty.

"Goddammit!" Steve shouted. "I can't believe she took off."

Diane slumped down on the sofa and began crying again. "We never should've left. It's your fault, Steve. You said she'd be asleep for hours."

"I thought she would be. You like to blame me for everything. You could've stayed." Steve was furious with himself too, and Diane's words didn't help.

"It's your fault," Diane said again.

"You're right. I should've made you stay." Steve was exasperated and angry.

The pills from the detox center were meant to calm Amanda down and help her sleep. Added to whatever she had taken on her own earlier, reason said the drugs together would render his daughter so high by now that Steve wondered how she could even drive.

"She must've gone back to Daniel's," Steve said as he flew out the door. "I'm going over there. Stay here in case she comes back."

How could I have let this happen? I feel like an idiot.

Steve called Amanda's cell phone as he drove, reaching only her voice mail. He speed-dialed Daniel's number. No answer. The next call was to the sporting goods store where Daniel worked. Just as someone answered, the call dropped. Steve swore under his breath as he pressed the redial button. Daniel answered on the fourth ring.

"Bait and tackle."

"Daniel, it's Steve. Amanda's pretty fucked up. She took off in the Mustang from my house. I can't believe she's even driving. Have you heard from her?"

"No, I haven't talked to her since I left for work this morning."

"I'm going to the apartment to see if that's where she

went. Do you know where else she might have gone if she's not there?"

"Hey, man, I have no idea where Mandy would go," he said, the irritation evident in his voice. "She does what she wants. I'm sick of her shit, Steve," he added, and hung up.

Steve continued on to the apartment, knowing Amanda could very well be there with a supply of drugs and just not answering the phone. Steve hoped that was the case. He swore again and redialed Amanda's number.

"Come on, Mand, answer!"

The call went directly to voice mail.

"Call me as soon as you get this message, Amanda. Your mother and I are worried about you."

Steve's breath whistled as it came out of his mouth. Fortunately, there was a parking spot on the street near the apartment. He jockeyed the truck in, jumped out, and sprinted to the door. He knocked impatiently. When no one answered, Steve pounded on the door, yelling, "Mandy! Open up!"

A guy from the apartment above stuck his head out the window. "What's going on down there?"

"Hey, man," Steve hollered up. "Have you seen anyone go into this apartment recently?"

"No. I don't think anyone's in there right now either. It's been quiet."

"Okay, thanks."

With his mind racing and foot to the floor, Steve drove home to the mess that was Diane.

"She wasn't at the apartment," Steve said as he walked into the house. "And I spoke with Daniel. He hasn't heard from Amanda since he left for work this morning. He indicated they'd been fighting, though."

Diane lit into him like a barn dog to a rabbit.

"Where is she, Steve?" Diane cried, her face burning red with rage. "It's your fault she left. We should've stayed home. You know Amanda has a drug problem!" Diane hardly got the words out coherently for the hiccupping and crying.

"Of course I know," Steve snapped at her. "Just about everyone who knows her knows. We've been dealing with this situation for at least four years."

Steve cracked his neck in an attempt to release some tension. "Look, Mandy's done this before. And as much as we hate how she takes off and makes us worry like crazy, she'll probably show up in a day or two all contrite."

Diane didn't respond.

"I've called her cell and left a message," Steve told her. "She's most likely with one of her friends, or maybe with someone we don't even know. She can't be thinking clearly right now, but we'll probably hear from her later tonight or tomorrow. I'll go get her then, wherever she is, and take her to Mar Vista."

"Drugs wreck everything," Diane murmured, wiping her eyes.

Steve nodded. "Let's go get something to eat and then call it a night."

The couple walked to a cafe a few blocks away. After picking at grilled cheese sandwiches and tomato soup, they returned home. Steve wanted to console Diane. He started to put his arm around his wife's shoulder, but she wasn't having any of it. She jerked away, looking at him with dark, tear-filled eyes.

Steve sighed and went to get ready for bed. "Please, God, let Amanda be okay," he prayed.

He did not have a good feeling.

By the time Steve came out of the bathroom and climbed

into bed, Diane was already in a restless slumber. He closed his eyes and hoped he'd be able to sleep, too.

CHAPTER 4
THE SEARCH BEGINS

The morning of day two in hell was bright and sunny, belying the dark feelings Amanda's parents shared.

"You were out like a light when I got into bed," Steve said to Diane. "I'm glad you were able to get some sleep."

"I'm worried, Steve. This isn't the way Amanda's acted in the past. We've always been able to find out where she was pretty quickly," said Diane. "And her taking off like that when she was so high makes me crazy."

"It's still too early to go crazy. Amanda could be anywhere. Let's call customer service for our credit cards to see if any one of them has been used. I haven't looked in my drawer where I keep them, but she could've snagged one for quick cash. It wouldn't be the first time."

Diane nodded. "Even though we've done it before, I don't think we should put a block on any cards right now. We would be able to trace Amanda's actions if she or one of her loadie friends has access to our information. If a card is used, then the paper trail could lead us to her."

"Good idea. Usage history is a powerful tool."

Steve called to check their cards for recent or unauthorized use. None was evident.

"The possibility remains that Amanda is out bingeing

somewhere. Anyone could be providing alcohol or drugs. We have to remember this isn't the first time Mandy's taken off. Once bitten, twice shy, as they say," said Steve. "Let's see how the day pans out."

Steve went to work as if it was any other day. Saturdays were often regular work days for him anyway. He arrived on the job site and parked his truck. Steve decided he'd focus on the job at hand once he made a few more calls. Dialing Amanda's cell phone for what seemed like the millionth time, he again got voice mail. Irritated, he left another message. Next up, Daniel.

Her boyfriend said he hadn't heard from Amanda and had "no clue" where she was. Steve wasn't sure he believed him. Daniel could be covering for her, as he hadn't sounded too concerned.

"Amanda has lots of different friends she hangs out with," Daniel said. "She could be with any of them. Gotta go."

"Shit!" Steve slammed his phone on the dashboard. Daniel knew how to piss a guy off. He punched in the number of Bloomingdale's at the Fashion Valley Mall where Amanda had been working for the past nine months. After a couple of failed attempts, Steve finally reached the MAC cosmetic counter. Maybe Amanda had showed up there. He was hoping her manager wasn't in; he didn't want to have to talk to her again.

"MAC Cosmetics. This is Traci. How may I help you?"

"Traci, Steve Tate, Amanda Tate's father. Do you know when she's scheduled to work again, by any chance?"

"Well, Amanda didn't show up yesterday, and she isn't on the schedule for today or tomorrow," said Traci. "That's all I know."

"Okay, thanks. If you happen to see or hear from Amanda, please tell her to call me."

"Sure."

Was this something Amanda had planned in advance? he wondered. *Couldn't be. Her disappearance happened too fast and too randomly. I'll try the mall again on Monday if we haven't heard from her by then.*

Steve hoped that wouldn't be the case, as both he and Diane would be nuts if the entire weekend went by without a word from their daughter. Steve ended up being so busy at the job site that he didn't have time to think about anything but work. Two of his four-man crews were setting tiles in bathrooms and kitchens in a new condo building. The building was part of a complex, and the men were happy for the continuing work. San Diego was a good place to be if you were in the construction business. Lots of money was put out for new office, retail, and condo complexes. Steve was good at bidding, and his company stayed busy.

In the back of his mind, Steve was fairly certain that at some point his cell phone would ring, and it would be either Amanda or Diane calling. There'd be some kind of a problem, sure, but he would deal with it and Amanda would be back.

When no one had called by the late afternoon, Steve placed a call to Diane.

"Hello," Diane answered. She didn't sound good.

"I'm guessing you haven't heard anything yet."

"No, obviously," she said. Diane's nerves were raw.

"Let's meet at the Venetian for dinner. We can decide how to proceed," said Steve.

"That's fine," said Diane. "To be honest, I don't care if I eat or not, though."

"I understand, but we have to eat sometime, and we both like the Venetian. Meet me there at 6:30, all right?"

That would give Steve enough time to swing by his office, check the mail, and shower. He always kept a change of clothes there.

"Okay."

Steve arrived at the restaurant first and waited outside for Diane. He wondered what kind of mood she'd be in. Lost in thought, Steve didn't even notice the fragrance of the beautiful gardenias and stephanotis that grew in the garden next to the restaurant. The Venetian was a popular eatery in Point Loma, and patrons often stopped to drink in the delicate scent of the flowers before going in to eat. Once inside, the mouthwatering aroma of garlic and spices took over.

Steve and Diane usually liked to dine on the covered patio outside, but tonight Steve wanted to sit inside. He wasn't thinking about romance; he was ruminating about all the daily crap that kept him and Diane at odds. Their relationship wasn't where it should be, and this latest situation with Amanda didn't help.

Diane arrived five minutes later. The couple went inside and was seated immediately. They ordered salads and decided to split an entrée. The portions were big, and neither of them was very hungry.

"I've had such a terrible headache all day," said Diane as she picked at her salad.

Steve nodded as he wolfed down his greens and garlic bread without really tasting them. The waitress brought a large portion of bubbling lasagna with two plates. Steve dug out a thick section of the layered pasta, put it on a plate, and passed it to Diane. He cut a hefty piece for himself. The supper helped them both feel better, giving credence to the theory of lasagna being comfort food.

"I have this uneasy feeling something is very wrong," Steve said between mouthfuls. "Amanda's taken off before, but we've always had an inkling of what she was up to. This time, nothing, unless we haven't spoken with the right people yet. What do you think?"

Diane set her fork down on her plate.

"I've been telling you all along I don't feel good about this. Amanda was too high to drive, and we have no idea where she went," she answered. "We have to find her, Steve."

"We'll find her. I suggest we call every single one of her friends, even the lowlifes. Especially them. If someone's covering for her, maybe he or she will get sick of us calling and pestering them, you know? Maybe they'll give up some information or tell her to call us. It's worth a try."

Diane nodded, drifting away in thought.

The distraught couple finished the rest of their meal in silence. Steve motioned to the waiter for the check and paid the bill.

"See you at home," Steve said as he climbed into his truck. "We'll compare notes."

"Okay," Diane said sullenly.

Inside his truck, Steve started calling Amanda's friends. No one was able to help. Diane and Steve arrived home about the same time. Steve asked for a rundown of Diane's calls, hoping her luck had been better than his.

"I only have a couple of numbers programmed in my phone. I talked to both Alexa and Sam. Neither knew where Amanda is, but said they'd let me know if they hear anything. I got Jenna's voice mail and left her a message." Diane sighed, looking dejected.

"I don't have anything good to report, either."

They sat down with their address book and called a few more names. Amanda knew a lot of people. They got nowhere.

"I'm tired and stressed to the max," Steve finally said. "You must be, too. What do you think about calling it quits for the night and starting fresh in the morning?"

"That's fine," said Diane. "I can't think now anyway."

I hate this, Steve thought as he got ready for bed. *If Amanda waltzes in like nothing's happened, I'll . . . actually, I'd like nothing more than for that to happen.*

CHAPTER 5
GO WEST, YOUNG MAN

Steve had been a hellion growing up. His parents had spent many a sleepless night worrying about their devil-may-care son. As he had gotten older, Steve regretted what he had put his parents through. He sometimes thought he was getting his just deserts with Amanda now because of all the hell he had raised.

Paybacks are a mother.

In high school, Steve's classmates all thought he had it made—good at sports and good looking. But there was that wild side. Steve's mother was certain he'd been born with an overload of testosterone.

Mucho macho, mixed with drugs and alcohol, made for one crazy SOB, Steve thought. He shook his head at the memories.

Steve actually hadn't done more than drink beer and smoke marijuana in high school. Just a little pot now and then to be cool—as if being a star in sports wasn't enough. No accounting for the male ego.

His football prowess had earned Steve a scholarship to Western Michigan University. While Steve loved the game, he didn't like pushing himself that hard. He liked to party too much. His poor work ethic caught up with him, and after two years, Steve was booted off the team for letting his grades fall.

School had become a drag for him. One night when Steve was smoking pot with a couple of his friends, he got to thinking about going someplace fun. He took a toke from the joint he was holding and said, "Man, I'd like to be on a beach, getting high. Somewhere fun, like Southern California." He blew smoke rings and smiled.

Steve's friends looked at him through bloodshot eyes and nodded in agreement. Going to California sounded like the best idea they'd ever heard.

"There'd be plenty of hot chicks, too," Steve added.

The promise of babes in bikinis sealed the deal. Within a week, Steve had dropped out of school and moved out to sunny Southern California. Two of his friends went with him. They instantly became beach bums, total party animals.

Steve's life soon revolved around various forms of drug activity. He bought and sold reefer—just enough to keep the buzz going and pay his few bills.

"Seemed like everybody was doing some kind of drugs back then," he said to a friend, years later. "The party lifestyle sucked a person in. You fell into it, got used to it, wanted it, needed it, whatever. Can't say I didn't have a great time, though. Especially those Jacuzzi parties. They were wild Southern California style. We used to call them 'shake and bake,' hoping for a small earthquake to stir things up."

For a few years, living on the edge had made for an exciting time. Steve couldn't believe all the people he met who were walking on the wild side—movie stars, pro athletes, models, sons and daughters of famous people, rich kids with nothing to do and all day to do it, people who used to be famous, people who were waiting for their big break to become famous, people who didn't care about being famous. You name it.

But not having a trust fund made it hard for the Midwestern guys to keep up after a while.

One of Steve's buddies finally went back to Chicago, finished his degree, and became a social worker. The other moved to Napa Valley to work for a winery. A California friend, Brian, with whom Steve had done most of his larger drug deals, ended up getting popped. He was killed in jail before going to trial. Steve figured somebody hadn't wanted Brian to talk. The jailhouse murder had been enough to make Steve rethink his vocation. He had met some of the big players, but hadn't wanted to get in deep with them. Steve was glad his ego hadn't taken over then and he had kept his distance.

With the handwriting clearly on the wall, the time had come for Steve to quit dealing drugs. He changed careers, first working as a bartender, and then as a used car salesman.

Steve's break came when he went into construction. Weary of sales, the job fell into his lap one day when a friend mentioned the construction company he worked for needed some part-time help. Steve had worked in his uncle's construction company in the summer between junior and senior years in high school, so he had a little experience.

Ripe for another change, Steve leapt at the chance. He worked hard, was very capable, and enjoyed what he was doing. Construction soon became his job of choice. Being outdoors was great, and Steve liked the work environment. The supervisor, Mick Casey, gave Steve more and more responsibility as time went on.

Finally, one day Casey pulled Steve aside and said, "You have too much brain matter to be breaking your back. I suggest getting more education. It'll help you get ahead."

"Sounds like a good idea to me," Steve had responded.

After taking classes at night to learn about management, marketing, financials, bidding jobs, etc., Steve began moving up in the company. He found he had a knack for working with people—those above him, and those he managed. Customers liked his knowledge and easygoing personality.

Eventually, Steve was ready for more. With careful planning, and using the savings he had managed to acquire, Steve went out on his own. His small company did fairly well for a couple of years, but he wanted to grow the company and get ahead. The American dream had worked for others; why not for him?

Competition was fierce in the construction trade. Steve approached his friend, Geraldo Perez, about forming a partnership and going after the minority contracts. Perez had been born in San Diego, but his parents were from Tijuana.

"I want to take my little company and make something of it," Steve had said. "There are big jobs out there just waiting to be plucked by guys like us. What do you say, Geraldo? Let's do something together."

"Okay, bro, I'm in. I think we should use my heritage to the fullest benefit," Geraldo said. "Why not, you know?"

Steve nodded in agreement. "We definitely have a shot at being awarded minority contracts by working together as partners. It'll double our opportunities."

Steve was excited at the prospect of increasing revenue and was thrilled that Geraldo was all for the partnership. The men chose Tate-Perez Construction, soon to be commonly known as TPC, as the company name. They hired a lawyer to take care of all legalities associated with the start-up. Within months, they were on their way.

TPC specialized in doing tile and finishing work for commercial construction and new housing projects. Some years they had so much work they could barely keep up. Those years granted both men the means and opportunity to make good investments.

Steve felt proud he was able to provide nice things for Diane and Amanda. The family had taken trips and attended plays, concerts, and other events. Amanda attended private school and had gone to Disneyland and Knott's Berry Farm several times with her parents while growing up. Diane wore the latest fashion, always looking terrific, and Steve liked that. They were living the good life. For a time, it seemed that nothing could go wrong.

CHAPTER 6
POLICE, HOSPITALS, AND MEXICO

D ay three in hell began with Steve finally falling into a fitful sleep around three o'clock in the morning. He woke up at five. It took almost an entire pot of java to clear his head. He sat at the kitchen table, reviewing the situation. The previous night he had called all of Amanda's friends listed in their address book, and no one knew anything. Or at least they weren't saying.

Someone has to know something.

Other occasions when Amanda had "seemed to vanish," someone had known where she was. This time, all of the players appeared clueless.

Steve rubbed his eyes and the tense muscles at the back of his neck, where a big knot had developed. He sighed. The whole situation just didn't make sense.

Where the hell is Amanda?

While Diane slept, Steve took a hot shower and got dressed. Then he slipped out to grab breakfast and make some early morning calls. Steve was ready to rattle some cages.

Mitch's Seafood on Scott Street was inexpensive and had a decent breakfast selection. Steve pulled in to eat and use his cell phone. One frustrating call after another made Steve want to pull his hair out. No one knew anything. No one seemed that worried, either.

Can't anyone get it through their thick skulls that this time Amanda really is missing? He was getting increasingly more angry and worried. *Someone should know something!*

Even though the food was good, Steve's stomach was in a knot, and he couldn't eat. He drank his coffee and tried to think. *Shit!* Couldn't do that, either. Frustrated, Steve paid the bill and left.

He called Amanda's cell phone again once he got in his truck and got a recording saying her voice mail box was full.

Something's not right. Amanda always checks her messages. She lives by those messages. What can I do?

Steve elected to go to Mass. Regardless of what he had said to his sister, he planned on getting God's help, too. Steve usually went to church alone. Diane wouldn't go with him; she hadn't been raised that way was what he figured. And Mandy rarely joined him once she moved out. Steve went directly to St. Agnes Catholic Church on Evergreen Street in Point Loma. The timing was right, 8:00 a.m. Mass was just starting. Even though he said the prayers he'd learned as a child and followed along with the service, Steve couldn't shake the feeling that something was desperately wrong. His voice cracked when he joined the congregation for the "Our Father." After that, he went blindly through the rest of the Mass.

Please, God, let Amanda be all right, he silently prayed.

Now hungry, Steve drove home by way of McDonald's for coffee and scrambled egg biscuits. The street was quiet when he pulled up in front of his house. He called out to Diane as he carried the provisions into the kitchen.

"Hey, babe."

"I'm up," Diane responded. "Where'd you go? Church?"

"I did. I also brought some coffee, tea, and biscuits," he said, placing the food and drinks on the table. "Figured we could both use something to eat."

Diane looked sad and drawn. "Thanks. Maybe this food will help numb the raw feeling I have inside."

"I don't understand how not one of Amanda's friends knows anything," Steve sighed. "Shit. She's social as hell. People don't just vanish into thin air." He paced while eating. "Her voice mail box is full, too."

Diane looked up, startled. "What? You know Mandy checks her messages like clockwork. It doesn't add up, Steve. I'm scared something bad's happened to her."

Steve's worried expression displayed both confusion and fear. He stopped pacing.

"I don't think we're going to get any help from Amanda's friends. We should call the police. It's been long enough, and we have no clue as to her whereabouts."

Diane went pale and started whimpering. "You're right. Call the police."

Steve looked up the number for the San Diego Police Department. He punched in the digits and resumed his stride.

"I've been transferred. Now I'm on hold," Steve said tightly.

Diane watched him try to get through to the right person as he circled the room.

When the call was finally answered, words spilled from Steve in a rush.

"Hello. My name is Steve Tate. My wife and I haven't heard from our daughter, Amanda Tate, in a couple of days, and we're very concerned. Do you have her name listed on any type of report?"

The officer on the line responded, "Hold a minute. I'll check our records for the name Amanda Tate."

Steve's anxiety level rose while he was waiting for the officer to check. After a few minutes, the officer returned and said, "No, sir. No one with the name Amanda Tate was arrested or involved in any kind of mishap during the night. Her name doesn't turn up on anything in the past few days, either."

"Okay, officer, I appreciate your checking. Thanks."

Steve had hoped his search would end with the call to the police, with Amanda in lock-up. At least then he'd know where she was and could get her the help she needed. He'd thought that the threat of jail would have been a motivating factor toward a successful rehabilitation.

"Guess I should call the hospitals now, too," Steve said grimly.

Ashen, Diane nodded solemnly.

He called both Sharp Memorial and Mercy Hospital, but no one matching Amanda's description or ID had been admitted in the past two days.

Steve stretched. His back hurt already. He tried Amanda's number again. The cell phone made a funny ring.

A man with a thick Spanish accent answered, "*Si*, hello."

Shocked, Steve asked, "Where's . . . where's Amanda?"

"This my phone, *pinche pendejo*," the man retorted.

Steve knew the phrase meant "fucking asshole" from listening to the men on his crew talk to each other.

"She's my wife. Fuck off!" the man added and hung up.

Steve's knees went weak. His heart pounded double-time. Shaking, he called right back.

A female voice answered, "*Hola*."

"Where's Amanda? I want to speak to my daughter!"

The woman hung up without responding.

Steve pushed the redial button. The call immediately went to the message, "This voice mail box is full."

"What happened? What happened?" Diane demanded.

Steve, pale as a ghost, whispered, "Amanda's in Mexico. Oh, God."

CHAPTER 7
PAM AND BENNY

Steve's sister, Pam, pulled her long blonde hair back in a low ponytail as she mulled over the conversation she had with her brother earlier that day. *What if something really has happened to Amanda? I'd feel guilty forever if I didn't try to help.*

Her husband, Benny, had been golfing when Steve called, so Pam had time to formulate a plan before her husband returned. She had all the best intentions of talking things over with Benny when he got home, but somehow she was never able to get the conversation going in the direction she needed it to.

"Hi, honey," said Pam when her husband walked in. "I prepared a tomato salad, baked chicken, and green beans for dinner. Are you hungry?"

Benny dropped his clubs at the door and slumped into the sofa. "Sounds fine, Pam. I'm beat."

"How'd golf go today?" Pam was aware her making small talk might seem annoying when Benny was tired, but she also knew he wouldn't be wild about the idea of her going to San Diego to help find Amanda. She needed the right window to approach the subject.

"The game stunk. I couldn't get in the rhythm and played like crap," answered Benny.

"So . . . your game wasn't up to par?" Pam teased.

Benny only glared at her, his reaction a big indication that it would be wise to wait until the next day to discuss her decision to go to California.

The next day, Monday, was very busy for Pam. She volunteered at Johnson's Children's Home one day each month, and this was her day. Pam decided she would tell Benny about her conversation with Steve when he came home that night. Though Pam was still not convinced Amanda was truly missing, she knew her brother was certain. Steve had left a message on Pam's phone saying the situation hadn't changed, and he needed her. Pam's mind was made up.

I have to help my brother. That's what families are for.

As she left the children's home, Pam called Angelo's Ristorante to order something for dinner. Angelo's was Benny's favorite Italian restaurant, and it had an extensive take-out menu. At least Benny'd have something he liked to eat while she told him about Amanda.

Pam's cell phone rang right after she placed the food order. She checked the ID. "Hey, Benny!" she answered.

"Hi, baby," said Benny. "What're you up to?"

Pam kept her voice neutral. "I'm going to pick up some pizza and caprese salad from Angelo's."

"You know the way to my heart!" he laughed. "I'll be home in thirty minutes."

"See you soon," Pam said and quickly hung up. She didn't want Benny asking any questions before she was ready to talk.

Benny smelled the pizza as soon he opened the front door. The aroma brought back memories of his childhood.

Pam knows me so well, he thought. *I know her, too, and*

I have a feeling something's going on.

Pam asked Benny about his day as they sat down to eat.

"It's been nonstop since early this morning," answered Benny. "I actually have to go back to New York this week for a few days. Would you like to go with me?"

"I'm not sure I can . . ." Pam often traveled with her husband, but now she had traveling of her own to do.

They were diving into the best pizza in town when Pam began telling Benny about Amanda. He listened without saying a word while she told him how sad and desperate Steve had sounded. Pam ended by saying she'd told her brother she would come out to help him.

Benny sat calmly finishing his pizza. The pie was delectable, and he wanted to savor every bite. Pam waited for his reaction.

"Do you feel certain Amanda is legitimately missing?" he asked. "I mean, she does have a history."

Pam nodded. "I was skeptical at first, too, I have to admit, but this time appears to be different. Steve said he and Diane have tried everything to find Amanda and have met with dead ends. If you could have heard the fear and anguish in Steve's voice, you'd understand I have to help him."

Benny sighed and rubbed his face with hands. He was a stubborn man, but his wife could be stubborn, too, especially when it concerned family. "I don't like the idea of you going out there for something like this without me, Pam. Who knows what the situation will turn out to be?"

"I have to go, Benny. Steve needs me there, and it's impossible for you to go now. You should have heard him. I believe him when he said this time was different."

They sat a few minutes in silence.

Finally, Benny said, "I understand how you feel. Steve and Diane must be very scared. I'd like to go to San Diego, too, of course, but I simply can't miss these meetings."

Pam said, "Thanks, Benny. I knew you'd understand." She gave her husband a hug.

They were cleaning off the table when the phone rang. Pam picked up the phone. "Hello."

"Hello, Pam?" Steve sounded panicked. "A Mexican answered Amanda's phone! She's in Mexico! We've got to get her out!"

"How do you know she's in Mexico? Couldn't a Mexican answer her phone in San Diego?" Pam asked.

"Cell phones from the United States make a unique ring when they're across the border, and hers made that sound just before a guy answered. He had a thick accent and said Amanda was his wife. We've got to get her! I'm going to Tijuana tomorrow."

Pam was stunned. "That's unreal, Steve. I don't know what to say."

Her face registered shock and Benny saw it. "I'm so sorry you and Diane have to go through this. I just can't believe it. You're in our prayers. Please be careful. I'll let you know what I'm going to do as soon as my plans are firm. I love you." Pam was shook up and talking rapidly.

"Thanks, Pam, be sure and tell Benny."

Pam said good-bye to Steve and then relayed the conversation to Benny.

Benny cleared his throat, and Pam could feel his apprehension before he spoke.

"I absolutely don't want you going into Tijuana. That

town is a crazy, dirty, unlawful place. I don't need to be worrying about you, too." He took Pam's hands in his. "Listen, baby, you can be a big help to Steve and Diane by making sure their clothes are clean and they are well fed. The basics. There probably will be phone calls and local errands you can help them with, too."

"I haven't given much thought as to what would be most helpful, Benny. I plan on being supportive, however I can," Pam said, a bit defensively.

"Don't go into Tijuana," Benny said flatly.

Pam hesitated, then said, "Okay," but she wasn't sure if she could actually honor the request.

CHAPTER 8
HELP AND NO HELP

Benny sprang into action first thing when he got into the office, calling Jim O'Brien, his company's head of security. O'Brien's previous job had been as a U.S. customs agent in New York, and he'd seen a lot. The man listened as Benny laid out the facts as he knew them regarding Amanda's disappearance in California. Immediately grasping the gravity of the situation, O'Brien provided the number of a firm in Washington, D.C. that had helped the company in the past with security issues in Central and North America.

"Listen, Ben, Tom Severs is the guy you should ask for when you call. Tell Tom I said for you to call him," O'Brien said.

"Okay, thanks," said Benny.

They discussed a couple of other issues the company needed addressed, and when they were finished, Benny said, "Thanks again, Jim. I'll give Tom a call and mention your name. We'll talk soon."

Benny dialed Severs' number. Severs mentioned he had heard of Benny through the channels. He said to give O'Brien his regards. The two men talked for several minutes, with Benny telling Severs what had happened in California, and what kind of help he needed. Severs was more than happy to oblige. His nephew, Billy, had died of a drug overdose five years earlier, and it had become Severs' personal mission to do anything he could to help in the war on drugs. Severs gave Benny the phone number of Alberto Reyes.

"Alberto Reyes is a retired detective and former California state trooper who works as a private investigator. He lives in a town near the Mexican border and has proved to be quite helpful to us in the past," said Severs. "Reyes has good contacts, is reliable, and doesn't get pushed around. He has experience in finding people, too."

"Sounds like my kind of guy. Thanks, Tom, I appreciate your help. I'll talk to you later," said Benny as he hung up. He held onto the phone and called Mr. Reyes.

"Reyes."

"Hello, my name is Ben Mandarino. Tom Severs gave me your number, said you could be of help."

Benny proceeded to describe Amanda's disappearance with what details he had. During the ensuing conversation with Reyes, Benny realized that many more teenagers and young adults in the United States went to Mexico for drugs than he'd ever imagined.

These kids don't realize they're playing with fire, thought Benny.

Reyes said, "Listen, Ben, this could be a very tough situation. You might not like what you find. Numerous kids disappear. Many are never heard from again. They might OD, or get arrested. The Mexican penal system is a circle of horror, and it's hard to get out of it. Some kids get killed by drug dealers. Having to tell parents you don't know what happened to their son or daughter is horrible. What's worse is telling them their kid is dead."

Benny shuddered to think Amanda had somehow gotten into this nightmarish situation. He told Reyes that his brother-in-law, Steve Tate, would be contacting him. They could work out payment and all the details when they talked.

"That's fine. I'll do all I can to help your family," Reyes promised.

As he hung up the phone, Benny thought again, *Pam doesn't need to go Mexico and get into the middle of this. I don't want anything to happen to her.*

* * *

It was noon when Steve heard someone come in. He suspected it was Mike, his good friend of many years. When he'd called Mike to tell him that Amanda was in trouble, Mike said he'd come right away. That was no surprise to Steve; they'd always had each other's backs. A tough ex-navy SEAL, Mike didn't rattle easily. It wasn't the first time Mike had gotten a call about Amanda, but this time Steve had sounded desperate.

I haven't had a good fight in a long time, Mike had thought. *I'm ready for this.*

"I'm here to help you, Steve," Mike announced when he saw Steve. "We'll find your girl."

"Thanks, man, makes me feel better knowing you're here," said Steve, giving his friend a bear hug. "The time has come to get the police in on it."

"I'm with you."

How the hell did Mandy get to Mexico? And why? Steve only had questions, no answers.

As Mike and Steve drove to the police station, Mike said, "Tell me everything you told me on the phone again. I want to be sure I didn't miss anything. Maybe her boyfriend, Daniel, is hiding something or covering up for Mandy."

Steve shook his head. "I don't think Daniel had any part in Amanda's disappearance. When I spoke to him, he only sounded fed up, not scared, or like he was hiding anything. The guy's basically a pussy. Mandy wore the pants in that relationship," said Steve. "I don't know why my daughter would be in Mexico, but I do know that people go there to buy drugs. If Daniel knew or thought Amanda had gotten drugs across the border, he gave no indication. Leads me to think if Amanda was crossing to score, it either wasn't a regular thing, or Daniel wasn't aware of it. She could have chosen to keep him in the dark, too."

Mike nodded.

"Maybe she was forced into crossing the border," Steve added. "We don't know anything for sure at this point."

"I have to chew on this a while," Mike said.

"No problem. Two heads are better than one."

I'll take any ideas at this point, Steve thought.

The men went to the Western Division Police Station on Gaines Street. That particular location serviced the Point Loma area. It was a good place to start.

As they walked toward the front desk, familiar beads of sweat formed on the nape of Steve's neck and began trickling down his back. His entire shirt would be wet before long. His nerves were raw, and he didn't know what to expect, or even what to hope for, from the police. After giving a brief rundown of the story to Officer Ken Mulvey, who was on desk duty, Steve paused expectantly.

"Does your daughter take off often?" asked Mulvey. "If history gives you reason to believe she may be somewhere with friends, then she'll most likely turn up in a day or two."

Steve grimaced at the officer's insinuation. "May I please speak to a sergeant?" he asked politely.

Mulvey pursed his lips and looked at Steve with barely concealed contempt. "Giving me your statement is sufficient at this time, sir. Your daughter is most likely on a bender and will show up any day. Some kids go to Mexico to have illegal fun. Happens all too often."

Steve could barely contain himself. He tried hard to keep his breathing even and explain in a calm, unemotional way that his daughter was basically a good kid from a good family who might have gotten into trouble.

"I don't know what happened to my daughter. The bottom line here is that she's missing. You're the police. I thought you'd be a little more helpful," said Steve.

Mulvey shrugged. "We can get involved if someone is missing here, but we've no jurisdiction in Mexico. Are you certain your daughter is there?"

Steve explained about the distinctive ring he'd heard from the phone, and the man who had answered Mandy's cell.

"Yes, I'm familiar with that ring tone when cell phones are across the border. You're right that she's probably in Mexico . . . or at least her phone is."

"Come on. We need some help here. What if this was your daughter?" Steve was in anguish and in no mood to give up.

"What do you recommend we do?" asked Mike, stepping in.

"I'd file a missing person's report," replied the officer after a minute.

"I'll do that right now," said Steve.

The officer handed Steve the necessary paperwork. Grateful to get something on record, Steve murmured, "Thanks." He figured written documentation might get them some help. Steve answered all the questions asked: height, weight, age, what she was wearing when last seen, etc.

As Steve was handing the forms to Mulvey, a sergeant approached him, but he only reiterated what Officer Mulvey had said.

"I'm sorry, Mr. Tate," said Sergeant Riley. "The department can work with law enforcement from surrounding cities and counties, but we're unable to do anything about what happens in Mexico. The missing person's report can be helpful, though. It'll be entered into the National Crime Information Center database. If you can provide us with a photograph, we'll add that to the report."

"I'll definitely bring a picture over here," Steve said. "But isn't there some way we can get manpower going on this too? Don't you have contact with the Mexican police?"

"I've explained what we can do at this time," Sergeant Riley answered patiently. "If you learn more information, we can determine a threat assessment. Or if the case becomes critical, the sheriff's department can bring the report to the attention of other outlets."

Steve fought to control his temper, but lost that fight as desperation set in. "Dammit!" he exploded, hitting the desk with his fist. "This is critical to me! My daughter's in Mexico and I need help. What am I supposed to do?"

Mike grabbed Steve's arm and tried to calm his friend. "Let's go. Diane can drop off a photo of Amanda later," said Mike. "We'll do some digging."

CHAPTER 9
AMANDA'S BAD DECISION

A manda was out of control.

"I can't stand my life anymore. No one understands how I feel. I need drugs. Where are the damn keys?" she muttered to herself.

She recklessly pushed pens, notepads, and books off the desk as she searched frantically, knowing her parents would be back at any moment. "Come on, come on. Ah . . . here they are. Yes!"

Amanda's voice had dropped to a whisper. Her hands were shaking and she was sweaty all over, but the keys were hers.

Now to get out fast, she thought.

Any momentary guilt Amanda felt due to putting her parents through so much over the years was quickly assuaged when she told herself that her parents should realize the drugs were making her act the way she did.

It's not my fault. It's the damn drugs. I'm going to stop using, too. Just not today.

Amanda spied her dad's change jar and dumped the contents into her pocket. Then she ran out. At the curb was her beautiful car. The Mustang was ready and waiting. Like it knew. Amanda felt queasy as she turned the key in the ignition and pulled out onto the street. She desperately needed some relief from the paranoia, shaking, cramps, and itching. Sometimes it felt like bugs were crawling on her skin and in her hair. The pain in her stomach was intense. And now, Daniel had said they were through. Tears ran down her cheeks.

How could he do this? He said he loved me.

Amanda thought she might lose her mind.

Having grown up in the area and knowing the side roads, Amanda drove as if on autopilot. Soon, the Mustang was on Highway 5 heading south. A convertible passed her. Speeding up, Amanda swerved into the left lane. Her mood swung, too, to one of bitterness and anger.

What the fuck is wrong with Daniel anyway? He's such a loser. Shit. I'd like to slap him.

The Mustang flew down the highway as Amanda forced herself to keep it together. She couldn't think about anything except scoring some drugs.

Pay attention here, Amanda reminded herself as she accidentally veered into the next lane and almost hit a car. *I just need to be cool enough to cross the border. I've done it a hundred times. I can do it. I can do it.*

Amanda was fourteen the first time she had gone to Mexico to have fun with some older friends. By that time, the teenager had already had her first taste of fame. Amanda's parents said their daughter was "blessed with a beautiful singing voice." They were right. She had loved all those early years of voice lessons. Singing was her passion. Amanda auditioned for the San Diego Children's Choir when she was ten, and made it. She sang with the Intermediate Choir for two years. The choir performed with the Danish Ballet at the San Diego Civic Center and did some touring in Southern California. Being part of a professional singing group had been a great experience for

Amanda.

Eventually, though, Amanda had tired of going to practice and rehearsals when she would've rather been hanging out with her friends. The turning point came at age fourteen, when Amanda sang the national anthem at a San Diego Chargers football game. She did a terrific job and had received minor recognition around town. Boys started taking an interest, too. Amanda was physically developed already, so lying about her age had been easy.

I have to lie, she had told herself then, *because all the cool guys are older.* Amanda drank up the attention.

I guess that's when it all started, the partying and the drugs, thought Amanda, as she let her mind slide into the past.

She'd been able to hide a lot from her parents during that time, which she liked. They had been so trusting, seldom checking out the stories she told them, alibis, really. Amanda and her friends had things worked out. They lied and covered for each other.

Amanda's high school years were a hazy memory. That she had even graduated from high school was practically a miracle, and Amanda knew it.

If it weren't for cheating, I probably wouldn't have passed half my classes. I knew I could do the work, I just chose not to. She sighed at the memory.

Amanda had actually liked school when she was in elementary and middle school at St. Didacus. *Seemed like I lived a more normal life then—it's almost hard to remember.*

In Amanda's defense, wealthy Mexicans had bought homes in San Diego so their offspring could attend school in the States. The kids usually went to private schools like St. Augustine's, the Academy of Our Lady of Peace, or the Bishop's

School in La Jolla.

Those kids lived really high on the hog, as my Grandma Tate used to say, remembered Amanda.

Many of these high school students lived only with their Mexican maids, who acted as "chaperones." On Fridays, the maids were driven back to Mexico by a driver and the weekend help was brought in. The American students who knew of these arrangements seldom told their parents.

The Mexicans had the best parties, too, Amanda reflected. *Nobody told them what to do.*

Amanda had occasionally gone to parties at the kids' parents' homes in the hills of Tijuana. Those residences were spectacular. Gated entries with guards and guard dogs, the families lived in virtual compounds. Amanda remembered one place in particular had caged animals like a person would see in a zoo. Lions, tigers, and bears. There also was an aviary. Some of the animals were kept behind glass.

The whole set-up is unbelievable and super cool, in a weird, shouldn't-this-be-illegal sort of way, Amanda had thought then.

Like some of the other students, Amanda had never shared any of her Mexican friends' lifestyles with her parents. They wouldn't have let her to go to the homes or to the parties. But lots of her friends went, and the parties were a blast. The wealthy Mexican kids had everything.   So crossing the border into Tijuana was no big deal; she'd been doing it for years.

Amanda was approaching the San Ysidro border crossing. She fought to stay lucid. She had to keep her cool long enough to pass from one country to the other.

Crossing into Mexico turned out to be a breeze. Amanda's demeanor appeared calm, and she sailed through to the other side with no problems. She had tried to control the shaking, and she knew she looked like crap, but the guards hadn't seemed to notice. Or care. *Does anyone? I feel so lost, but the drugs will help. Help me. Help me.*

Amanda was convinced that she desperately needed OxyContin to quell the pain that was rapidly invading every inch of her body.

* * *

Mike and Steve drove back to the office to chug coffee and brainstorm.

"Maybe we missed something. A clue of some type," said Mike. "Can you think of who might know where Amanda would go in Mexico? And why? That is, if she went there of her own volition, I guess."

"If she did go on purpose, then I figure Tijuana, but where, exactly? I have no clue. We've called so many of her friends and keep reaching dead ends. It's hard to believe that virtually no one would have any clue what happened to Amanda. Could she have lost her phone? Maybe she traded it for drugs." Steve racked his brain. "I know Amanda didn't have any money with her. Shit, she was desperate enough to take the change out of the jar."

"Just doesn't sound good, Steve," Mike said. "Let me try calling some of her friends. Maybe a fresh voice would help."

The two men spent the better part of the afternoon throwing out ideas and making phone calls.

"I don't know how many times I can call some of these so-called friends of hers," Steve said. "Frankly, I'm getting sick of it."

Daniel was still no help. "I just called her stupid boyfriend, Daniel, again. He seemed almost pissed. I'd like to go over there and shake him up, you know? But what good would it do? I'd probably get tossed in the can, and that wouldn't help anyone."

"We can't let our tempers get the best of us here. You'd think Daniel would be more concerned, but if they've been fighting, he might just be angry about that," said Mike.

"I think I'll report the Mustang as stolen," Steve said suddenly. "At least the law will be involved then. Maybe we'll even get some help from the police."

"Good idea," said Mike. "Someone may have forced Amanda to drive to Mexico. We have no idea what happened at this point. At least by filing a report, the police will be on the lookout for the car, and the border guards will be made aware."

Steve called the police to file the stolen vehicle report, and then punched in the number for the automobile insurance company to inform them. Just then, his cell phone died.

"Fucking battery," he said, frustrated.

Steve's head was throbbing. He rubbed his face and neck. *Where the fuck is she?*

Hearing Mike's stomach growl, Steve looked at his watch. "Guess we should think about eating something," he said, bouncing the truck keys around in the palm of his hand. "I'll call Diane and let her know we're on our way to take her to eat with us. I can juice up my phone's battery on the way."

"Sounds good," said Mike, as he closed his notebook.

The men left, stopped to pick up Diane, and then headed to a restaurant.

Diane barely acknowledged Steve and Mike during dinner. She sat with her head lowered, picking at her Caesar salad with shrimp.

Steve felt bad about how things had gotten between him and Diane. At times they seemed to be living parallel lives in the same house. *Our strained relationship doesn't need any help making it unravel,* he thought. *I blame myself.*

Now they shared a goal; find Amanda and help her rid herself of the demons in her life. Those demons had affected the entire family.

"Diane," Steve said when Mike excused himself to go to the men's room, "we have this common thread in the fabric of our day-to-day existence, but we are not a real couple. Not by a long shot. Something's missing and has been for a long time. I want us to get back to where we were . . . to where we can be. How do you feel about that?"

"You have to ask me about that now?" Diane snapped. "All I care about is finding Amanda."

Steve looked crestfallen. "You're right. I shouldn't be thinking about us right now. Shit. My head is all over the place. I just want to go to sleep and wake up with all this behind me."

Mike returned to a couple obviously in pain. Diane was staring off into space and Steve's head was in his hands. Mike felt for them and hoped they'd be able to locate Amanda soon.

Later, on the drive home, Steve was lost in thought. He set his jaw determinedly and promised himself, *If we don't get concrete answers by morning, I'm going to Tijuana to look for Amanda myself.*

CHAPTER 10
SERIOUS PROBLEMS

D ay three in hell. Steve woke up in a sweat at four in the morning from a dreadful nightmare. Tossing and turning, he couldn't sleep, and didn't want to try. The nightmare of reality was as bad as—or worse than—the one he had just experienced. He had to find Amanda.

Getting up quietly, Steve tiptoed to the kitchen to make a pot of coffee and review his "to do" list. He read:

1. Call the hospitals again.
2. Call the police. (Maybe they've heard something.)

He was too fidgety to continue. Steve paced the room as thoughts jumped about in his mind. What could he do that would help most?

Light was starting to peek in through the windows; dawn was breaking. Steve stretched and twisted his torso. He checked his cell phone for messages. No calls relating to Amanda's disappearance.

His business partner, Geraldo, came over at seven. Steve told him that someone had answered Mandy's cell speaking with a thick Spanish accent. Together they called the number again, with Geraldo holding the phone. When someone answered, Geraldo spoke in Spanish, waited for the response, and then yelled at the person on the other end as he hung up. Geraldo called back, but no one answered.

"You have serious problems, my friend," Geraldo said. "Turns out the *hombre* who answered Mandy's phone said she is 'his' now, and the phone is also 'his.' The shithead laughed and hung up."

Steve's face flushed red with rage, though his eyes showed fear for Amanda. "What the hell's going on, Geraldo? Who is that man? Does he . . .have Amanda?"

Steve's muscles tightened as he spoke through clenched teeth. "He's probably in Tijuana. We've got to go to there."

"Mexico's a tricky place, man," said Geraldo.

"I know, I know," Steve said.

A heavy silence fell on them like thick cement out of a truck.

Finally, Geraldo said, "We could use some inside help. My cousin Amado is a cop in San Diego, but he was born in Tijuana. Maybe he could help us. He's got some connections, too. Most of his family still lives in Tijuana."

"Okay. Sounds good," Steve agreed. "Call him."

Geraldo's next words made Steve's heart stop. "We should check out the morgue, too. I'm sorry, Steve, but you never know."

"Fuck, Geraldo," said Steve, fighting back tears and practically choking on his words. "I can't even think about the . . . morgue!"

"I'll take care of it," Geraldo assured his friend. "Don't worry. I'm going to call Cisco and take care of a couple of other things too."

He bear hugged Steve and turned to leave. "Later, bro," he said.

The look of sadness in his friend's eyes cut Steve to the

core. *Is this really happening?* Steve's mind spun.

All of a sudden, Steve felt extremely tired—drained, as if someone had let all the air and energy out of his body. He stumbled over to the sofa to stretch out for a few minutes.

The sound of a phone ringing woke him out of a twitchy sleep. He looked at his watch. Ten o'clock. *Dammit!* Steve jumped up and reached for the phone. Caller ID let him know it was Pam. He picked up the receiver, paused to take a deep breath, and said, "Hey, Pam."

"Hi, Steve. I can't be there until Thursday, but all the arrangements have been made. My flight will arrive at 9:45 a.m. on USAirways. Will you be able to pick me up, or should I just hop a cab?"

"I can get you." *If you only knew how much I need you here.*

"Great! Benny's calling someone he knows in law enforcement to get a lead on a private investigator. We should hear back later today," said Pam.

A private investigator. Good idea. Steve's hands were clammy and his head was pounding. *How could I have let Amanda go?*

His thoughts tortured him, but he managed to say, "Thanks, Pam. You don't know how much I appreciate you guys. E-mail me your flight info, and I'll be at the airport to pick you up."

"Maybe you won't even need me to come out when Thursday rolls around," said Pam. "Amanda could be back by then."

"I hope you're right," Steve said quietly. "Tell Benny I'm grateful for anything he can do. He's the best brother-in-law. Geraldo has a cousin who's a cop, and we're going to see if he can help too."

"Okay, good. How's Diane?"

"Upset, of course. We're both sick with worry, and the cops here say their hands are tied. I feel like tying some hands myself."

Steve replaced the receiver. He could hear Diane getting up and went to the kitchen just as she walked in. Diane immediately started brewing tea.

"You could have had some tea ready for me. It's the least you could have done," grumbled Diane.

Their relationship was one of either intense love and passion, or full-out fighting. The roller coaster of emotions made life difficult, and both Steve and Diane had entertained thoughts of leaving. Diane liked Steve to wait on her, but the more he did, the more she wanted him to do.

"We create our own monsters," Steve always said.

On a normal day, Diane would've taken the tea that Steve had freshly brewed for her and curled up on the sofa for a lazy morning with the paper. She didn't have to be at work until 10:00, and Steve usually left for work by 6:30. Steve loved his wife, but they seemed to have more differences than similarities.

Steve and Diane's daughter had bits of both of them, although she was her own person as well. Amanda had way too much energy and temperament for her mother to handle; consequently, they butted heads a lot. Steve had been better able to deal with Amanda on a day-to-day basis during her formative years.

Amanda's parents made sure she had the opportunity to attend good schools, they provided her with great singing teachers, and Steve had taken her to church. The family did things together, too. Steve and Diane always thought they had done a good job raising their daughter, but at age twenty-one, Amanda was still a challenge.

Diane started to cry and hiccup, so Steve held her for a few minutes. He could barely keep it together himself. Diane finally wiped her eyes and said, "We need to do something more proactive, Steve. I can't take it."

"You're right. Let's start by going over my list."

He pulled a paper from his pocket and handed it to Diane. She unfolded it and read:

1. Call the hospitals again.
2. And the police. Maybe they've heard something.
3. Call the TV stations, especially channel 9. The show, "Around and About San Diego," sometimes broadcasts pieces on missing persons.
4. Call both of Diane's brothers.
5. Call the radio stations.
6. Call the insurance company.

"The thing is, we still don't know how Amanda ended up in Mexico," Diane said. "Was it by force, by going with a friend, by driving herself, or what? We don't even know for certain that she's there. Her phone is in Mexico, that's all."

"I'd say there's a good possibility Amanda's in Tijuana. The city's close. Someone could have stolen her phone and is using it in Mexico, but then, where's Amanda? So I think she's somewhere in Tijuana."

Even though Amanda had considered the Mustang "her" car, Steve had paid for it, the car was in his name, and he had been making the insurance payments. Steve had let Amanda drive the car, using it as leverage to help her stay clean and sober.

Obvious how well that plan worked, Steve thought.

"Hello, State Farm? This is Steve Tate. I need to report

my car stolen." Steve walked back and forth while he spoke with the agent.

"Well, that's done," Steve said as he ended the call. "Now the license number will be put on a list. At least it's something."

"I just had an idea," Diane offered. "We can make posters with Amanda's photo and information on them. I have can have them made at work. Then we can go to Tijuana and tack them up all over the place. We can pass them out, give them to the cops, make sure they're everywhere. Seeing Amanda's picture might jar some memories."

"Great fucking idea!" Steve exclaimed. "Geraldo can help us with the Spanish translation. We should have some posters printed in English, too. We can put them up in San Diego and near the border. Give them to the police here. You never know what might click."

Let this lead to something, Steve prayed.

CHAPTER 11
AMANDA'S IN TIJUANA

Amanda drove into Tijuana and turned right at the first corner. She knew a *farmacia* was located just down the block. Druggies frequented the pharmacy because they were able to get all kinds of pharmaceuticals without much fuss. She'd met up with friends there several times in the past few months.

Amanda felt like throwing up and opened her window for some fresh air. She knew she looked as bad as she felt but didn't care. Relief was near. Eyeing the *farmacia*, Amanda pulled over and parked.

"Hey, *chica*! Want some shit?"

A nice-looking young Mexican leaned on the door and looked in at her. He stole a sideways glance at the other Mexican male with him as she answered.

"Yes, oh yes." Amanda choked out the words.

"Okay, give me twenty dollars."

"I can't. I . . . don't have that much."

Amanda was shaking, obviously in need of a fix.

"How much money you got?"

The men opened the car door and pulled Amanda out. One reached in and grabbed her purse. In broken but understandable English, he said, "Come on. Let's go get high."

Amanda nodded. The desire for drugs was stronger

than rational thinking. Consumed by a physical need for opiates, Amanda ignored her gut feeling that told her she shouldn't be going anywhere with these strangers.

The men practically dragged her down the street. She turned and looked back at her car just as someone was driving it away.

"My car . . . what is . . . ? Where is . . . ?

Amanda caught a glimpse of the driver, a young Mexican male. She tried to stop, but the men had strong grips on her arms and forced her to continue walking with them.

"Don't worry," said the taller man. "We'll take care of the problem for you. You can have the car whenever you want."

His accomplice remained silent.

Amanda, focused on getting high, thought, *Alright. I'll worry about the car later.*

CHAPTER 12
STEVE PUTS THE WORD OUT

Craig and Dave were Diane's brothers. Born ten months apart, they were often referred to as "Irish twins." Good looking guys, neither one of them was able to stay with one woman for long. Craig owned a well-known restaurant, the Windjammer, in Manhattan Beach. Airline personnel frequented the place. Craig made sure the female flight attendants were always well cared for. The restaurant was a fun and popular hangout, but as far as Steve was concerned, Craig was a jerk. They'd never seen eye to eye on anything.

"Amanda's always got some kind of drug problem," Craig had said when Steve called about her disappearance. "She'll turn up, like usual. I'll let you know if she slides in here. Talk to you later."

"Yeah, thanks," said Steve. *Asshole.*

Dave was more laid back and much easier to get along with. He worked "in the industry," as he referred to show business. He had dated a lot of starlets, and even seemed like he might stay with a petite blonde who had a bit part in a show he was on, but the relationship fizzled out when the show got canceled. His best gig to date was a recurring role on a soap opera, but that had ended three years ago. Dave paid his bills with radio spots and commercials. He did whatever he could to get by, sometimes even manning the bar for Craig at the Wind-jammer.

Dave had had his own troubles with drugs too. He liked to "walk on the wild side," as he often said, but he was clean now.

At least, thought Steve, *the last I knew of it, Dave was clean.*

Steve hadn't heard anything to the contrary lately, and word traveled. Steve called Dave.

"Hey, bro, I need your help. Amanda's missing. I've tried to track her down, but I just can't find her. You wouldn't have any idea where she is, would you?"

"No, man, I don't know where Amanda is. I'll put the word out, though. She likes to hang out here sometimes," Dave said. "You know how the party crowd is in West Hollywood. Everyone seems to know everyone."

Amanda had done a month at the posh Wonderland Rehab Center in West Hollywood. She had met a lot of famous and semi-famous people there.

Lot of good it did her, mused Dave.

But there was a chance someone might know or have heard something about Amanda, so Dave said he'd do what he could.

"Thanks, Dave. If you hear anything at all, let me know." Steve was exasperated. "Seems like all I do is hit dead ends."

One of the great things about San Diego, Steve knew, was that even though it was a big city, it operated like a small town on some levels. When Steve contacted channel 9 television, the people couldn't have been nicer. Since a police report had been filed, the station manager agreed to air a bulletin on the local evening news about Mandy being a "missing person." Steve e-mailed a photo and the information about Mandy to the station manager. A Spanish-speaking television station, Telemundo, was willing to air Amanda's photo, too. Licensed out of Tijuana, the station had operating affiliates in San Diego and surrounding areas. It was a great station for people who spoke only Spanish. Steve was hopeful a lead might be generated since there was a lot of back-and-forth traffic between San Diego and Tijuana every day.

Somebody has to have seen Mandy somewhere, sometime, Steve thought. *With posters all over, and her face on TV, maybe someone will come forward with some information.*

Steve called the police again. They hadn't heard anything, but said they'd be willing to distribute the posters so the officers could be made aware of Amanda's missing status. There was no news at the hospitals, either, and Steve refused to think about the morgue. Diane, with her boss's help, had done a terrific job with the posters. Elena Medina, who worked in the office, did the translating, so they hadn't needed to call in Geraldo. The two hundred posters—fifty written in English— would be ready by 6:00 p.m.

Diane had found a photo of Amanda, taken when the family was in Puerto Nuevo, Mexico. They'd gone to Rosarito Beach first, then headed south to Puerto Nuevo for the delicious, and cheap, lobster dinners. When Diane had first looked at the photo of Amanda, smiling and wearing her lobster bib, she had burst into tears. Her daughter looked so happy, but now . . . Diane wouldn't let herself think too deeply about Amanda's possible situation; it was too frightening.

Amanda's dark looks make her almost look Hispanic, Steve thought when he looked at the photo. *I hope her complexion won't make her more difficult to find in Mexico.*

Mike showed up around two o'clock, and the three began what would be the first of many trips to Tijuana.

"I have cash to help loosen lips," said Steve, patting the eight hundred dollars he had in his pocket. "Money talks everywhere, but especially in Mexico."

"Got that right," agreed Mike.

Steve said a silent prayer that they'd be able to find Amanda soon. Not knowing what had happened to her, or even worse, what *was* happening to her, was making everyone crazy. Amanda's disappearance was pulling Diane and Steve together, and pushing them apart at the same time. Steve's stomach was in a constant state of agitation, and Diane moaned as they drove. He drove as fast he could to Tijuana.

About fifteen minutes into the drive, Steve's cell phone rang. It was Benny.

"Hey, Steve, I have the number of a private investigator. He's a former California state trooper of Mexican descent, and he's bilingual. Name's Alberto Reyes. He said he's available to aid in the search for Amanda."

"Thank you so much, Benny. We need every bit of help we can get."

Benny gave Steve the phone number, which he relayed to Diane as he drove.

"Talk to you soon, Steve. You all are in my prayers."

"Thanks. I'll call now."

Steve gave Diane his cell phone so she could punch in the numbers for him. She handed it back to him as the call began to ring.

"Hello, Bert Reyes here," the male voice answered.

"Bert, Steve Tate. Benny Mandarino gave me your

number. I'm calling about my daughter, Amanda, who's missing. We believe she's in Mexico."

"Hello, Steve. Benny filled me in somewhat already. I'm available to meet with you tonight. I'm finishing something up this afternoon."

"That's great. We're on our way to Tijuana now to look for Amanda. I can't tell you how desperate we are, or how scared. Sure hope you can help us."

"I was able to free up my schedule for the next few days," Alberto said. "We'll find her."

"Thanks. I needed to hear the confidence in your voice. I'll call you again in a few hours and we can set something up."

"Sounds good. I live in National City; I'm sure you know where that is. Talk to you later."

"I'm glad we have another person helping us," Diane said when Steve finished his call to Alberto.

Steve felt a little better, too, knowing they were going to get some help. He hadn't wanted Diane to see the fear in his eyes; he didn't think she could handle it. Steve's jaw clenched as he gripped the wheel. They continued heading south, not sure what they would find.

CHAPTER 13
DOING DRUGS WITH THE WRONG PEOPLE

Amanda couldn't believe a stranger had driven away with her car and she'd done nothing. While upset by this, she remained consumed by her desire for drugs.

I won't freak out, Amanda thought, trying to calm herself. *These guys said I can get my car back when I want. I'll just have them take me to my car after I get high.*

Amanda noticed one of the men, the cuter one, was looking at her. He seemed vaguely familiar, like maybe she'd seen him when she bought dope in Tijuana before.

He's probably okay, she assured herself.

"Where are we going?" Amanda murmured, desperate for drugs. She knew she was in bad shape.

Neither man answered. They could see that the girl was too messed up for the question to matter. The odd trio traipsed down an alley and stopped at the back entrance of a *farmacia*. The Mexicans glanced around and then quickly pulled the door open. Inside was a musty storage room packed with boxes. Some were full, some empty. There were two interior doors. Held back by the taller man, Amanda watched as the other went to the door on the left. He knocked and said something in Spanish.

Amanda was shaking pretty hard by then. Her clammy skin was itching like crazy. She had intense cramps that almost doubled her over with pain. *Hurry up,* she thought.

The door opened, and they went in. A man was chopping pills into powdery lines on a counter. Another guy with dark hair and thin lips stood behind him. Both were Mexican.

Amanda had done drugs in the back rooms of *farmacias* before, but she had always been with someone she knew. Most often her friend, Jeanette, whom she'd met at the rehab facility, Phoenix House, in Venice Beach, had accompanied her.

I learned some good tricks in rehab, remembered Amanda. *Like where and how to get the drugs you want.*

She had learned the places to go to in Tijuana for drugs and which *farmacias* were "cool," meaning they'd sell anything to just about anyone.

Amanda was in such desperate need of a fix, the powder on the counter looked like a taste of heaven to her.

Could be Percocet or OxyContin, she thought, barely able to stand up. *I'd like heroin, but this'll do.*

"*Aqui, chica.* Here," said one of the Mexicans as he handed her a straw cut down to about three inches.

The tall guy pushed a wobbly Amanda toward the counter. She grabbed the corner to keep from falling.

"What is this?" Amanda mumbled.

The question was ignored. Amanda felt the tall man's firm hand on her back. She took the straw in her trembling hand, leaned over the counter, and snorted the coarse powder deep into her head. The drug burned like crazy, but her extreme need drove Amanda to immediately inhale a line into her other nostril, as well.

Soon, she felt good. Real good. Amanda looked at the strangers. Her legs were weak and she tottered. One of the men steadied her while another gave her something to drink. It tasted funny.

I don't even care what I'm drinking, thought Amanda. *I'm good now. Time to score some dope and head back to San Diego.*

Amanda smiled weakly. Her eyelids were heavy and her tongue felt thick.

"Can I get . . . my car now? I have . . . to get back." Amanda's head tilted to one side as she spoke. She was fading fast.

The guys in the room laughed.

The tall one said, "Just be happy you're high, *chica.*"

The man with the razor blade started cutting up more pills. Another two men came in. One, a big, muscular guy with tattoos and blonde, stringy hair, looked American. He was obviously strung out.

Do I look like that? Amanda wondered.

Then she passed out.

* * *

Amanda woke up on a mattress on the floor. She didn't have any idea what time it was, where she was, or how she had gotten there.

"Hey! Somebody . . . "

Amanda tried to yell, but the effort alone made her feel as if her aching head was splitting wide open. She struggled to sit up.

It hurts everywhere. I feel sick.

Amanda's bleary eyes started to focus. She peered around in the dim light and realized she was in a small, desolate room. A vent at the top of one wall let in a small amount of natural light, but did nothing to lessen the putrid smell hanging in the stale air.

Amanda wanted to scream when a tiny lizard ran by her foot, but no sound came out of her parched mouth. Her lips were dry and chapped. Seeing her purse, Amanda reached inside with a shaking hand for lip gloss to moisten her lips. She coughed, and the movement radiated pain throughout her body. She poked her hand back inside the bag to get her cell phone but couldn't find it.

Where's my phone?

Amanda felt panicky. Her head was swimming. She was nauseated and in pain. *Again. Always in pain.*

Lying back down, Amanda closed her eyes. She tried to think about what had happened and where she might be. It didn't make any sense for her to be in this godforsaken room. She strained to hear someone or something, but her ears were met by dead silence, which in itself was scary.

Amanda had difficulty locking in a clear thought. Try as she might, she couldn't remember anything. Random thoughts floated through her aching head. She had no strength. She was cold, and her body shook. Expecting to vomit, Amanda could already taste the nasty bile in her throat.

I just want some drugs and to go home. Really, going home would be enough, she thought. *I'm fucked up.*

Amanda began to cry, and through her gulps, heard something break the eerie silence. The sound got louder. Someone was coming.

The door to the makeshift prison banged open. Two burly men, dressed in combat fatigues and steel-toe boots, stomped in and glared at her. Without a word, the men walked over to the petrified Amanda and kicked her hard in the side. First one, and then the other.

The shock of the unexpected kicks was almost as bad as the pain. Amanda screamed in misery and terror. One kicked her again. Amanda's piercing screams filled the room. She was so weak; it had been like kicking a rag doll. The men showed no emotion as they watched the tortured young captive writhe in agony. Satisfied after a few moments, they left.

Amanda spit up blood. She thought she might die from the unbearable pain the strangers had inflicted upon her. Amanda hadn't prayed in quite some time, but she did now.

Dear God, help me. Oh, please, please, help me. I beg you.

Amanda sobbed in agony and fear until finally, mercifully, she passed out.

Time passed. Eventually Amanda came to.

Dirty, thirsty, and badly in need of some drugs, Amanda had never been this afraid. Excruciating pain emanated from every pore. Cramps engulfed her and convulsions sent sharp jabs like stabbing knives throughout her body. The pain from the kicks was so intense that Amanda was certain her ribs were broken. She gagged, which caused spasms.

Petrified, Amanda forced her mind to work. The last thing she clearly remembered was getting high in the back room of the *farmacia*.

How did I get here? Who were those guys? What do they want with me? Why are they hurting me? The questions swirled around in her head.

Amanda shook from fear and pain. Almost delirious, her mind wandered back in time. A deep chill came over Amanda as she remembered her friend, Valeria Perez. Known as Vali, the wealthy girl had been born in Mexico but lived during the school year with her parents and grandmother in a large house in

San Diego. The Perez family had wanted their children to attend school in the United States. They also maintained their mansion in Tijuana and spent much time there. Amanda had been to their Mexican *hacienda*. It was an amazing place.

Vali, her sister, Vera, and her brother, Eduardo, didn't want for anything. Vali had even had a nose job when she was sixteen because she didn't like her profile. Her parents never said no to Vali. Amanda had been certain Vali's family was involved in dealing drugs on a large scale, although she had never asked Vali anything directly. Sometimes, though, Amanda had overheard things when she was with Vali at the Perezes' house in San Diego—conversations that sounded suspect.

There were times when Amanda had visited that there'd been a lot of action at the house. People, both Mexicans and Americans, were inside and outside the place, as well as all over the property. Vehicles of all types came and went. It was during those times when Vali would ask if she could spend the night at Amanda's. Vali told Amanda she didn't like being home when there were so many strangers there. She didn't feel safe, although Vali didn't realize then what power her father actually possessed. He wasn't the top guy in the Mexican Mafia, but he could get things done. Since Vali always had more than enough money, and there was often an unusual amount of activity at her house, Amanda figured the stories about the drug dealing were probably true.

Since the Perez family situation hadn't affected Amanda directly, it never bothered her. And Vali had seemed like any other friend. Any other super-rich friend.

The girls weren't as close now that they were out of high school. They'd only gotten together a few times to "party down." And that was before the murder.

Amanda had heard through the grapevine that Vali's mother, Rosalba, had been brutally slain in Tijuana a few months earlier. Amanda was horrified. When she heard the grisly details of Rosalba's tortured body being found in the trunk of a car, Amanda couldn't imagine how Vali must've felt when it happened, or how she could go on living after her mother's vicious murder.

Her hands and legs bound, and her throat slit, Rosalba had been left to bleed to death in the trunk. The assassins had left a despicable message on Vera's cell phone that included the sound of her mother screaming, then gasping and gurgling, as she was being killed. The car was found four days later in downtown Tijuana. Rumor had it that Vera had been suffering from screaming nightmares ever since.

The story of the sadistic murder had been on the news, both in Mexico and in Southern California. The killing clearly was meant to "send a message." It did. Vali, Vera, and Eduardo had immediately gone into hiding.

Amanda hadn't talked to Vali since the murder, nor did she know where Vali and her siblings had gone. She didn't know what had happened to the father and grandmother. Vali's cell phone had been disconnected, and Amanda had quit trying to get a hold of her friend after a few failed attempts. Truth was the slaying had so scared Amanda that it had given her nightmares, too. They had lasted for weeks. *At least Daniel was a comfort during those night terrors,* she thought.

Amanda felt terrible for Vali and her family, but her fear of the Mexican Mafia had made her keep her distance from them. Though Amanda's parents had heard the sordid details of the slaying on the news, they were unaware their daughter knew Rosalba Perez. They knew Vali was a friend of Amanda's, but they had never met Vali's parents or known their names. Steve and Diane had been blissfully unaware of the horror and panic that had gnawed on Amanda's insides.

The memory of the killing deepened the fear Amanda now felt. If drug dealers could do something so horrendous to someone's mother, and she remembered Mrs. Perez as being beautiful and kind, then what would they do to her? Amanda was convinced she had been taken to this hellhole by the cartel.

They probably think I know something about Vali or the Perez family, even though I don't, she thought. *I'll just do whatever I have to, so they'll give back my car and I can leave.*

In fear and misery, Amanda cried herself into a restless, painful, terror-filled sleep. She had no realization of the passage of time.

Five hours would pass before anyone would come back to her prison. Five hours of torment for Amanda. But it was only the beginning.

CHAPTER 14
THE DEADLY CARTEL

Enrique and Jorge sat at the table with an American known as "Ice." Skinny and unkempt, the man looked like a junkie. The nickname had been given to him because of his addiction to the powerful stimulant, methamphetamine. Methamphetamine, or crystal meth, was often referred to as "ice" on the street. Ice had been working for Jorge's boss, Javier Morales, for over four years. During that time, he'd met the *jefe* only once.

Not many people were allowed to meet Javier. Everyone had heard his name, however, and certainly knew his reputation. "Don't fuck with him," about summed it up. Javier was one of the leaders in the human smuggling trade. Coldblooded, brutal, and merciless, Javier reveled in having absolute control. He ruled by terror. Javier was known to personally slit the throat of anyone he thought was screwing with him, sometimes first cutting off the tongue of the offender as a reminder to everyone to keep their tongues still. Javier's henchmen maintained a list of several horrifying execution techniques that could be applied at their boss's whim. One favorite was cutting off an arm or leg a few inches at a time, which elicited increasing and unending pain for the poor soul on the receiving end of this barbaric tactic. Stories of the torturous deaths of Javier's rivals and enemies kept many at bay. Police, city officials, army officers, business owners—no one was exempt from the ruthless tentacles of the *jefe* known as Javier.

Numerous police and city or government officials were on the cartel payroll, and millions of dollars were paid monthly in bribes. Word on the street was that if you didn't pay up, you *would* pay—with your life. It was practically impossible to know whom to trust in Mexico.

Javier's top men were no better than he. Jorge's temper was legendary. Known as *bastardo despiadado,* ruthless bastard, Jorge liked to torture for pleasure. Enrique could, and would, do whatever he had to do, too. Meeting Javier face-to-face wasn't necessary to force compliance by scare tactics. Javier's soldiers in the cartel did his dirty work just fine.

Ice knew better than to fuck up. He'd seen what had happened to those who did. Besides, he liked his drugs, and, even if he didn't, he was in too far with the cartel to go anywhere. He had often thought about getting out, but Ice knew he was stuck.

For now, at least, he liked to think.

"It's time for another run. The *pollos* are ready to go," said Jorge.

"Okay, bro. I'm ready," Ice replied.

Ice hated being a coyote for the *pollos.* He even hated the terms the cartel members used. A coyote was a human smuggler, and *pollos*, or chickens, were the cargo. The ruthless smugglers called the illegal immigrants "*pollos*" because they were considered without value beyond what they could bring on the open market. The immigrants were considered expendable until transported across the border and the tariff was paid.

Ice would rather have been transporting drugs, but, of course, he had no choice. Ice did what he was told.

The irony was that the *pollos* were sometimes driven across the border in trucks carrying crates of live chickens. These trucks had false backs, and the humans were packed in the small compartments like sardines. Without water and sufficient ventilation, there were always a few who didn't survive the trip.

Ice had a more personal reason, however, to hate the term *pollos*. Two Mexicans he had gotten to know fairly well while hanging out in Tijuana years earlier doing drugs and such were in a group of *pollos* he had seen lined up the month prior. Ashamed of where they had ended up, the men had avoided Ice's eyes.

Life is hard, Ice had thought, *but there's no time for sentiment, or I'll end up a pollo myself. Or worse.*

Still, Ice had felt bad about seeing his old friends in such a demeaning situation.

Javier's human trafficking ring operated alongside the thriving drug trade. In fact, his cousin, Carlos Morales, belonged to one of the major drug cartels in Tijuana, and they were deeply intertwined.

The cartel was one of three that distributed and sold multi-ton quantities of cocaine, marijuana, and heroin. The cartel also had begun dealing in methamphetamines. Meth was a very popular street drug in the United States and brought in an easy dollar. Or many dollars, as it turned out.

Carlos was near the top of the organization and poised to take the highest post eventually. As one leader got killed or arrested, there was always someone in line to step up. Often a battle ensued for the coveted lead position, but Carlos was ready. He'd earned his chops in the business and had looked death squarely in the eye on more than one occasion. He'd caused others to do the same, only they hadn't lived to tell about it.

Superstitious locals wondered if there was something in the DNA of the Morales family that bred violence. As cruel and unfeeling as Javier was, Carlos was far worse. He grew up torturing dogs, chickens, birds—anything living he could get his hands on. Even Carlos's own siblings weren't free from his cruelty. When he was eleven, Carlos had gotten into a fight with his older brother, Santos. When it seemed like the older brother was going to win the fight, Carlos grabbed a brick and beat Santos in the face and head with it. As Santos lay bleeding on the ground, Carlos kicked him and twisted his arm around his back until it snapped.

Santos lost his front teeth and the vision in his left eye. The broken arm never healed properly, causing him pain for the rest of his life. Their mother, Luisa, had gone into a deep depression when she saw what Carlos had done. Santos had been her favorite child of the eight in their family. Santos was a good child, and she couldn't understand what had possessed Carlos to beat his brother so savagely.

"*El diablo!* The devil," Luisa said when someone asked about Carlos. She would often cry and beat her chest when his name was mentioned.

Carlos would laugh when his mother referred to him as "the devil." His apparent inability to feel compassion or remorse had soon become his trademark. From that time on, everyone, even family members, had been afraid of Carlos. Maybe he *was* possessed.

Carlos's temper and acts of viciousness worsened as he got older. At thirteen, he became leader of a gang known for its fearlessness and brutality. Carlos became adept with a knife during that time. He also carried brass knuckles, the kind with points, which he loved using. When he was fifteen, Carlos was invited into the Morales Family Organization, known as the MFO, as a soldier. An honor not awarded to many fifteen-year-olds, Carlos was determined to make his mark within the cartel.

The MFO, Arellano-Felix Organization (or AFO), and the Mexican Mafia were the largest and most feared drug cartels in the Baja area of Mexico.

"I'm going to help make the MFO the biggest, baddest, and best," boasted Carlos more than once. He was well on the way to that goal by age twenty.

Carlos had cold, black eyes; thick, dark, wavy hair; and bright white teeth. The outlaw wore a mustache and had a habit of pulling on it when he was angry. No one liked it when Carlos got angry. The mere act of reaching for his mustache was known to strike terror in those who witnessed it.

Ice had worked for Carlos for three years before Enrique was ordered to turn him over to Javier. The American had gotten so good at smuggling that Carlos decided to move him to trafficking humans. Carlos liked the idea of moving good "soldiers" around after a time. He felt it kept them on their toes. He knew that Javier would appreciate having someone like Ice, who was experienced at smuggling, being "given" to him. Javier would then feel beholden to Carlos for being so generous with one of his best workers. Carlos liked having people owe him favors, so the deal was a win/win for the cousins.

Ice had never exhibited fear or stupidity while smuggling. The Morales family liked that a lot. Also, since Ice's drug habit was so strong, the cartel wasn't worried that he'd bolt, or turn. The bosses were therefore comfortable with increasing Ice's responsibilities. Ice got paid just enough to support his habit and pay for living expenses. As a bonus, the family supplied him with women. Ice had sometimes thought about eventually quitting the business and "getting the hell out of here," but so far it had only been a vague dream, usually felt when he was very high. Truth be told, Ice was fearful of both Javier and Carlos.

The cousins, well known for their brutality, had no conscience. They both preferred torturing a turncoat before allowing him to die. They even kept a medical doctor on hand for the purpose of administering enough drugs to keep the traitor alive, just so the torture could last longer.

Ice had never actually witnessed someone being tortured to death, but he'd heard the stories. One night, a couple of years ago, when he was at Carlos's hacienda waiting for his orders, Ice had heard piercing, gut-wrenching screams coming from another area of the estate. The desperate wails had made his skin crawl. Those sounds of hell had resonated in his head long afterward. Ice had made himself a promise, right then and there, that no way would he ever take on the Morales family.

CHAPTER 15
RETRIBUTION

Two of Carlos's men, Juan and Hector, stood outside his home office, waiting for the word to go in. The men would be happy to report they had the girl sequestered, as told. Certain she was the same pretty one they'd seen several times over the past few months coming to Tijuana to buy drugs, they knew Carlos would be pleased with their work. Who could forget such a *chica bonita*?

The girl had been so messed up when they had taken her that it had been almost too easy. What kind of fool woman would come alone to Tijuana in search of drugs?

Juan was on the thin edge of feeling the unyielding wrath of Carlos, and he knew it. Everyone knew it. No one wanted to be around when something happened. Juan had gotten too close to one of their mules, a raven-haired beauty from the States who they were using to transport drugs across the border. Juan had actually fallen for her. He had even talked about having the girl move in with him. Juan had broken an unspoken rule about fraternizing with the captives, and he was worried he'd have to pay for his foolishness.

Carlos was forced to have the mule taken out when she started acting like she was something more than she was. He didn't want to have to worry about her knowing too much, or talking to the wrong people. Or talking at all. Carlos was angry that Juan had been so stupid. How could he have fallen for a mule? Next to go would be Juan, if he wasn't careful. He had been given a break because he was the cousin of Carlos's wife, Solana, and she had begged Carlos not to hurt her aunt's son. But even Solana knew Juan's days were numbered.

Carlos wouldn't even be talking to these guys, Juan especially, because they were too far down the food chain, but Carlos wanted to keep an eye on *el bastardo*. In Carlos's mind, Juan had been a problem for years. He was always straddling the line between doing his job and doing something stupid and self-serving. Juan played too fast and loose with the rules, proving he ultimately could not be trusted.

I've no time for shitheads, Carlos thought. *I won't risk losing everything over a stupid shit like Juan, just because he can't keep his dick in his pants. Solana will get over it. Her aunt will, too. Have to.*

Hector, on the other hand, was a good worker who kept his nose clean. He could be counted on to do what it took, without complaint, to get a job done. Like Enrique, Hector didn't take anyone's shit.

Si, Hector's good, thought Carlos, as he turned toward the door.

"Now!" he shouted. "Open the fucking door and get in here!"

Hector and Juan opened the door quickly and went in. They described snatching a fucked-up Amanda from her car on the street in Tijuana in broad daylight. Julio had driven her car away as planned. They had also taken her phone.

Carlos listened intently as the men explained exactly how they had taken Amanda. He was pleased there had been no complications.

"Grabbing the chick was easy, even in the middle of the day," Juan boasted with a cocky smile.

"Shut up," Carlos growled through clenched teeth.

"I think it'll take a good dose of powder to keep this girl coasting. She's obviously done a lot, judging by how often she's been seen in Tijuana. Her tolerance level's gotta be pretty high," said Hector. "But I'm not worried about it. We have the best shit."

Carlos nodded.

"*La chica* will be dreaming most of the time. No sweat," Hector added.

"Easy job," Juan said again with a smirk.

Carlos noticed that Juan had that look in his eye when he talked about Amanda. *His dick's what's killing him,* thought Carlos. *His dick, and soon, me.*

Carlos told his soldiers to go back to the holding house and give Amanda a big hit of the "good shit."

Hector knew Carlos was referring to the stash of China white, the high grade of heroin they kept for "personal" use.

"That blow will knock her out for a while. Have her suck you, Juan, when she gets high. The blow job will be great for both of you," he sneered.

Carlos stared at the men through steely eyes for a long minute; then he told Juan to go ask Eber for some dust for the latest captive.

Juan couldn't believe his good luck. *Solana must've succeeded in turning Carlos's anger around. The new girl gets to do some hard blow, and I get a blow when I'm hard.* He laughed at his own joke.

Juan was gone only ten minutes, but it was long enough

for Carlos to tell Hector what he had to do. Hector nodded grimly. He reminded himself not to fuck with Carlos.

The kidnappers drove the dirty open jeep down the back roads of Tijuana, past the sounds of loud music, Mexicans yelling at each other, dogs barking, and the general noises of the city. Before long, they were out of town, heading to a remote area, each man thinking of what was going to happen when they reached the house. They finally turned on the long gravel road that led to the holding house where Amanda was captive.

Juan's heart was beating fast, both from his encounter with Carlos and the thought of having his dick sucked.

I like that shit, man, thought Juan. *This is going to be good.*

Hector's thoughts were more goal oriented. He knew he was a good soldier. His star was rising. Hector planned to follow orders until the time came when he would be the one to give orders. The thin flicker of a smile slid across Hector's lips.

My time will come.

"Hurry up," Juan directed Hector. He could already feel himself getting hard, and Hector wasn't driving fast enough to suit him.

As the jeep approached the house, the men scanned the area to see if anything looked out of the ordinary. Nothing did. They drove up to the front of the old place, parked, and got out.

Dust and tumbleweeds blew past them. The air felt hot and dry. The parched earth was cracked beneath their feet.

Glad I'm not forced to stay in this shit hole, Juan thought as he wiped dust off his face.

Hector kicked in the door, scaring Amanda all over again. She looked up at the men with panic and dread in her eyes.

Hector felt pity for a second, and then remembered that such an emotion was a luxury he could ill afford. He stood by the door as Juan went to the girl. The smarmy look on Juan's face disgusted Hector.

Amanda was frozen with fear.

Juan pulled a baggie containing fine white powder from his shirt pocket. He reached in his pants pocket for a little spoon. After gently opening the baggie, he dipped the spoon in and filled it. Juan stared deep into Amanda's eyes as he held out the spoon to her.

As fearful as she was, the possibility of getting wasted seemed like a heavenly escape to Amanda. She inhaled quickly and deeply. *Oh, that familiar burn. Hurts so good.* Amanda let her head drop back. She rubbed her nose while Juan then refilled spoon. Amanda snorted the powder into her other nostril. She enjoyed the rush, which was immediately followed by the soothing feeling of being lost in space. Amanda's eyes drooped and she started to float. The intense pain that had been her constant companion was vanishing into thin air.

This is why I like to get high, Amanda thought.

Suddenly, she felt Juan's hands prying her mouth open, followed by his pushing with his big, hard dick. Shocked and repulsed, Amanda jerked her head around trying to fight what she was afraid might be happening. She twisted, squirmed, and pushed, but her thin, weak arms were useless against the man. He was strong, and determined. For a moment, Amanda felt like she might be sick. Heroin often made her throw up, and what this man was trying to do added to the wave of nausea that washed over Amanda. She resisted with what little might she had. The feeling of queasiness passed as Amanda slid out of the present and into the great abyss.

Disgusted by Juan's display, Hector left the room and waited outside the door.

Juan was close to climaxing. He groaned loudly as he clumsily tried again to force his organ into the girl's mouth. Amanda's body went limp and her eyes rolled back in their sockets.

Juan dropped Amanda's head as his hands grabbed his pulsating dick. She fell lifelessly to the ground, unaware of Juan's sexual actions.

"*Mierda*! Shit!!" Juan hollered as he came, shooting his juices partly on Amanda's face, but mostly all over the floor. Exhausted and breathing hard, Juan was angry the kidnap victim had been unable to suck him like he wanted, but he knew he'd be back.

Next time, she'll have to give me what I want before *she gets her drugs,* he thought. *Even if I have to tie her up first.*

The sizable hits of the powerful heroin, coupled with the girl's small size and weakened condition, would keep the captive out of it for hours.

Juan looked at the girl as if for the first time. *She's beautiful, even this fucked up.*

He wiped himself off with a ratty blanket he picked up off the floor, and then, in an unusual display of tenderness, Juan wiped Amanda's face.

Maybe I'll have to stop by and check on her a lot, he thought, zipping up his pants. *We can have some fun. I'll just tell Hector that I'll go ahead and take charge of monitoring this one.*

Smirking, Juan felt pretty damn good as he kicked open the door and walked out.

Ready to tell Hector of his plan, Juan looked up at his partner in crime just as Hector aimed the AK-47 directly at Juan.

Juan's protests were obliterated by the gun's powerful blasts. His chest exploded as the bullets hit, driving the remainder of Juan's body back against an old pillar. Bloody bits of flesh and bone were sent flying everywhere.

So much for pissing off Carlos, thought Hector.

He walked away, knowing Carlos would send in a cleaning crew. *I'll get pussy on my own time. Safer that way.*

Hector jumped into the jeep and pulled out his cell phone. "Done," he said, then flicked the phone shut.

CHAPTER 16
AMANDA'S MOTHER, DIANE

D iane knew she had issues.

Who wouldn't, with two alcoholic and emotionally absent parents?

Diane was the eldest of three children. Her dad, Bud, had worked in sales. He was gone a lot when she was growing up, maybe even more than he had to be. Bud had the lethal combination of being both good looking and a bald-faced liar.

Daisy, Diane's mom, was something else, too. Her given name was Thelma, but she hated the very sound of it. She liked to be called "Daisy," because it made her feel "as pretty as a flower."

Bud and Daisy had eloped when they were teenagers, mostly to piss off their parents. The fun had lasted about two years, until Diane was born. Daisy found out real fast how much work it was to care for a new baby.

The couple didn't have a lot of money, and their being broke made a bad situation worse. They fought a lot.

Bud usually reeked of alcohol whenever he was home. He had a hair trigger temper, and no one wanted to be around him. He found a way to be around Daisy, though, and she got pregnant with Craig when Diane was four. Almost as soon as baby Craig popped out, Daisy discovered, to her dismay, that she was pregnant again.

Bud's reaction wasn't surprising.

"Why'd you go and do a fool thing like that?" he'd asked. "As if two kids aren't enough."

Little Diane was a doll. She rarely cried, but Daisy didn't care. Things between Bud and Daisy went downhill fast after Diane was born. By the time the two boys were toddlers, Daisy was drinking pretty heavily, too. Straight vodka made her as mean as a snake. She dished out discipline with her father's old leather belt. Life had become a nightmare for the kids, only getting worse as they grew up.

"Di," Daisy would yell, "go get my cigarettes! And give those boys something to eat."

When Diane was about eight, she got the hiccups. They lasted for two days. The constant hiccupping drove her mother crazy.

"Stop it, stop it!" she'd screeched.

Daisy had tried to beat the hiccups out of Diane with a wooden spoon. Of course it didn't work, and Diane had been plagued with hiccups on and off ever since.

When her boys were young, Daisy would lock them in the empty back bedroom when they "misbehaved." There were nights when she left them locked in the dark room overnight, without supper. The boys would cry and pound on the door until they passed out from sheer exhaustion. "Those wild ones need to learn a lesson," Daisy would say. As the boys got older, the old leather belt was given a real workout.

"I'm surprised my brothers don't have permanent welts on their legs from that belt," Diane had told Steve when they were dating.

No, Diane didn't have a fun childhood, and she hated

being called "Di." It brought back too many bad memories.

Diane loved Steve. He knew how to take care of her in the way she had always wanted her parents to care for her when she was a kid. Diane also hated Steve. He expected her to do what she considered to be too much.

Haven't I had a hard enough time? Diane thought with self-pity. Her feelings for Steve were always conflicted.

Diane had done so much work as a child, taking care of her brothers, that when Amanda was born, she didn't bond with her baby the way most mothers do.

Steve was the one who wanted a baby anyway. It's only fair that he does his share, Diane had thought then. *I deserve to have it easy now, after all I've been through.*

Over the years Diane had convinced herself of this point.

And now this!

CHAPTER 17
TIJUANA

O n day five in hell, the travelers waited in the long line to drive into Mexico. Tension in the truck was building. Beads of sweat popped up on Steve's forehead.

I hope to all that's good and holy we can find our daughter. Please God, Steve prayed.

"I can't take it," cried Diane. "I'm scared we might not find Amanda. And we don't know what's happening to her."

Diane covered her face with her hands as the hiccups started. Steve gently put his hand on Diane's shoulder and rubbed her back for a minute. *I'm scared, too*, he thought.

Steve remembered the many times he, Diane, and Amanda had driven into Mexico. He thought about how they'd enjoyed going to the beach area, Playas de Rosarito, and then to the Puerto Nuevo district for the twenty-dollar lobster dinners and the dollar margaritas. He choked up.

Those happy days seem like a million years ago now.

Driving into the town of Tijuana was a different story altogether. Steve had seldom driven to Tijuana just to spend the day. It was much easier to park in the States and walk over. The last off ramp on Highway 5 before the border was the Camino de la Plaza exit. Impossible to miss, the highway sign even read, "Last U.S. exit." Only a few minutes' walk to the border, along with the cheap parking rate, made it an attractive stop.

But today they drove in. While drivers didn't need special paperwork to cross the border, the Mexican government recommended that tourists purchase Mexican auto insurance, the only kind of insurance recognized there. Should a driver have the misfortune of being involved in an accident, automatic jail time was imposed if the driver didn't have the designated insurance.

Steve chose to forego the insurance and take his chances. With the hope of finding Amanda, the group had decided it would be easier to put her in the truck with them and drive back across the border than to stand in the USA entry line for what could easily be hours. The line going into Mexico always moved fairly quickly. The ones opposite, going into the States, were agonizingly slow.

We'll worry about the long lines later, Steve thought.

As they crossed into Mexico, Steve was struck by the difference a few hundred feet made. As soon as they crossed the border, virtually everything was different. Tijuana didn't resemble San Diego in the least.

Steve found a parking place near a McDonald's, but even the fast-food joint didn't give the city an American feel.

Dust and extreme poverty were the first things that screamed out at them. Poor children ran up to everyone, begging for money or candy, and mothers with blank expressions sat on the side of the street holding their babies. The infirm sat on the sidewalks with their cups set in front of them. Beggars approached the tourists with their hands out.

Third world country just down the street from one of the most bustling cities in America, Steve thought.

Seemingly oblivious to the abject poverty were the street

vendors. With their goods displayed on sidewalks and streets to entice tourists who had come for a bargain, the vendors stayed busy hawking their wares. They ignored the locals, the invisible poor among them.

Taxis were in abundance, ready to take tourists to other areas of town, where more stores featuring clothing, statues, and trinkets awaited. Tijuana had beautiful churches to admire, and offered many restaurants to choose from. Food venders fried up the ever popular *orejas,* elephant ears, and the smell of hot oil and sugar permeated the streets. Colorful striped blankets and sombreros hung outside shops and garages, attracting shoppers.

Velvet wall hangings were commonplace, but as Steve glanced at them, he didn't see any of Elvis. He felt a pang as he remembered how he and Amanda used to joke about buying an "Elvis on velvet" blanket to take home. Steve glanced at Diane. She looked resolute as she adjusted her hat. With determination driven by hope, the trio walked up to the *farmacia* on the corner.

"This place is as good a place as any to begin our search. Maybe someone inside here has seen Amanda," said Steve as he held the door for his companions.

The *farmacia* was bursting with customers, most of them American tourists. They no doubt had heard about the lenient rules in Tijuana. Almost any drug or pharmaceutical could be purchased over the counter in Tijuana, even drugs that required a prescription in the States. Women sought Retin-A, body builders were after steroids, older folks wanted cheap meds, and druggies craved their dope.

The *farmacia* was neat, clean, and very professional looking. Glass shelves were well stocked, and several locked cabinets were visible on the back wall. Behind the first counter stood a smiling man with a big moustache, wearing a white lab coat. He appeared to be about forty years old. Two young, beautiful women in white jackets and short skirts walked around the store, asking if anyone had questions. They spoke in Spanish, but alternated with broken, heavily accented English. Standing guard by the door was a large, muscular man with a perpetual frown.

He looks like he could kick ass and take names, Steve mused. In the back of the store, Steve saw another counter with a door behind it. *Probably the storage room,* he thought.

Steve made his way through the shoppers to the front counter, while Diane asked if anyone had seen Amanda. She held up a picture.

"No, no, *senora*."

"Sorry," said a tourist. "Is she lost?"

Diane nodded, blinking back tears. Steve turned as the smiling pharmacist spoke to him.

"*Hola, senor.* What do you need?" The man's accent was thick but understandable.

"We are looking for our daughter, Amanda. She's been missing for two days. Here's her picture. Do you remember seeing her?" Steve asked as he slipped the man a twenty.

The pharmacist took the money, looked briefly at the photo, and quickly shook his head. Turning, he immediately grinned at the next customer.

Would he admit if he had recognized Amanda? Steve wondered.

On the way out, Steve asked the guard if he'd seen Amanda. The mountain of a man barely glanced at the photo before shaking his head. There was something about the guard that Steve didn't trust.

Once back outside, the three stopped passersby to ask if

they'd seen Amanda. No one had. Steve was getting frustrated. *Where is she? Everyone looks guilty, and no one does. Who can be trusted?*

The trio continued going into area businesses near the border area of Tijuana, asking if anyone had seen Amanda. Steve dropped cash all along the way in his effort to get information. So far, the only thing he'd gotten was poorer.

"We can work better once we have the 'missing person' posters," Mike said.

He was a man of few words, but they were usually spot on. "It'll seem more legit to people who don't know us, and maybe someone will cough up some information."

Diane's hiccups had become pretty steady.

After about two hours, Mike suggested they head back. The private investigator would be waiting to hear from them.

"Diane," said Steve, "things will start rolling once we get the PI on board."

Steve sounded confident, but inside he was sick with thoughts of what could be happening to Amanda. *I hope my imagination is worse than her reality. I pray that.*

The trio walked back to their vehicle, scanning the area as they walked. Mike made mental notes of what he saw.

"Do you think she can see us? Is Mandy wondering if we're going to come for her?" Diane voiced what they all were thinking.

Steve unlocked the doors to his truck. The heat in the truck was overpowering, but no one complained. They climbed inside and drove around the block to get in line for the trek back across the border.

"I guess it's a good thing we didn't wait any longer to leave, because the rush back to the States will be starting soon," noted Steve.

The lines moved along, and after about ten minutes, it was their turn with the border guards. The three showed their driver's licenses and car registration.

"What were you here for?" the customs agent asked.

"Just some shopping," Steve answered. "We were looking for Elvis on velvet."

The guard let them through.

Steve didn't generally like the Mexican border guards, nor did he have any faith in them. He thought they acted like God with guns. He had heard too many rumors about them being on the "take" with drug cartels, and didn't think now was the right time to tell them what they were really doing in Tijuana. He didn't want to take any chances with trusting the wrong people.

"I don't think the guard would've been any help," said Steve, seeing the inquisitive look on Diane's face. "And I didn't want to be held up, having to explain anything. I just want to meet Alberto Reyes and get things rolling."

Once they were on the highway, Steve made the phone call.

Reyes and Steve agreed to meet in a little restaurant in National City. It wouldn't take long to get there, and riding in the air conditioning was a welcome relief. Diane leaned her head against Steve's shoulder and fell asleep. Mike stared out the window.

Ten minutes later, Steve saw the exit and followed the directions Reyes had given him. He found a parking place around the block and took it. As if on cue, Diane's eyes popped open. Mike blinked and slid out of his reverie. They were all anxious to meet Reyes and hear what he had to say.

Mike, Diane, and Steve entered Paco's Eats. Reyes was

waiting for them. Steve picked him out immediately. Though not tall, Reyes was well built and had a steely look. Steve liked him right away. *We need someone who isn't easily intimidated,* Steve thought.

Reyes approached Steve.

"Alberto Reyes," he said, extending his hand. "Call me Bert."

"Good to meet you. I'm Steve; this is my wife, Diane, and my buddy, Mike."

Diane murmured, "Hello."

Mike nodded as he shook Bert's hand.

"Let's sit down and order something to eat," Bert said. "Got to eat when you can. Even though it's not fancy, Paco's has the best Mexican food in National City. Hope you don't mind eating here."

"No, this is fine," Steve said as he looked around. It was a small restaurant with no frills, but Paco's was packed with people, either eating or waiting to eat.

Bert had already lined them up with a table, and they were seated right away. The waitress brought water. Steve and Mike downed their glasses at once. They were parched, and the water was cool and refreshing.

They were ready to order when the waitress returned, bringing chips and salsa. Taco salad for Diane, two beef burritos with refried beans for Mike, and chicken chimichangas for Steve and Bert.

"Kids from the States go missing in Mexico all the time," Bert said. "It's terrible. They usually cross the border for drugs, or sometimes just to party, and disappear after that. The longer they're gone, the harder it is to find them."

He dipped a large chip in hot salsa and put it in his

mouth. "Working with the Mexican *policia* isn't easy. First of all, there are several factions of police, and they don't all work together like law enforcement does here in the States. Some of the *policia* accept bribes, and some are on the payroll of the drug cartels. But there are good officers in Mexico, too. They have it the hardest, trying to work and do the right thing amidst so much corruption. So this won't be easy."

It was well known among those in the U.S. government that bribery ran rampant in Mexico. The conversation had come up many times in police circles when Bert had been with the department. They often discussed how officials of all levels, as well as many in the Mexican military, were in on the take. Sadly, corruption appeared to be commonplace, and honest Mexican officials lived in constant fear for their lives. There was a saying in Mexico, "*plata o plomo*" ("silver or lead"), indicating a choice between accepting a job on the criminal payroll, or taking a bullet to the head. Those words had encouraged many in Mexican law enforcement to make an unlawful decision. Bert thought it wise not to mention all of this to Steve and Diane. They were worried enough.

Steve and Mike looked at each other with sadness after Bert spoke. Diane wiped tears from her eyes with her napkin.

"Have you had any experience looking for Americans who had disappeared across the border?" Steve asked.

"Sure have," Bert answered. "I've probably worked on at least fifteen cases over the past five or six years. Three in the last year alone."

Steve had expected Bert to keep going, but he didn't. Steve was hesitant to ask his next question, but he had to.

"What's the success rate?"

"We've been pretty lucky. We've found ten of the fifteen Americans alive, and brought them back. Another was murdered, although no one was ever charged with the crime. We were able to locate the body and bring it back to the States, though. The victim was a twenty-year-old male who had gone to Tijuana to drink and have fun with his friends. He had gotten into a fight with the wrong guy, from what I heard. His wealthy parents flew in from Virginia to claim the body. It was in the news two years ago. Maybe you saw the story."

"What about the others?" Steve asked.

"Never found them or what happened to them. Three girls and one guy, all young adults. The male was twenty-five. One girl was eighteen, one was twenty-two, and the other was twenty-five, I think. All separate occurrences. We heard on the street that one of the girls was killed by a drug cartel. Don't know about the others. These are only the cases I've been directly involved in. There've been many others."

The waitress brought their food, and they all fell silent as she placed their orders in front of them. Bert took a swig of his ice-cold *cerveza*.

"I've assisted on many missing person cases involving people who've disappeared in Mexico. Unfortunately, more often than not, they don't have happy endings." Bert wiped his mouth. "I just want you to know up front what you're facing. But we'll do the best we can, and not a lot of time has passed, which is in our favor."

Diane looked like the wind had gone out of her sails. Mike sat tight-lipped, and Steve was numb. They realized the odds didn't look good for Amanda.

Rubbing his neck, Steve asked, "What do you recommend we do?"

Bert paused to take a bite. He chewed slowly while mulling over his response, knowing he had to choose his words carefully. Finally, he said, "Let's start with you telling me what you know, from the beginning."

CHAPTER 18
PARTYING IN THE HILLS

D ave felt a twinge of guilt about all the partying he'd done, especially the many times he'd let Amanda and her friends join in.

Shit. Who would've thought Amanda would get so wrapped up in drugs? I sure hope Steve doesn't ever learn about my involvement, Dave thought. *It could ruin a good friendship. Best to keep some things to myself.*

Dave continued cruising down Melrose toward West Hollywood. There was always action in West Hollywood. He pulled into Ago Restaurant and flipped the valet his keys. Strutting in arrogantly, he nodded hello to a man standing by the door. Friendly and fun, the man had appeared on *The Sopranos* TV show, and was often at Ago. Spying a couple of buddies at the bar, Dave sauntered over as he scanned the room.

"What's up?" he asked his friend Brett.

"A kick-ass party later in the Hills. We're going to Forty Deuce first. You down?" Brett was one of the regulars, too.

"Yeah, dude."

After a few drinks and flirting with a couple of bar groupies who were hoping to see celebrities, Dave left. His drinking buddies weren't far behind.

The girls won't be disappointed, Dave thought as he eyed

Bruce Willis entering the restaurant. On his tail were Michael Keaton and a friend. There was always someone famous at Ago.

Forty Deuce was jammed, as usual. Simply making their way to the stage area took some doing. Hot bodies were everywhere, and everyone wanted to be seen. Dave noticed that some patrons appeared spaced out, high on something. *Wild night already,* he thought.

The girls who performed were awesome. They were often foreign, and always very sexy. Forty Deuce was Dave's favorite place.

"It's a bitch working our way over here, but worth it!" shouted Brett over the loud music as they locked into their spots near the stage.

Brett grabbed a waitress and ordered drinks. She laughed as he whispered in her ear.

Something dirty, no doubt. Dave smiled as he watched his friend in action. *Tonight's going to be a good night . . .*

Dave liked Brett for a host of reasons. He had movie star good looks, which always helped with the ladies, and he was one of the few guys in the area who had no aspirations of being a "star." Brett was content with dealing drugs to the stars.

"Easy money, dude," he'd say. "And there's always somebody wanting something. Good job security."

Yeah, if you don't mind worrying about being ratted out and arrested or something, Dave had thought. *Not everyone has the balls to deal. Or is crazy enough to do it.*

Dave sighed. He loved drugs, and he hated them. Loved them while he was using, hated them when he was trying to come down, or trying to score when he needed a buzz, or when he was too fucked up to remember to go to an audition. Dave had lost two agents in the past year by not showing up for a scheduled audition.

Chasing the high can kill you or cause you to lose an acting job, he thought bitterly.

"You're too undependable, Dave," his first agent had said. "Doesn't matter how good you look, or even how good you are. If you don't show up, they're going to quit calling."

"But . . ." Dave wanted to try out his prepared excuse.

"You're just not that big of a star to be pulling any kind of shit," the agent interrupted as he showed Dave the door.

After his second agent stopped returning his calls, Dave vowed he would make it to auditions, no matter what the night before had held. So far, he'd been doing okay with his promise. He hadn't been cast in any big parts lately, but he was able to pay his bills and he had a good shot at a new TV pilot that was in the works. Dave's agent, his third, and, hopefully last, said the casting director had liked Dave's last read. He was scheduled for a call back next Wednesday. *I absolutely can't miss this one,* he thought.

The guys stayed at Forty Deuce for a set. With eyes glued to the stage, they were mesmerized by the undulations of "Miss Dakota." She shimmied, thrust her hips, and rolled around the raised floor to the beat of the music, all the while taking off pieces of clothing. Whipping her head around, her thick brown hair flew past them like strands of silk in the wind.

"I want to touch that hair," Dave said to Brett.

"I want to touch more than that," Brett answered.

The music was sexy and hot, just like the dancer. Miss Dakota's red lipstick made her white teeth shine like polished pearls in the stage lighting. As she ran her hands down her writhing body, the heat in the bar intensified. Miss Dakota had many fans, and they were screaming for more.

"Man, I love this shit!" Brett yelled over the music as he threw back a shot and then downed a beer.

Miss Dakota finished her routine with one leg up against the wall, and her body bent back, eyes looking directly at Dave. Feeling himself fill up, Dave knew it was time to either leave for the party, or just go ahead and pick someone up right then and there.

As the dancer exited the stage to the roar of the crowd, Dave, Brett, and a couple of Brett's friends began making their way back through the bar to the outside. The guys were pretty jazzed and ready for a good Hollywood Hills bash. On their way out, Brett and Dave saw several people they knew and stopped to say a word.

"Party time in the Hills," shouted Brett as they finally went out the door.

Leave it to Brett to ensure a good crowd at a party.

Dave zoomed around the curves and up the hill in his black 645i BMW. Brett and his two friends were in their vehicles, right behind him. Brett's friends, Chuck, a stunt double, and Jake, an MMA (mixed martial arts) champion, were party regulars. Having seen them at several parties before, Dave was continually amazed at how much alcohol and drugs the two guys could consume and still hold onto their jobs.

Big and tough, neither guy liked to be messed with. Chuck, born rich and good-looking, was confident his looks were going to take him from being a stunt double to a star.

"It's just a matter of time," he'd tell whoever would listen. Even though he was vain and not well liked, Chuck was always around, probably because he often footed the drug bill. Dave didn't like Chuck much, because even though the guy was twenty-eight years old, his parents still gave him whatever he wanted.

He wanted a Hummer; he got one—brand new and totally pimped out. Being spoiled only adds to Chuck's overall wonderful personality, Dave thought as he drove.

Jake zipped along behind in his vintage Spider. A couple of his MMA friends were going to be at the party, too. *The more the merrier.* Jake smiled, anticipating a good hook-up.

One of the better known MMA fighters, the German Bulldog, was considered a top contender. "A beast with the best chin," was how he was referred to in the press. A local favorite, Bulldog was well known in Southern California, both for his fighting skills, and because of the threat of his losing everything due to his increasingly heavy drug habit. A good-looking guy in a big, brutish sort of way, Bulldog sported the requisite tattoos on both biceps. One tattoo was a snarling bulldog, the other was stars and lightning bolts. Bulldog said they told his story.

"Everybody's ink tells a story," Bulldog always said when asked. "But mine is special. Want to hear about it?"

Bulldog's given name was Greg. Originally from La Jolla, he was a rich dude with too much money and too much time. Greg would've been great in college football—only problem was, you had to get into college first. Bulldog didn't like school and had barely graduated from his exclusive high school. His parents had bought him a decked-out black Escalade when he turned eighteen and sent him on his way.

Bulldog often went into Mexico to score prescription drugs with a couple of his loadie friends. The trips to Mexico had begun when he wanted to get steroid injections.

"No way you could get this big and strong on your own, unless you had some killer genes, and even then," he'd let on to his buddies.

Sometimes he and his friends would hang out in Mexico

for a couple of days just getting wasted. "It's so easy to party in TJ," Bulldog would boast.

Both Jake and the Bulldog had won a lot of money and titles, but kept pissing the riches away.

Brett drove a Ferrari and wasn't afraid to cut loose. He always had someone with him, usually a hot chick, or maybe two. Tonight was no exception. He'd found two "starlets" at Forty Deuce who were ready and willing.

"Hop in ladies," Brett had said. "Time to roll."

Giggling, the girls had squeezed into the front seat, and off they went.

I have to remember to ask if anyone has seen Amanda, thought Dave as he drove to the party. *Where the hell is that girl? Maybe she'll be at the party. Now that would solve a lot of problems. If I found her, I'd be the hero for a while. And if they've already reported her missing, there could be some good press involved. Yeah, hope she'll be there. For both our sakes.*

Dave gripped the wheel and stared at the road. One by one, the cars screeched around the final curve to the house. A few cars were there already, an X5, a Hummer, a 250Z, a couple of Mercedes, Jags, and a Maserati.

Should be a killer party, Dave thought. He was ready.

CHAPTER 19
THE CLEANUP

A manda woke up and instantly threw up. Able to quickly turn her head to the side, she saved herself from choking on her own vomit. The room was dank with the faint odor of sex. Amanda tried to recall what had happened, but couldn't hear her thoughts over the pounding in her head.

I need help, Amanda felt desperate. *Who can help me?*

Fear wound itself around the captive like a boa, squeezing ever tighter. Tears made tracks down her cheeks. Amanda had no idea where she was, or how long she'd been on the floor. Writhing from pain and need, Amanda eventually returned to a restless sleep full of nightmares. She dreamed about running, being chased, figures lurking behind trees, falling, and seeing someone holding a knife over her. Amanda screamed in her sleep. The sound of her shrieks woke her up. Sobbing, her ribs wracked with pain, Amanda eventually slipped back into sleep from sheer exhaustion.

Evening had settled in when the old jeep pulled up in front of the cabin. The engine's rattle and hiss broke the silence of the desert, jarring Amanda awake. Weak from hunger and thirst, Amanda couldn't be sure if she'd really heard the sound, or if it was just in her head. The head that felt like a sledgehammer was inside, rapidly pounding away.

Paco stepped out of the jeep and looked around. Everything was quiet and undisturbed. *Bueno,* he thought. Silently, Paco strode around the perimeter of the house. He was able to walk on dried cactus and desert plants without making the slightest crunching sound. His *compadres* felt Paco possessed the talent to move around soundlessly because he was descended from the revered K'miai tribe. K'miai, one of the original inhabitants of the area, was part of the larger Yumano tribe. Paco's family had heard stories of their roots passed down for generations. Proud of his heritage, Paco got a modicum of respect for his lineage. It set him apart.

Paco was sure his special talents and loyalty to the Morales family would help him rise to the top of the organization. He had plans. He didn't like the ruthlessness of the Morales family, and knew that when he was *jefe,* he'd be the best ever. Paco planned on incurring the loyalty of everyone by being tough, but fair. He believed it was in his native blood.

But for now, Paco had a job to do. He motioned for Emilio to get out of the jeep and take the hose, broom, and rags with him. Paco walked back to the jeep and reached inside for a bag. Quietly, he walked to the front portico. What was left of Juan's body after the assault rifle had done its job was sprawled out in a bloody mess. Paco took gloves out of his pants pocket and put them on. Even though Paco was not a big man, he was strong and swift. Situating the bag over the blown up body, he skillfully scooped the bloody pieces of corpse into it. He quickly picked up the nearby larger chunks of body parts, adding them to the bag. Paco tied the end and heaved the bulging bag over his shoulder.

Emilio watched wordlessly. He waited for Paco to head back to the jeep with Juan's remains before making a move.

Emilio still couldn't believe Hector had shot Juan. He knew Carlos had ordered the hit, but he thought Juan had been given another chance. Solana's words must've fallen on deaf ears.

Emilio was young and had a lot to learn. The first rule, according to Paco, was to follow orders. Juan had forgotten, and it had cost him his life. Not anxious to meet a similar fate, Emilio did what he was told. At age seventeen, he knew it would be a while before he'd be anything more than a soldier.

Emilio carried the hose to the faucet on the side of the building and screwed it on. He turned on the water and went back to the portico. After hosing down the entire area, Emilio used the broom to force the water and bloody debris off the portico and away from the front of the house. He thoroughly watered down the portico again, wiping away any residue with the rags. When Emilio was certain all traces of the killing were gone, he undid the hose, coiled it up, and took everything back to the jeep.

Paco inspected Emilio's work. The area looked clean, with nary a sign of the recent killing. Paco nodded as he got into the jeep.

"*Muy bien,*" he said as he started the engine.

"*Gracias,*" answered Emilio.

The men drove toward the mountains where Juan's body would be burned, along with the rags and broom. No one would ever admit to knowing about Juan's fate. Emilio had passed his first major test. Paco was proud of his cousin.

CHAPTER 20
BACK TO TIJUANA

B y day six in hell, Steve still hadn't gotten much sleep, but it didn't matter. All he wanted was to get his daughter back home. Diane was struggling, too. The couple tried to stay positive, but fear and dread were knocking on the doors of their minds. The parents forced themselves not to voice the unthinkable.

"I need almost an entire pot of coffee just for myself," Steve said. "I tossed and turned all night. I'll make you a cup of tea."

"I didn't sleep well, either," Diane said. "It's impossible not to think scary thoughts."

"I know." Steve chugged his first cup of coffee, then poured another. "We can pick up the posters on the way to meeting Bert. Once we get those posters plastered all over Tijuana, something will click."

"Is Mike going to go with us?"

"No. He said he was going to stay in San Diego and get some things done." Steve hadn't asked what that meant; he didn't want to know.

Diane and Steve sipped their drinks in silence for a few minutes. They both looked like hell, and with good reason. Steve finally suggested they say a prayer together.

Diane said, "You say it."

Steve closed his eyes and prayed, "Dear Lord, we implore you to help us find our daughter, Amanda. It is only with your guidance that we will find her. Please keep her safe until she is returned to us, her loving parents. This we ask in Jesus's name. Amen."

Diane mumbled, "Amen."

Steve took Diane's hand and looked her in the eyes. "I commit to you that we will not give up. Have faith. We'll find our girl."

Diane nodded, tears in her eyes. Steve's eyes burned, too. It was time to get ready for their second trip to Tijuana. In less than an hour, the couple was climbing in the truck for the trek south.

Steve jumped right back out.

"I'm going to get some bottles of water for the drive. Want anything?"

"No, I'm okay," Diane answered.

The phone rang while Steve was in the house. It was Mike.

"I'll have my cell phone with me all day, Steve, so call it if you need anything. Let me know how it goes with Bert. I'll call if anything comes up you should know."

"Okay. I appreciate everything. You know that, right?"

"You don't need to say anything."

"Thanks, Mike. Talk to you later."

Steve walked back out carrying both the water and a heavy heart. "Let's hit it," he said to Diane.

The truck snaked through the neighborhood, heading south out to the 5 toward National City. Traffic wasn't bad yet, and Steve's mind began to wander. He didn't like where his thoughts were going. Lost in his personal clouds, Steve almost missed the exit. He and Bert had agreed on meeting at the Starbucks on McKinley in National City. Easy off, easy on. As the truck pulled into the parking lot, Bert came out of the coffee shop. Nodding hello, he hopped in the backseat with his large coffee and a bag of muffins.

Taking a sip of coffee, Bert said, "I got you guys something to eat. A blueberry muffin for Diane, banana nut for you, Steve."

He handed Diane the bag and then settled back in his seat.

"Thanks, Bert."

"Yeah, thanks."

"I made a few calls last night to people I know on both sides of the border. Everyone's eyes and ears are open."

"Want to see the posters?" asked Diane. "I brought thumbtacks, tape, everything. We can put them up all over Tijuana." She hiccupped.

Bert took a poster and looked at it closely.

"Amanda's a beautiful girl. Looks like she was having fun here." He caught Steve's eye in the mirror. "The Spanish is well written. These will help a lot."

Steve filled Bert in on the previous conversations with Daniel and some of Amanda's friends. "I didn't go into it last night at Paco's, because there were more important fish to fry then. I figured we'd be together today, too, and would talk more."

Bert agreed that Daniel didn't sound like a likely suspect. It appeared to him that Amanda had been living a double life. And the one with drugs had taken over.

While driving, Steve checked his home phone for

messages. Nothing from Amanda. There were some calls from friends and relatives who were worried and were offering prayers and suggestions. He told Diane about the messages. His work crews left reports about their efforts. No one mentioned the morgue, and Steve hoped it would never come to that.

They sped toward the border.

CHAPTER 21
DEEPER IN HELL

Light was peeking through the filthy window. Amanda realized it must be daytime.

I wonder what time it is. Or what day it is.

She wanted to cough, but her throat was too dry. Amanda vaguely recalled a nightmare she'd had about someone shouting, and a gun blasting. The dream had seemed so real, but nightmares often do, especially drug-induced ones.

In the next instant, Amanda heard a vehicle pull up to the house. She was petrified.

Hector and Omar got out of a pickup truck, walked up to the portico, and inspected the area. No remnants of Juan were visible anywhere.

Hector, satisfied with the cleanup job, said, "Okay. Let's get her."

He kicked the door open to the musty room, where Amanda lay curled up in a fetal position, moaning. She looked thin and frail.

Amanda's ribs hurt, her head hurt, her throat hurt—everything hurt. She was hungry and thirsty.

The men looked at their captive without emotion.

Hector said, "It's time to go."

Omar leaned down and put his arm around Amanda's

waist to help her up. She cried out in pain. He put his other arm under her legs and picked her up.

"I got the bag," said Hector, grabbing her purse.

The men quickly scanned the room, then left. Omar carried the limp, whimpering young woman out to the truck. Hector followed. He tossed her bag in the truck and took a bottle of water out of a cooler.

Hector opened the bottle and held it out to Amanda to drink. "Here, you probably need this."

Amanda's hands were shaking so hard she couldn't bring the bottle to her lips. Hector slowly guided the bottle to her mouth. The first sip went down hard. Then her body screamed out for more. Amanda sloppily drank the rest of the water.

Omar laid Amanda down in the backseat.

"Don't talk or make a sound," he ordered.

Amanda had no strength to move, let alone cry out loud enough for anyone to hear. She was too weak to care who these men were or where she was going.

The new destination can't be worse than the one I'm leaving. Can it?

They drove for about half an hour. The men rarely spoke, but when they did, every word spoken was in Spanish. Amanda didn't understand the men, but it didn't matter. She tried only to withstand the bumps she felt from the road. Lying in pain in the backseat, she didn't know what she needed the most—food, medical assistance, or drugs.

I probably need food the most, Amanda reasoned, *because the odds of seeing a doctor right now are remote, and a person could do drugs until they croaked. Depending on what's waiting for me, maybe the third option would be the best.*

Tears rolled silently down Amanda's cheeks. After a

while, she could see buildings out of the truck's window. They must be in a city now. *Are we in Tijuana?*

After a few turns, Hector stopped the truck, and the men got out. Omar opened the door to the backseat and pulled Amanda out. She was very weak, but with one man holding each arm, she managed to stumble along, her aching ribs screaming with each step. They walked slowly about half a block down an alley, then entered the back door of an apartment.

The flat looked like someone's home. *Who lives here?* Amanda wondered. *Why did they bring me here?*

Omar led a hesitant and wobbly Amanda to a small room with a mattress on the floor. He helped her sit down.

"I'll be back," he said, shutting the door as he left.

Amanda was too afraid, and in too much pain, to move. She sat in a slump and waited. Her side ached terribly, and that was the least of it. Before long, Omar and Hector returned. Omar handed Amanda a banana and a small bag of chips. She stuffed the food into her mouth like a starving animal. Hector gave Amanda another bottle of water, and she immediately gulped down most of the water. He then reached in his pocket and took out four pills.

"Here," he said. "Take these."

Amanda was happy to take the pills, regardless of what they were. She was suffering intense pain in every inch of her body, and drugs could only help. *I would like to pass out and wake up at home,* she thought. *Maybe this whole thing is just a bad dream.*

But as much as she hoped what was happening to her was a bad dream, Amanda knew it was real. She was being held captive.

After Amanda swallowed the pills, Omar produced a

small baggie of pure-grade heroin and a tiny spoon from his pocket. Amanda looked at him quizzically.

"Quality heroin," he announced proudly. Omar slowly dipped the spoon into the fine white powder, making sure none spilled.

Flushed with anticipation, Amanda's eyes were fixed on the spoon. *This is what I really need,* she thought. *It'll help me get by.*

Omar held the spoon up to Amanda's nose. Snorting deeply, Amanda felt the familiar burn, followed immediately by a rush. *Feels so good. Almost heaven.*

Omar held out another spoonful. Amanda quickly inhaled the powder. Moments later, her eyes rolled to the back of her head, and she fell back onto the mattress.

"*La chica es lo nuestro ahora,*" Omar said with a nasty grin.

The men looked at each other and smiled.

"Yes, the girl is ours now," agreed Hector.

Satisfied that *el cautivo bonita* would be "out of it" for a while, the men left. Between the heroin and the pills, the girl would practically be in a coma.

Many hours later, Amanda began stirring. *Did I hear something?* She wasn't sure.

Before Amanda could register a clear thought, the door opened, and Hector walked in. He gave her a quick nod and said, "I have something for you. You seem to like these."

He handed her a few pills and a bottle of water. Without question, Amanda took the tablets and downed the water.

"I'm hungry, and I want to go home," she said weakly. "Please let me go home." Amanda started crying.

Hector didn't respond. After a few seconds, he simply

turned and walked out.

Amanda gingerly lay back down and cried until she drifted into the restless semi-consciousness brought on by drugs. In her fog, Amanda thought she heard the door open again and someone with a firm stride come in. *One of the men from before, maybe?*

Looking up at him through glazed eyes, Amanda couldn't tell for sure who he was. Too drugged to focus or move, Amanda could only wait to see what he wanted.

Without a word, the man unzipped his pants. While staring into her eyes with a menacing look, he reached down and tugged at Amanda's jeans. Horrified, a feeble Amanda tried in vain to fight back, repeating hoarsely through her dry throat, "No, no! Stop!"

No one heard her faint cries of terror. The would-be rapist continued to roughly pull her clothes off. Amanda struggled with all her might, but she was no match for his brute strength. Amanda thrashed about until the combination of fright and the effects of the drugs took over, and she passed out.

Much later, Amanda woke up, crying and shaking. She had had a horrible nightmare, one that seemed very real. Scared, hungry, itchy, and dirty, Amanda's head was pounding and her side ached.

What happened before? Amanda forced herself to think. *I kind of remember a man coming in and . . .*

Amanda then realized she was wearing an old T-shirt and nothing else. She curled up into a ball under the thin blanket that covered her and sobbed.

Time passed. The tortured captive drifted in and out of a painful consciousness. Eventually, Amanda became aware of a stomping sound. The pounding came nearer and nearer. The frightened girl slowly turned her head toward the door as it was kicked open and banged against the wall. Two men stood there, glaring at her.

"*Hoy esta amuermada*," the first one said. (She looks wasted today.)

"*No basta*," the other replied, laughing. (Not enough.)

A woman stepped around them, carrying a plate of beans and a tortilla. She also had a small bottle of soda.

"*Debe tener hambre*," the woman said. (She must be hungry.)

Amanda looked at the food. She was starving, but also weak and scared. Amanda thought of her parents and started crying again. Her crying angered the taller man.

"*Callate!*" he shouted at her. (Shut up.)

The men spoke in rapid-fire Spanish, gesturing wildly as they spoke. Amanda thought they were arguing, but she couldn't be certain. The woman looked at Amanda and shook her head. She said something to the men in a quiet, but stern, voice. The shorter man yelled back at her. All Amanda understood was a name, "Maria." The men looked angry as they stormed out of the room.

The woman named Maria helped Amanda to stand up. Too limp to walk on her own, Amanda leaned heavily on the woman as they went to a bathroom across the hall. The room was filthy and harbored a nasty smell. A grimy, broken mirror hung over the dirty sink. Amanda groggily stared at the mirror and saw a sad, gaunt, almost lifeless young woman with a dirt-streaked face, and greasy, stringy hair.

With a gasp, Amanda realized it was her own reflection.

Maria turned Amanda away from the mirror and gently helped her sit down on the toilet.

It's hard to pee with someone watching, thought Amanda, but she was too weak to protest the lack of privacy. *Why does it hurt so much?*

Amanda struggled to remember what had happened to her. All the drugs she had ingested made thinking difficult. When she wiped herself, Amanda saw blood. She knew then the nightmare had been real. Amanda wanted to scream, cry, throw up. Leaning her head against the wall, she felt the life going out of her. Amanda wanted to give up. Then she saw her family in her mind's eye.

This can't be how I'm supposed to die, Amanda thought, choking back sobs. *Not here, not like this. I will survive. God help me, I will survive.*

Slowly, she pulled herself up to the sink. Maria held her in place while Amanda washed her face and hands. Then Maria gave Amanda a small, rough cloth to dry herself. When she was finished, Maria tenderly guided Amanda back to the room.

This is my prison, thought Amanda. She whimpered as she sat back down on the blanket. *What are they going to do with me?*

Maria spoke to Amanda softly in Spanish, but Amanda couldn't understand. Slightly comforted by the gentleness of the woman's tone, however, Amanda looked directly into her eyes and saw a hint of compassion.

"Chica," Maria said to Amanda. *"Por favor,* eat."

Amanda ate the beans and tortilla. She tried to remember when she had last eaten anything, and what it was.

A banana, maybe? Some chips? When was that? Was it here?

Amanda's head was throbbing, and there was too much confusion swirling around inside to think clearly. After indicating she was thirsty, Maria gave her a Pepsi. The drink was warm, but Amanda was oblivious. She drank it all.

Maria knew why Amanda was there. *She's like all the others.* But something about this young woman touched Maria. She felt sympathy for the wounded, pretty girl. Maybe it was because this dark haired beauty reminded Maria of her sister, Bettina. Bettina didn't have to live like she did. Or die like she did, either.

Maria bit her lip to keep from crying at the memory of her sister. She decided to help this newest victim as much as possible. First, the poor girl needed something to wear. Maria sighed. She wondered if this girl remembered why her clothes were gone. *Better if she doesn't,* she decided.

Maria left the room but returned soon after with some faded blue jeans and a thin, long-sleeved shirt. It was apparent Amanda had been crying again, but Maria pretended not to notice.

"Chica, por favor, it's okay. Here."

Maria laid the clothing she had brought on the bed next to Amanda, and motioned for her to put it on.

Amanda was grateful for the tenderness of the woman. She wondered briefly what had happened to her own clothes, but continued sobbing at the memory of the man yanking them off as she'd struggled.

The woman gently helped Amanda get dressed. After a few minutes, Amanda's sobs turned to whimpers. She looked up at the woman. Fairly certain she had heard the men call the woman by name, she said, *"Gracias,* Maria."

Maria flinched, then nodded. *"Como se llama?"* she asked Amanda.

Even though Amanda had lived near the Mexican border all of her life and had gone to Mexico many times, she couldn't speak Spanish and didn't know much more than hello, thank you, and good-bye in the language. She guessed, however, that the woman was asking her name, so she responded, "Amanda."

They both knew the special moment was over when they heard footsteps approaching the room. The door flew open, and the taller man entered. He looked at the two women suspiciously, then barked, "Maria! *Tengo hambre.*" (I'm hungry.)

"Si, Enrique," Maria responded as she quickly got up and left the room.

Enrique looked hard at Amanda. He spoke to her in heavily accented, but quite passable, English.

"You are with us now. No one knows where you are, and no one cares."

At that, Amanda burst into tears again. Too frightened to respond, she thought, *I know my parents care! But will they be able to find me?* She wrapped her arms around herself and rocked back and forth.

"Don't worry," Enrique continued, stopping her motion with his hand and turning her face up. He stared at Amanda with a look that shot fear to her soul. "We'll take care of you. You just have to do your job, and everything will be okay," he sneered, letting her face drop.

Straightening up, Enrique turned his head toward the door and shouted, "Maria! Bring the pills."

Maria returned with a plate of food for Enrique and the pills he ordered for Amanda. Glaring at Maria, he took the pills, turned, and held out his hand to Amanda.

She had no idea what the pills they kept giving her were, but maybe they would make the pain and throbbing stop.

What difference does it make what they are anyway?

Amanda swallowed the pills with the glass of water

Maria handed her. A panicky feeling had been eating at Amanda, making her stomach burn like hot coals were inside. She had a nagging fear that no one would ever find her. Even she didn't even know where she was.

Amanda lay back down on the mattress, her body heaving with sobs. Enrique's eyes steadily bored into her, filling Amanda with dread. Finally, he left, taking Maria with him.

Soon, Amanda's body felt light, as if she was floating. The mattress was suddenly soft and very comfortable. She tried to think, but couldn't get control of her head. It felt like a hurricane was whipping around in her brain. Storm clouds reigned. Then she was out.

Later, when she awoke, Amanda felt nothing but confusion.

How long have I been out this time? Too scared to move, she tried to go over everything in her mind. So many blanks. *What is going to happen to me?*

Amanda tried making sense of something that didn't make any sense at all.

CHAPTER 22
DRUGS RULE

The party in the Hills was good, if you like drugs and sex. Who doesn't, right? That's supposed to be a joke. A joke on me, I guess. When am I going to learn which head to think with?

Dave usually enjoyed ruminating about a big bash; that is, if he could recall it. The last thing Dave clearly remembered about this party was putting the rolled up C-note in his nose and inhaling.

It was killer, too, he thought. *So was she. Red hair and red hot. Music blaring, bodies and mind-altering substances everywhere. Fuckin' great!*

Red Bull and vodka had been the night's drink of choice, at least at first. At some point, when it was time for most of the partiers to crash, the drugs and drink morphed into something like China white (a very pure form of heroin), marijuana, and beer.

"Just a little bit more," or "One more hit," were the words heard most of the night.

Dave pulled himself up from the sofa. He wondered for a minute whose house he was in, and how he got there. He closed his eyes and took a deep breath. Picturing the tantalizing redhead, Dave realized she was probably gone by now.

That's okay, he thought, *I don't have time for the morning after the night before with some chick I don't know.*

Dave's BlackBerry was still in his jeans pocket.

That's a miracle, he thought. Powering it on, he was immediately alerted to messages of all types. *Wonder what's cookin'. . .*

Glancing up, Dave saw a couple still locked in some kind of sexual embrace on an oversized chair in the corner. They felt his gaze and returned it. The guy said, "Dude," then went back to the brunette.

Dave recognized the house as one he had partied in before. He wasn't sure whose place it was, though. Dave shrugged. *Doesn't matter.* There had been lots of people and lots of drugs and lots of sex. *Helluva party, even if I can't exactly remember what happened or how I ended up alone.*

Dave stretched and scratched his stomach. His throat felt like the Sahara, so he ambled toward the kitchen for something to drink.

Amanda hadn't been at the party. Or at least, Dave hadn't seen her. He had glanced around for her when he first arrived, but once the drinking and drugs started, all he had thought about was himself. And the redhead.

I'm like every other self-absorbed druggie. I need to stop this shit. Dave sighed.

He still held out hope he'd be the one to locate Amanda.

If I'm the one who finds Amanda, it'd be super for her, super for the family, and totally awesome for me, he thought.

Dave didn't appreciate how his thoughts only added greater meaning to the term self-absorbed.

CHAPTER 23
FRUSTRATION IN TIJUANA

S teve, Diane, and Alberto Reyes arrived at the Mexican border around noon. Since Alberto had been a California highway patrol officer for several years, he was still allowed to use his credentials to get into the government lot. The lot was adjacent to the border on the American side. It was very convenient.

Steve took the last exit ramp off Highway 5 and turned into the government parking lot. They were let in with no problem when Alberto showed the guard his badge. Steve quickly found a spot to park, and they disembarked. Diane took a stack of posters, giving some to Steve and Bert. She put tape and tacks in her backpack, placed her wide-brimmed hat squarely on her head, and took a deep breath.

"Let's go."

The three walked through the parking lot and out the gate. They joined the line of people going into Mexico on foot.

"I feel like I'm part of a giant centipede," said Steve.

They arrived at the turnstile separating Mexico and the United States in no time. Once in Tijuana, the trio went to work immediately.

Diane taped the first poster to a sign post. Steve said a silent prayer as he put one up on a pole near the Dairy Queen. Bert spoke in Spanish to the natives, asking if anyone had seen the girl pictured on the poster. A few people walking by looked at the three as they tacked up the posters on every available pole they could find, but most paid no attention to them. It was hot and dusty, and everyone had their own agenda.

After about an hour of talking to people, going into businesses, and putting up posters, Bert suggested it was time to go to the authorities. "I have to remind you about the Mexican *policia*. The department here doesn't operate like the one in the States. You may get frustrated."

"We'll deal with it," said Steve. "Have to."

They began with the American Consulate, which was about six blocks from where they were. After walking the distance, they discovered the consulate office was closed for the day.

"The frustration begins," lamented Steve.

The trio took a cab to the nearest police station. After waiting in a long line to sign in, they had to wait in another long line before their number was called to be helped.

Diane looked as tired as she felt. She sighed heavily, "This is exasperating. And it's so hot in here."

She looked around at the people sitting in chairs and waiting. Sweaty and cranky toward each other, they looked like they'd been there for hours.

"I need to go to the ladies room. I'll be right back," she said.

Diane went to the door marked "*Mujer*" in the back of the room. Steve watched to make sure no one followed her in, or even looked at her funny. He didn't trust anyone or anything in Tijuana.

Several minutes later, Diane came out and sat down next to Steve. He thought his wife looked like she'd been crying.

Steve put his arm around Diane's shoulder. She leaned against him for a minute; then said, "It's too hot," and pulled away.

They had nothing to do but sit and wait. Twenty minutes later, it was finally their turn, and an officer called them up to the desk.

Bert did most of the talking. When Steve tried to add his two cents, the officer ignored him. Steve could feel his blood pressure rising. The man behind the desk was perspiring and looked irritated.

After a few more words in Spanish with the officer, Bert said, "Come on. They won't be of any help to us here."

The officer had suggested going to the *oficina de policia* about two blocks away and inquiring there.

Tired, hot, and exasperated, Steve said, "I don't get it. Why is he sending us to a different police station? Couldn't the officer here call over there? Can't they understand our daughter is missing and every minute counts?"

Steve was ranting and he knew it. He didn't care. He turned and smacked the wall with his hand, wishing it'd been someone's face instead.

"I warned you that the process here would be frustrating," said Bert. "We just have to work through it."

On the way to the other station, Steve and Diane held up posters for passersby to look at. They asked if anyone had seen "*este chica.*" No one had. Some people wouldn't even take the time to look at the poster.

Diane cried softly. Steve listened for the familiar sound of hiccups he knew would soon follow. Meanwhile, tension bubbled up inside him like hot magma. He felt like a volcano about to erupt.

CHAPTER 24
AMANDA'S UNCLE CRAIG

Everyone thought Diane's brother, Craig, had it made. He looked good, didn't have any trouble with the ladies, and his wallet wasn't empty. Owning a popular restaurant and bar didn't hurt, either. Photos of celebrities coming and going from his establishment were always in the newspapers and magazines, which ensured good business. Patrons enjoyed rubbing elbows with the rich and famous. Craig had learned a lot of secrets about show business and the stars over the past six years, but he knew how to keep his mouth shut.

Plenty of straight-acting people came into the bar to have fun. Thursday night usually brought in the closet gays, mostly actors, agents, and others in the business who worried their careers would be ruined if their "secret" got out. Even though many gays in Hollywood had long ago come out, there were still plenty of denials. Some in the party crowd were switch hitters. It was often hard to tell if a person was truly bisexual or just liked whatever he/she could get that night. Craig had "covered" for people too many times to count, but now he could count on their business. One hand washed the other.

I've been lucky this been a hot spot for so long, Craig mused. *If the walls could talk, we'd all be in trouble.*

Sometimes the flame of popularity flickered out fast.

But like a great kiss, a trendy restaurant and bar was all about location. The eatery was only half a block away from the beach, and it had a very private VIP room. Those two things helped to keep the Windjammer in high demand.

Unfortunately, Craig was never sure if a hot chick was eager to be with him for his looks, his money, because he was the owner of a popular business, or for himself as a person. His ego told him, "It's you, man," but inside he knew better. Still, Craig had women, plenty of money, and access to all kinds of party material.

I can have a different chick every night if I want, sometimes more than one. Hef has nothing on me. Sex, drugs, and rock 'n' roll.

Craig had moments when he thought about finding "the one," the special lady who'd be there with him through thick and thin. But how could he expect a woman to be true, when he knew he couldn't be?

It's definitely not my fault that I have the morals of an alley cat, he thought. *Dad was a drunk and had women all over the place. Mom finally started drinking, too. She eventually had a couple of "friends" who would come over to "fix stuff." We kids knew what needed fixing.*

Their parents finally divorced when Craig and Dave were nine and ten. Diane, fourteen at the time, was crushed, as she had been her daddy's favorite. Not that being his princess meant much. The best thing was it had spared Diane the rod. But after the old man left, she got it, too.

Two years of miserable "family" life later, their mother, Daisy, married a burly-looking construction worker named Pete. He let Craig and Dave do whatever they wanted, which included getting into minor trouble along the way. The brothers' lack of responsibility had clearly begun in their early years. Pete had a wandering eye, too. The eye seemed to stop on Diane at times, but Craig didn't know if anything had ever happened. Daisy also noticed how Pete looked around, but she just looked the other way.

We had such a miserable home life. I figure our horrible upbringing explains why we're all fucked up in our own way, Craig rationalized.

Both Craig and Dave were happy when Diane and Steve got together. They wanted someone who would take care of their sister. Steve was good for Diane in a lot of ways, and he seemed to love her a lot. When Amanda was born, the couple appeared thrilled and started spoiling her right away. Diane wasn't a strict mother. The brothers thought that maybe Diane was trying to make up for the tight leash she'd been kept on as a child.

Craig had watched Amanda go from a young student singer to total wild child. She got in with a fast crowd at an early age. Amanda liked drugs and never lacked for male company.

Pure party girl, Craig thought. *Amanda and her girlfriends were gorgeous too. Sometimes it seemed like they just didn't care about anything. Maybe they didn't.*

In the beginning, Craig had tried to rein Amanda in when she and her friends would come into the bar, but Amanda was headstrong and could create a fuss. Craig didn't need the hassle, plus Amanda was fun and witty, and he liked being in on the party.

Craig's guilty conscience is what kept him from getting too close to Steve. Craig didn't want to have to look Steve in the eye and "fess up" about Amanda's activities—and his own part in them. So he stayed out of Steve's way as much as he could.

Hope nothing's happened to her. Amanda's not a bad kid, and she is my niece. I guess I could ask around some. Steve acted pretty worried this time.

Craig decided to do a little digging.

CHAPTER 25
A LEAD

The *oficina de policia* wasn't a very welcoming place. Two uniformed officers stood near the doorway and watched, stone-faced, as Steve, Diane, and Bert passed them on the way in. Bert gave a greeting in Spanish. One of the officers nodded. Looking around, they saw that at the end of a short hall was an office. Bert held up his hands to stop the other two, and went on to the office alone. Diane and Steve waited in the hall outside the door, nervously pacing. After a few minutes, Bert came out and shook his head.

"What happened?" Steve asked anxiously. He couldn't help but see the unhappy look on Bert's face.

Bert muttered, "Things don't work the way you want them to here."

Diane tried not to cry. "I'm so discouraged. What do they expect us to do?"

"The *policia* suggested we go to as many *oficinas de policia* as possible, because each one is run individually," said Bert.

"How the hell do they operate like that?" Steve asked dejectedly.

Bert shrugged. "It's just the way they do things here."

Bert had suspected this would happen, but knew that

Steve and Diane needed to experience for themselves how the police department was run in Mexico. Still, someone might know something they didn't know they knew, and Bert was always trying to make more connections within the department, too.

"Did you offer them cash?" Steve asked Bert.

"No. It's not that easy," he answered. "You can't just walk into a police station and offer cash. Those kinds of things are done on the side."

Diane stifled a yawn, which prompted Steve to check the time.

"It's getting late," he said. "Time to head back to the border and get the truck."

"Maybe we should take opposite sides of the street tomorrow when we tack up the posters," Diane offered as they walked. "Seems like we could cover more ground much faster that way."

Bert frowned. "I don't like the idea of the three of us splitting up, even if we're only on opposite sides of the street. We could get separated, and it isn't safe. We haven't even scratched the surface of crime here in Tijuana."

"But . . ." Diane tried to interrupt.

"And you, especially, Diane," Bert continued, "need to be with someone at all times. It's not worth the risk. Last thing we need is to have something happen to you, too."

Bert spoke matter-of-factly, but his words landed with a thud. Diane's face looked like chalk. Steve took her hand. Though he felt drained from the stress, heat, and frightening thoughts, Steve put up a strong front for Diane.

"Bert's right. We'll still be effective putting up the posters tomorrow, working as a team," Steve said.

It took thirty minutes to make their way back to the

border, and once there, they had to wait in line in the hot sun with the throngs of people anxious to cross into the United States. All types of people were in line—tourists, college kids, various stoners, and a lot of Mexicans. Babies cried, parents were frazzled, and there was nowhere for anyone to sit down. But everyone had one thing in common—they all looked at each other with mistrust.

"Sit tight while I go speak with someone," Bert said.

He went up to a guard, spoke in Spanish, and flashed his badge. Those in line eyed the couple with a mixture of envy and suspicion.

Steve didn't make eye contact with anyone. He noticed Diane was too tired to focus on anything. She had a vacant look in her eyes, one that saddened her worried husband. Frustrated with the turn of events, Steve rolled his head, cracking his neck.

I should be able to take care of my family, my wife, my daughter. I don't even know where the hell Amanda is, and Diane is close to losing it. I am, too, if truth be told.

Steve gulped several deep breaths. *I have to hold it together,* he told himself. He flicked drops of sweat from the end of his nose, knowing the sweat wasn't just from the blistering heat of Tijuana.

A guard motioned them over to the far left side and through a turnstile that had been roped off.

Alright, thought Steve, *saved us all from burning up.*

"Thanks for getting us through like that," he whispered to Bert.

"My pleasure," Bert answered.

They made their way to the parking lot where the truck, now covered with a thick layer of dust, awaited them. The hot air inside the truck was stale and unmoving.

"I feel like I'm climbing into an oven," Steve said as he lowered himself onto the front seat. "Still feels good to sit down, though."

"I'm so thirsty," whispered Diane.

The bottles of water they'd left on the floor of the truck were now too hot to drink. They'd have to wait to relieve their parched throats. Steve started up the truck and pulled out of the lot.

"People will see Amanda's face on those posters," Steve said confidently, "and someone in Tijuana will recognize her. I know it. Tomorrow's another day."

Steve's cell phone rang as he turned onto the highway toward National City. "Hello," he said, gunning it.

"This is Bill Mulvey, auto insurance agent from State Farm Auto Insurance. Is this Steve Tate?"

"Yes." Steve's heart was pounding.

"We received a call from the Mexican authorities in Tijuana," Mulvey said, "telling us a vehicle registered in your name has been found. A 2003 Ford Mustang."

Steve almost drove off the freeway.

"That's my car! Where'd they find it? What condition is it in?"

Steve's passengers were instantly alert.

"The car had been stripped. Not much left," Mulvey answered. "It was found on a side road by a police officer who called it in."

Where is the car now?" Steve motioned to Diane to get ready to write down some information. His body prickled with electricity at the thought of retrieving the car.

"The vehicle's been towed to an impound lot on the west side of Tijuana, where it's being held for you. As I understand it, you have to go to the police station at Eighth and Constitution to pay the towing fine first. They'll give you a receipt to take to the impound lot. Make sure you have valid ID when you get to the police station," Mulvey instructed.

"I will."

"We're taught to remind our clients in these types of situations that Mexico isn't the United States. You'll have a harder time getting answers there. And be careful when you get to the lot. The guys who run those impound lots are not easy to deal with. They don't care about your problems. They don't care where the vehicles came from or how they happened to be brought to their lot. They just want money. We've seen this before."

As Mulvey dispensed instructions, Steve repeated them to Diane so she could take notes. He glanced over at her and she nodded.

"Okay, we got it," Steve said. "Do you know when the car was brought to the lot?"

"I'm not exactly sure. The Mexicans don't give up information very readily. You'll likely learn more when you go get the car," the agent said.

"Okay, thank you." Steve set the phone down. "Holy shit!"

Diane started hiccupping and sniffling. Steve reached over and squeezed her hand. She squeezed back. It was the first nice moment they'd had in a long time.

"A lead!" Steve shouted. A jolt of what felt like hope ran through his body. "I'd like to turn around right now!"

Bert placed his hand on Steve's shoulder. "It's best we go home, get some rest, and plan on tomorrow being an intense day."

"I guess you're right," said Steve. "Remind me to get more cash to take with us tomorrow, Diane. I've doled out all I brought, trying to get answers today. We didn't get much information for the money, but it's still flowing through my fingers like water. But the phone call from State Farm sure was something."

"I look at this as a solid break," said Bert. "I'll talk to some of my contacts inside Mexico. We might get more information once we ID the car."

Maybe tomorrow will be the day we find Amanda! Steve was pumped.

After they dropped Bert off and agreed to the modus operandi for the next day, Steve and Diane rode in silence for a few miles.

Finally, Steve said, "I'm looking forward to having Pam come." He stole a quick peek at Diane, who looked like a whipped puppy. His heart ached. Diane said nothing. "It's good news about the car being found," Steve said, trying to engage her in conversation.

Something in Diane had changed. She looked at Steve like he was from another planet. "I suppose you think hearing that Amanda's car was stripped and towed is good news. But what good does it do us? Finding a shell of a car doesn't tell us where Mandy is, or what's happened to her. Why did we leave her alone in the house that night?"

Diane gave Steve an accusing look. This time, he was quiet—he couldn't argue with the truth.

They passed a Subway and stopped for a quick bite to eat. After they finished, the distraught couple rode the remainder of the way home in silence. As soon as Steve pulled into the driveway and cut off the truck, he felt completely drained. Even getting out of the truck was an effort. Steve forced himself to walk to the other side and help Diane, but once her feet hit the ground, she pushed him away.

"I'm tired and scared," Diane said.

"I know," Steve responded.

They went into the house and got ready for bed. Steve stood in the shower for a good ten minutes, trying to wash away his worries along with the dirt. The dirt went down the drain, but the worry piled up in his head like mounds of snow after a blizzard.

As he got into bed, the realization that Amanda was in Mexico with no car and no phone suddenly hit Steve like a punch in the gut, literally taking his breath away.

Mandy couldn't leave, or even call, if she wanted to, he thought dismally.

Steve put his head on the pillow and squeezed the water from his eyes. The tears rolled down his cheeks. His mind was tormented.

Dear God, Steve prayed in the dark, *please help us find Amanda before something terrible happens to her.*

It looked to be another long, sleepless night.

CHAPTER 26
GETTING PREPPED FOR THE JOB

Maria slipped into Amanda's room and watched her sleep. *The beautiful girl doesn't know,* Maria thought. *Today is the day.* She leaned over Amanda and whispered, "Chica . . . chica."

Amanda slowly opened her eyes and tried to focus. Seeing Maria, Amanda wanted to say something, but her throat was too dry. It hurt to swallow, and her head was throbbing. Every part of her body hurt. Before Amanda was able to respond to Maria, the door banged open, and two men strode purposefully in.

"Today you do something for us," Enrique barked at her. "We want you to drive a van. You can do that, no?"

He stared down at Amanda, who was too afraid to move. Enrique then nodded to his companion and said something in Spanish. Then he turned to Maria.

"It's time. Get the girl cleaned up and ready to go," he ordered Maria. He and the other man quickly left the room.

What does he mean, I will do something for them? And can I drive a van? Amanda had no one to ask.

Maria went into the bathroom to get a glass of water for Amanda, who gratefully drank it all. Maria then motioned for Amanda to follow her. Too unsteady to get up by herself, she was pulled up by Maria. Together, they walked gingerly to the bathroom. Every step was painful for Amanda. She carefully sat down on the toilet and started to pee. It burned like fire, and then she remembered her real nightmare. Amanda looked up at Maria and saw the truth in her eyes. Tears welled up and spilled down Amanda's thin face.

Be here with me, Lord, she prayed. *I need you.*

Amanda pulled herself up to the sink. Maria helped Amanda wash her hands with the cold water and dry them with the rough cloth.

While Amanda leaned against the sink, Maria took two yellow tablets out of her pocket.

"*Debe tomas estas pildoras,*" she said, putting the pills in Amanda's hand and then giving her a glass of water.

These look different than the ones she gave me earlier, Amanda thought. *But what does it matter?* Silently, Amanda took the pills.

Maria brought Amanda back to the "bed" and left the room, returning shortly with a plate of beans and cheese, a few tortillas, and a Coke.

Famished, Amanda immediately devoured the food. When she was finished, Amanda unabashedly licked the plate. Maria took the dish away. A few minutes later, she returned with a towel and some clothes. As Maria motioned for Amanda to follow, a little boy stuck his head in the door. He looked to be about six.

Smiling, he asked in Spanish, "Who is she? She is very pretty."

"Go!" Maria scolded. "I will see you later."

The boy remained at the door for a minute, but the stern look he got from Maria made him turn around and leave.

Amanda was stunned to see the little boy. He seemed so out of place with what had been happening to her. She wondered who actually lived in this place, and how they were linked. Trying to wade through various scenarios, Amanda was unable to connect the dots. She let her mind wander over to her family. What were her parents thinking? Did they realize she couldn't contact them? What was Daniel thinking?

He probably doesn't even care I'm gone, the bastard, Amanda thought. She felt sick inside. *What is going to happen to me?* Amanda clutched her stomach as a rack of spasms rolled through.

After a moment, Maria again signaled for Amanda to follow her and began helping her get up. The motion brought the captive back to the present. As she stood up, Amanda noticed that she felt surprisingly stronger. Together, they walked down the hall to another bathroom.

This *cuarto de bano* was slightly larger than the other and contained a shower. Maria gestured for Amanda to go in, handing her the towel and clothing. Amanda narrowed her eyes at Maria, who only turned and left the room. While she was excited at the thought of finally getting to take a shower, Amanda was cautious as to why they were letting her get cleaned up.

What did he mean by asking if I could drive a van? It doesn't make sense.

As Amanda undressed, she saw blood on her legs. Another reminder of the violation in the night. A cry stuck in Amanda's throat. She turned the water on and climbed in. The shower felt like the best she had ever taken. It didn't matter that the water wasn't very hot, or that the pressure was barely more than a sprinkle. She gratefully let the light spray wet her body and run down her skin. Amanda wanted to wash away the filth, pain, and humiliation she had suffered over the past few days. A small bottle with *"champu"* written on it was leaning against the wall in the corner of the shower. Taking it, Amanda poured the liquid into her hand. She washed her hair and body. Amanda reached down to wash her between her legs, wincing at how raw and tender she was. The lather burned, and she bit her lip. Gently, Amanda cleaned every part of her body. As she rinsed the suds off, she put herself in a mindset of self-preservation.

I will do what I have to do to get out of here alive.

Amanda turned off the water and stepped out of the shower with new determination.

I can't believe how awake I am. Has to be those pills. Amphetamines, probably. Feels great.

Amanda dried off and gingerly put the clothing on. Her ribs hurt, but being clean felt so good. She towel dried her long hair and ran her fingers through it.

Not like home, but better than nothing.

Leaning over, Amanda shook her head and felt her long hair whip about. When she stood up, her head spun, and everything went black for a few seconds. Amanda had to grab on to the sink to keep from falling over.

"Whew. I need to take it easy, or I could hurt myself," Amanda spoke aloud. She immediately recognized how crazy her words were.

After what I've been through, hurting myself probably shouldn't be my biggest concern.

Amanda realized she had to take things easy. Her body had been through a lot. She was suffering mentally as well as physically. Taking a deep breath, Amanda opened the bathroom door and walked out to the new fate that awaited her.

CHAPTER 27
PAM HEADS WEST

P am had gotten up earlier than usual. The combination of excitement and nerves regarding her trip to San Diego had made for a restless night. She jumped into the shower. The hot water raining down on her body had a calming effect. She blew-dry her hair and applied makeup, all the while wondering what was going on out west. Dressing quickly, Pam gathered her purse, carry-on, and suitcase and deposited them by the front door.

Maybe there'll be good news when I arrive, she thought.

Pam went into the kitchen and got the coffee pot going. She put two whole wheat English muffins in the toaster for a quick breakfast as Benny walked in and sat down to join her.

"Call me when you land in San Diego," he said. "Don't get talked into doing anything crazy when you're out there."

Pam nodded as she put peanut butter and jelly on the toasted muffins.

"Bert told me the situation isn't good, but he's remaining positive."

"I'm going out there to help my brother," Pam reminded him. "I'll be careful and not take any chances, though." Pam meant what she said, but knew in her heart she'd do whatever was asked. "I don't know how Steve and Diane can take it. I'd be losing my mind if I was in their situation. It's just unbeliev-able."

"The circumstances might be horrible, but, like Steve and Diane, you'd do whatever it took to find your child. There's no point in going crazy. Now's the time for clear thinking and utilizing all the resources available."

Benny's ability to stay calm and think through a situation was one of the many things Pam loved about him. He was the one she wanted around in a crisis.

"I packed last night, so I'm ready to go," Pam said. "Just say a prayer we find Amanda. And soon. We need a good ending to this mess."

"I will do that. Keep me posted. Love you." He kissed Pam good-bye as he left for work. Benny didn't have a good feeling about the situation.

* * *

Steve was pouring coffee and brewing tea when Diane came into the kitchen.

"It wasn't necessary for you to sleep on the sofa."

"Didn't want to bother you, Diane. Seemed like you didn't care anyway."

"I don't care about anything right now, except for find-ing Amanda." Diane poured a cup of tea and sat down. "What time does your sister get in?"

"Just before ten, I think. I have to check for the exact time, but my plan is to pick up Pam, get Bert, and drive on to Mexico. I talked to Mike, and he's going to go with us tomor-row, if we still need him. I'm hoping for a break of some kind today."

The phone rang as Steve was double-checking Pam's arrival time. It was Geraldo.

"Hey, boss. Just want you to know I made some calls yesterday but found out nothing. In some ways that's good, considering the places I called."

Steve winced. "Thanks, *amigo*."

"Anything special you want me to do today?"

"It'd be helpful if you continued running the crews. I'll be out of touch for a while, you know. But you can always call my cell phone. Leave a message if I don't answer. I'll check my voice mail periodically. Tell the guys I appreciate the good job they're doing."

"Okay, Steve. We'll be praying, too."

"Thanks."

Steve took a big swig of coffee. He felt the hot brew slide through his body.

"Baby, we have to be strong and positive. There are people helping us. The *policia* found the car. I think we'll get somewhere today."

Hoping to lift Diane's mood, Steve leaned over and hugged her shoulders. Diane shrugged off his embrace.

"I'm numb. You have to understand that. I feel like I'm living a nightmare."

She went over to the counter and cut a piece of coffee-cake. Obviously distraught, she put the cake down after taking only a bite and went to shower.

Steve put his head in his hands. *I'm living a nightmare, too.*

CHAPTER 28
AMANDA'S ASSIGNMENT

E nrique was leaning against the wall outside the bathroom when Amanda walked out. He straightened when he saw her. "*Venga*. Come on. We have work to do."

The strong Mexican took Amanda's arm and held it tightly as they walked down the hallway. Immediately, her nerves were on edge. The young boy Amanda had seen earlier skipped down the hall past them. He was singing a song in Spanish. The scenario seemed so out of place to Amanda, given her situation.

I wonder if the woman, Maria, is the boy's mother, Amanda thought. *And who's the father?*

Amanda remembered the sympathetic look she'd seen in Maria's eye and was hoping that maybe Maria would be able to help her. When the time was right, she was going to try and communicate with Maria.

"*Hasta luego*," the boy said as he darted by again. Enrique's lips parted in a slight smile.

Something about the way Enrique moved reminded Amanda of what had happened to her in the night. She cringed. *Is this the man who raped me?* Her body stiffened under his grasp, and Amanda was able to keep her composure only because she was cranked up on amphetamines.

They entered the kitchen, and Enrique pushed Amanda toward a chair. Two men were sitting at the table with Maria. One was Mexican; the other looked American. Enrique stood in the doorway. Maria got up to get Amanda a Coke and motioned for her to sit. Amanda saw her purse on the table, but didn't say anything.

The American spoke first. "Here's the plan. Do it right, and nothing happens. Fuck it up in some way, any way, and you won't make it back home. Your parents won't miss you, though, because they'll have had an unfortunate accident. You get what I'm saying?"

The cold shock of the man's blunt words almost knocked Amanda off the chair. Her heart raced so fast she thought she might have a heart attack.

Maria returned and set the drink down in front of a stunned Amanda. The captive's hands shook as she picked up the Coke to take a sip.

"We've made copies of your driver's license and credit cards," the man continued. "We know where you live and who your parents are. You could never run far enough from us," he added, driving the point home.

"What . . . am I supposed to do?" Amanda's voice was a whisper.

"It's simple," interjected Enrique. He moved close and leaned on the table, facing Amanda. "You drive a van across the border, then you come back. Easy, no?"

"I don't understand."

"Explain it to the bitch, Travis."

"Look. Drive to the border; show the guards your driver's license. Say you were in Tijuana to buy souvenirs, if they ask. Flash your smile. Do nothing to suggest anything's out of the ordinary. Drive on into the U.S. Understand?"

The American named Travis didn't smile. He was youngish, probably early thirties, and muscular. His cold demeanor and strong build made it apparent the man wasn't afraid of a fight, and could definitely kick ass.

Amanda was frozen with fear.

"You've come over here a hundred fucking times, so this should be easy as shit for you. You don't want anything to happen to you or your family, do you?" Travis asked menacingly. His face hard and emotionless, Travis looked every bit the cold-blooded person he was.

All eyes were on Amanda as she processed what Travis had said.

She knew then her life was in danger, and not only hers. Amanda realized she was trapped, hostage to their demands. She hung her head and tried to think, but her brain wouldn't cooperate. The drugs, and lack of real sleep and food, were taking their toll. She took another sip of her warm, flat soda.

"Who'll be in the vehicle with me?" Amanda finally asked.

Enrique laughed wickedly. "Mary Jane and the lady. Tell her, Travis."

The burly American put his hand on Amanda's shoulder, squeezing so hard it made her cry out. "Don't fuck up," Travis snarled. He gave her a look that sent shivers down her spine.

"I won't." Amanda wanted to cry, but no tears came out. Her emotions were locked up. She knew she was in deep trouble. *How did I ever get messed up in this?*

Although Amanda hadn't yet been told of her exact assignment, she was to drive across the border in a van containing several packages of high-grade heroin. Each kilo, 2.2 pounds, would be wrapped in plastic and then put inside a plastic bag that was liberally sprinkled with baking soda to absorb the smell. The package would be encased in another plastic bag and secured with duct tape. The bags would be concealed behind panels in the van's walls. Eight kilos of cocaine would be making the trip, along with a good amount of the highly addictive OxyContin. Two hundred small baggies would be filled with the prescription painkiller. Bound similarly, the painkillers would bring a good tariff in the States. The increasingly popular and habit-forming drug, "Oxy," was making addicts out of many. The painkiller was becoming a big part of the gravy train for the dealers.

The men spoke of all this to each other in Spanish. Amanda didn't understand what they were saying, but she figured the activity they expected of her would be illegal. Amanda surmised the van would be holding drugs of some type. She was sure she'd heard the men use the word *cocaina.*

Is this why they abducted me? To have me run drugs for them?

To mix things up, the smugglers occasionally had mules transport drugs into the States via Garita de Otay, the Otay border crossing. Roughly six miles east of the more popular, and busier, San Ysidro crossing, Garita de Otay was used mostly by commercial trucks, and tourists who frequented the Tecate or Rosarita areas of Mexico.

It was decided that Amanda would be driving through San Ysidro. The cartel was busy boring out an underground tunnel near Otay that was destined to be used to smuggle illegals as well as drugs. A sophisticated operation, the tunnel had great potential. The leaders of the cartel weren't going to take any chances of a mistake made by a mule bringing unnecessary heat to the area.

Once across the border, Amanda was to continue to Camino de la Plaza, turn right, go the short distance to east San Ysidro Boulevard, and turn right again. A Jack-in-the-Box restaurant would be on the left. Since travelers were allowed to park in the fast-food parking lot for up to eight hours a day for five dollars, it was a good location for the smugglers to conduct their drop-off operations. Vehicles were in and out all the time, and no one paid any attention.

"Make a left turn into the parking lot and park in the back. Got that?" Travis sucked something out of his tooth and spit.

Amanda nodded numbly.

"Four guys will meet you. Don't worry about finding them. They'll see you. Stay in the vehicle until they tell you to get out. Understand?"

Amanda nodded again.

One American, two Mexicans, and one Mexican American would make up the four meeting her, although Amanda didn't know that yet, either. The plan was that two of the males would drive the van away immediately, with another guy following the van in a separate vehicle. One of the men would remain to walk back across the border with Amanda. They said his name quickly, and Amanda wasn't sure what it was. Gary, maybe.

"You'll be given a shirt to change into. Tie your hair back and keep your sunglasses on. Don't attract any attention. You'll be just another American couple walking across the bridge on Camoines Way to Tijuana for some fun," said Travis.

The plan sounded too simple to Amanda. *What about the policia and customs agents? And the U.S. police. Won't everything look suspicious?* Amanda was nervous. *Will I be able to keep my cool?*

Amanda's body shook, and she took a deep breath before she asked, "Aren't there dogs sniffing cars and trucks for drugs at the border? What about the *policia* and the customs agents? And the United States police?"

The words came out in a rush as Amanda questioned her captors. She was scared. Scared to do what they asked of her, and scared not to.

"Random searches, that's all. We have it wired for today, sugar. Don't worry, the guards won't be searching you. Just don't fuck up." Travis's piercing eyes bored into Amanda. "You don't need to be concerned about anything but your part. We've done this many times before. It's been months since we've used the Jack-in-the-Box parking lot, so there shouldn't be any extra heat or anything right now. It'll be an easy exchange. You can get all the drugs you need after the job is done. And tonight you won't have any trouble falling asleep."

Travis's eyes caught Enrique's. The men looked as if they were sharing a private joke. Then Travis yanked Amanda up. "It's time."

"Take your purse, bitch," said Enrique.

Maria let her eyes rest on Amanda's face. She knew the plan could work; it had many times before. She also knew what happened if the mule didn't do her part. It didn't matter if the screw-up was intentional or not, the consequences were the same. Maria remembered one girl from several months ago. The young, pretty girl had a drug problem, just like all the others. And that problem had led to others.

* * *

Marnie was the girl's name. From Wisconsin, she had moved to the Ocean Beach area of San Diego with her boyfriend, Nick, to get away from being poor in a small town. Nick, a good-looking guy, was a Class A jerk. He had found work as a bartender while Marnie waitressed at a breakfast restaurant. Their hours didn't mesh, and it wasn't long before Nick was having too much fun at the bar. He slept with one of the waitresses and a couple of patrons. Soon, he added selling small amounts of drugs to his job description. For Nick, every day was a party. Marnie had suspicions of what was going on, but Nick, a fast talker, had denied everything. Nick always made sure they had a nice stash of drugs at home. Marnie had fallen into doing more and more drugs herself to dull the reality of her messed-up situation.

One day when Marnie and Nick were both off from work, they had gone to Tijuana for a little club action and to score some hard drugs. They were having a drink in a dark, smoky bar where known dealers hung out when Marnie left to use the ladies room. She didn't come back, and Nick never saw her again. No one did.

Manuel and Oscar Fuentes were at the bar that night. While drinking *cerveza* and doing shots of tequila, they spied an opportunity to get another mule. The girl was hot, which they knew would make it easier to get her past the border guards—the guards not already in their pocket. And the girl was drunk. They quickly grabbed her as she was coming out of the restroom and slipped out the back.

Marnie was pretty, but she wasn't street smart and scared easily. After keeping her fucked up for several days and raping her repeatedly, the Fuentes brothers had told Marnie of the plan. She didn't like it and cried a lot. Marnie was too scared to participate in smuggling, no matter how much they threatened or slapped her around. She had almost lost her will to live.

Her lack of cooperation had pissed off everyone. Enrique's temper was out of control, and he almost killed her. Javier, on the other hand, was certain he could make money off the pretty girl, so he sold her to the Martinez family in southern Mexico. The Martinez men put Marnie to work in the prostitution trade. Word on the street was she was bringing in big bucks.

Sometimes the kidnapped girls were sent to Russia or another foreign country for prostitution. Lots of money was made in the selling of kidnapped girls for sex. The flesh trade was plan B for the girls who either wouldn't cooperate with the smugglers, or who already had, and after they'd made a few trips, doing more would get risky. The cartel didn't want anyone to get recognized and jeopardize their operation.

Maria remembered that Marnie was lucky in a way. One girl who had refused to follow the plan and had been brutally beaten found out the hard way there's only so much beating a body can take. The MFO had disposed of her battered remains somewhere south of Rosarito. Maria shuddered at the memory. She hoped Amanda would cooperate.

CHAPTER 29
PAM JOINS THE SEARCH PARTY

Steve and Diane left for the airport in time to pick up Pam outside the baggage claim area. Pam knew the drill. After disembarking, she put on her sunglasses and walked the long, bright hallway to the steps that led down to baggage claim. Not knowing what to expect when she arrived, Pam had packed an assortment of clothes. She was prepared to do whatever would be needed of her. Digging in her bag, Pam located the cell phone and turned it on. She called Benny to tell him she had arrived safely. He was already in New York.

The bags were reaching the tarmac as Pam arrived at the carousel. Pam's suitcase was one of the first out of the hatch.

My bag hasn't been first out in a long time, Pam thought as she hoisted the valise. *Maybe it's a good omen.*

She grabbed her carry-on, threw her purse over her shoulder, and trudged outside pulling the huge bag she had nicknamed "Big Red."

"Pam!"

Right on time, Steve's truck pulled up in front of the airport terminal just as Pam was exiting. He parked, jumped out, and gave Pam a huge hug. She could feel Steve's emotion spill out of his body.

"I can't . . . thank you enough . . . for coming." The

words caught in Steve's throat.

Diane climbed out of the truck to give her sister-in-law a hug, breaking into sobs.

"I'm here to support you guys and give you any help I can," said Pam, trying to comfort Diane.

Diane cried and hiccupped quietly as Steve drove away from the airport. Pam asked questions and took notes as her brother brought her up to speed on the events of the past few days.

Diane was alternately angry and scared as Steve spoke, showing her emotions through sighs and facial expressions.

"You may not remember this, Pam, but Amanda sustained a head injury when she took a bad fall a few years ago," Diane interrupted, her voice shaking.

"I don't think I knew about the fall. How did it happen?"

Diane shook her head. "We don't know exactly. She was at a skating rink, doing some tricks with her friends when she fell. She was rushed to the hospital where the doctor determined she had sustained a concussion and a severe sprain in her neck. Amanda suffered with terrible headaches for quite a while after that. The doctor prescribed Vicodin to give her some relief." Diane stopped to wipe her eyes.

Steve continued with the story. "The worst part was whenever Amanda quit taking the Vicodin, the headaches would come back, worse than ever. She finally came to us and said she had a problem and needed help. By then, Amanda had been taking so much Vicodin on a daily basis that she was afraid she was going to die."

"We sent her to rehab right away," Diane said between sobs.

"The first of several rehabs," sighed Steve.

"Where did she go for rehab?" Pam asked. She realized there were things about Amanda's past she wasn't aware of.

"We sent her to Cry Help a couple of times, Ronald McDonald House, and another place in West Hollywood that I can't remember right this minute," said Steve as he ran his hand through his hair. "Oh, and Phoenix House."

"Ronald McDonald House is a rehab?" Pam asked, surprised.

"Actually, it's a detox center," replied Steve.

"No, the name is Scripps McDonald Center. It's in La Jolla," said Diane.

Steve shook his head. "You're right. This whole thing with drugs . . . and now she's missing . . . I can barely think straight."

"Amanda's want for drugs is probably in her genes," Diane piped up. "I mean, look at your past, Steve. And you weren't exactly an angel either, Pam." Diane sat up tall on her high horse.

"You've got to be kidding me to talk like that, Diane!" Steve spat out, mortified. "Pam came out here to help us. She hasn't been here five minutes, and you go crazy and say stupid shit like that."

Pam's jaw dropped, momentarily stunned. But she held her tongue. *No point in getting into it with Diane right now. She needs to be given a break, considering what she's going through*, Pam thought.

Diane turned her head and looked out the window. A cold silence filled the truck. Finally, Pam asked, "Where are we going?"

"Mexico."

Benny will be thrilled, Pam thought grimly.

"We're going to pick up Alberto Reyes on the way. He's a private investigator. Bilingual. Has contacts on both sides of the border. Benny turned me on to him," said Steve.

"Sounds like he could be very helpful. I look forward to meeting him." Pam's thoughts turned to Benny. *He won't like this at all, but what can I do?*

Pam was tired from the flight and now they were going to Mexico. "Is there a Starbucks or some kind of coffee shop near here? I need a good jolt."

"There's one at the exit where we're meeting Bert. I'll get something, too. What about you, Diane?"

"I'll have a chai latte and a blueberry muffin," Diane replied stonily.

"Pam, we have a lead," Steve said, hoping to change the mood in the truck. "The Mustang was found in Tijuana and towed to an impound lot on the west side of the city." Steve glanced at Pam in the rearview mirror to see her reaction.

"They found her car! Wow, how did that happen?"

"I had reported the car stolen, both to the police and to the insurance company. The call came from the insurance company. They said the car had been completely stripped. No surprise there. Thieves will take anything they can pry loose. We'll go to the lot today and see what we can come up with."

CHAPTER 30
AMANDA'S UNCLES

D ave knew his career would never take off, or even get on track, unless he made a few changes. The first change would have to be with the man in the mirror.

How long can a guy party like there's no tomorrow if he's hoping there's going to be a tomorrow? Dave had asked himself.

He decided to call Roger Gallagher, his agent, to check in. He wanted Roger to know he was serious about working. Roger's secretary said he was in a meeting, so Dave left a message with her. He hoped he'd stressed strongly enough how important it was that Roger get back to him. He also hoped that Roger really was in a meeting and not just dodging his call.

If Roger doesn't return my call by tonight, I'll call him again.

Dave needed all the information he could get about the call-back audition. He wanted to nail it. Dave was determined.

Now it's gym time. Gotta keep looking good. He drove with a smile on his face. As he pulled into L.A. Fitness in Westwood, Dave thought about Jake, the MMA champ. *Maybe I should work out where Jake does, get to know some people, learn some stuff, and add "mixed martial arts" to my list of proficiencies. Might help me get some jobs.*

Mixed martial art, or MMA, as it was commonly known, was the hot item everywhere. Dave had been to a few fights and was surprised at the size of the crowds in attendance. Lots of chicks there, too. He was certain that was the way to go.

Dave had seen Jake at a few parties where Amanda had been over the past year. *I just ought to give Jake a call. You never know who might know something. It's another excuse to talk to him, too. Jake could be a good guy to get close to for lots of reasons.*

Dave's mind was on overdrive. He parked, picked up his BlackBerry, and sent a text to Brett: "Gr8 party. Still recovering. Need Jake's # Call me."

Dave hopped out of his car feeling pretty good. *Maybe things will start going my way for a change. Now it's time to sweat.*

As he entered the gym, Dave saw his brother near the free weights.

"Yo, bro!" he called out.

Craig looked up in surprise. He had planned on giving his brother a call all day. "I'm done for today," he said, "but I was just going to call you. Did you hear Mandy's gone again?"

"Yup. Steve called. He said Diane was too shaken up to talk. Mandy's cell phone got answered by some guy in Mexico, I guess. Damn, that girl is messed up."

Craig nodded as he wiped the sweat off his face and neck.

"I put a call in to one of my guys to see if anyone knows anything," Dave continued. "Maybe Mandy's down there with someone to cop some drugs and lost her cell. I know a couple of MMA guys who are pretty heavy partiers, you know? They go down there a lot." Dave liked to act like he had "connections" for everything—Hollywood style.

Not to be outdone, Craig jumped in, "I've seen so much shit at the Windjammer, you wouldn't believe. Buying, selling, using. Seems like half of Hollywood is fucked up. The other half is either going in or coming out of rehab."

Dave nodded.

"Heroin's everywhere, too," Craig continued. "Way too easy to get hooked, and that shit can totally fuck you up. I know Mandy's done it. She came in one night with the dude from the new beer commercial who thinks he's all that, you know who I mean, and they were both jacked up. I'd say speed balling. I pulled her aside and told her to watch out. That dude's such an asshole, you know? A player and a user. Mandy's eyes were dilated. She was spaced out. I know she didn't catch what I said at all."

"Think we should call him? What's his name? Justin? I can probably get his number through my agent. Could be she's on a binge, and he might know about it."

"I don't want to get involved," Craig said. "You can check it out if you want, but leave me and my bar out of it, man. I'm known for having a discreet place, and I don't want to lose that rep."

"Okay. I'll just keep my eyes open. Sure don't want her to OD or anything. Oh, I went to a kick-ass party in the Hills. Ended up with a super-hot redhead. Her natural color, too."

They both laughed.

"Hope I bump into that one again! Well, I'm going to go bust my ass. Later, dude."

"Later."

Craig strode out with the attitude of a guy who felt pretty good about himself.

CHAPTER 31
EXECUTING THE PLAN

Enrique, Travis, and Amanda left the apartment. Travis held his captive's arm as they walked quickly down the alleyway to the street. Amanda glanced around but couldn't see a street sign.

As if reading her mind, Travis said, "Keep your head down, and don't be looking at shit. Don't talk to anybody either." His grip on her arm tightened so much that she gasped. "Shut up!" he said.

Pale and apprehensive, fear was written on Amanda's face.

Not interested in attracting undue attention, Travis tried a softer approach. "What's your name? Amanda, right?"

Amanda nodded. *It's on my driver's license.*

"Nothing's going to happen to you. Just do your job. It's all good."

Amanda stole a glance at Travis. She noted he was kind of good-looking, in a beat-up sort of way. Enrique just looked mean.

The trio piled into a dirty white station wagon. Travis drove to the east end of Tijuana and parked in front of a house. Enrique exited the car. He glanced around before entering the house. Travis stayed behind with Amanda.

"It's cool, sugar," Travis said, smiling at Amanda. "People in the States got to get their drugs too, you know. And we're here to help."

Amanda didn't react.

"There'll be a cell phone next to you on the seat of the van. Don't touch it. The speaker will be on, with the group walkie-talkie activated. We'll be able to hear everything you say to anyone." Travis paused to let that sink in. "You can talk to us only if necessary. We'll reach out to you if we have to. Just drive through the border, and go to the Jack-in-the-Box parking lot. You know, like we talked about. When you return, there'll be lots of good shit waiting for you. You can get totally wasted then, baby."

Amanda couldn't believe she was going to be driving drugs from Mexico into the United States. *I could go to prison if I get caught,* she thought. Amanda also knew if she tried to tip off the border guards that these guys would come after her and her family. It was a terrifying realization.

Amanda wanted to cry, but couldn't. *Damn speed. Without it, though, I wouldn't be able to do this, that's for sure.*

She thought again about crossing the border as a mule. *I've read about people smuggling drugs internationally. And now I'm going to do it. Holy shit.*

Travis looked at Amanda for any signs of trouble. "You got any problems with this?"

Amanda's heart was pounding double time. She shook her head. *I'm so messed up. I'm sorry I ever did drugs. I wish I could run away right now.*

Enrique and Hector exited the house. When Travis saw them, he got out of the car and said, "Come on," to Amanda. They walked together about half a block, then went around to the back of a house. A dark blue, older-model minivan was parked on the street.

Hector asked Travis if Amanda was ready.

Travis answered, "Oh, yeah. She's good to go."

"*Esta bien.* It's all set," said Hector.

"Don't fuck up," Travis reminded Amanda.

White with fear, Amanda barely nodded. She was scared. Scared of the men, scared of jail, scared for her parents. Just plain scared.

"Get in the van and follow me to the border lines. When we get there, I'll signal which lane you should get into. Doesn't matter how long the line is or anything; just do as I tell you. Remember, we know you've been here many times to score, so crossing the border shouldn't be hard for you." Hector stopped talking and looked long and hard at Amanda. She glanced away. "We don't need any problems," he said threateningly.

Amanda tried not to shake.

"Enrique and Travis will be in the car behind you. You know we'll be watching you at all times. This goes right, everything will be okay. You know what'll happen if you try anything funny. Got it?" Hector stared coldly into Amanda's eyes.

Her face was frozen and her body numb. *I just want the job to be over,* Amanda thought, trying not to show her fear. *Over, so I can take something to make me drift away. Maybe for always.*

"I got it," she answered.

Enrique opened the door of the van and beckoned to Amanda. As she started to climb in, Enrique grabbed her arm and pulled her close enough so he could whisper in her ear.

"Remember the other night, bitch?" he asked with a sneer. "See you later." He gave Amanda a firm shove into the van.

Amanda said nothing as she got behind the wheel. Her heart was pounding even harder, and her hands were shaking. Now she knew for sure. Enrique was the one. She hated him with every ounce of her being. Fighting to keep her composure, Amanda asked God to keep her strong enough to survive her captivity. She knew her parents loved her and would search for her. She blinked back tears and stared straight ahead. *Let me live through this.*

Feeling itchy, Amanda could tell she was coming down from the speed she'd been given, and would need some narcotics. Soon. She was going to have to pull from deep within to complete the mission and not mess up. *I don't want my life to end at the hands of these savages.*

Enrique laughed as he slammed the door shut. Amanda wanted to scream.

Hector got in on the other side and set the cell phone next to Amanda. He wrapped a sweatshirt around the edges of the phone so it wouldn't roll around. He looked at Amanda for a second as if he was about to say something, but didn't. Amanda held her breath, not moving a muscle. Then Hector hopped out and got in a jeep that was parked near the van. Amanda turned and saw Enrique and Travis running down the street to where they had left the station wagon. Her nerves were on edge, and she was starting to sweat.

Suddenly, she heard Hector's voice, "We'll wait here until we see the wagon pull up. Then I'll go first, you follow, and they'll be behind you."

When Amanda didn't respond, Hector shouted through the phone, "Answer me!"

In a daze, Amanda glanced at the phone. Snapping back into reality, Amanda said, "Yes, yes, okay." She needed to pee,

but she'd have to hold it. The trip across the border was about
to begin.

CHAPTER 32
POSTERS IN HAND

Pam was thinking about what Amanda's situation might be. "Steve, what do you think we should do first when we get into Mexico?" she asked.

Diane responded. "I think we should go to the impound lot, I mean, the police station, first, to get the paperwork or whatever, and then the impound lot."

"I agree," Steve said. "We can put up posters all along the way. I'd like to give the police department copies to pass out to their officers. If people can see Amanda's face, we'll have a better shot at getting a tip. Maybe someone will notify the police if they've seen her."

Steve added that Bert would probably have some ideas, too. "We have plenty of posters, so it's not a problem."

"May I see one?" Pam asked.

Diane handed Pam one of the posters. On the poster was a big color picture of Amanda. A lobster bib covered her white top. She was holding a lobster in her hand and smiling. Amanda's long, dark hair was pulled back into a high ponytail, and she was wearing large silver hoop earrings. The top of the poster read: *"PERSONA EXTRAVIADA."*

Seeing Amanda's picture and the words "MISSING PERSON" written in Spanish took Pam's breath away. "This makes Amanda's disappearance hit home," she said sadly.

The entire poster was written in Spanish, and Steve explained that Amanda's name, age, eye and hair color, height, and weight were printed on the poster.

Mandy's small, only five foot two, and so pretty, thought Pam.

The poster stated when and where Amanda was last seen, the make, model, and color of the vehicle she was driving, and the license plate number. It included phone numbers to call.

"Wow," said Pam. "It's incredible to see this. I just can't get over that Amanda is missing and in Mexico."

At that, Diane started crying. Pam instantly regretted her words. "I'm so sorry. I don't even know what to say. You know Benny and I have been praying for Mandy's safe return."

Diane, sobbing into her tissue, only nodded. Steve glanced at her and his heart broke. *Why is this happening?*

They approached their exit, Steve signaled, and then he turned off the expressway. He saw the Starbucks on H Avenue in Chula Vista, pulled up, and parked. Bert was outside, talking on his cell.

Everyone got out of the truck to use the bathrooms and get provisions. Steve performed the introductions.

Bert said, "Nice to meet you, Pam. By the way, your husband, Benny, is very well thought of."

"Thanks," Pam responded, shaking Bert's hand. "He said the same about you. I'm glad you were able to make time in your schedule. Hope you can help us find Amanda."

Bert nodded and got in the car with them. They drove the remaining few miles to the Mexican border in silence, each lost in his or her thoughts.

Pepper the town with posters. Give some to the police,

Steve thought. *Go to the impound lot. Get leads on Amanda's whereabouts. Let today be the day of a major breakthrough. Please, God.*

I hate Steve for letting Amanda go, Diane thought. *I'm so scared for my daughter! We need to find her and bring her back home.*

Bert was more pragmatic. *Sure hope some of my contacts come through with something. Amanda could be anywhere doing anything. Or worse, she could already be dead.*

Pam's thoughts included her concern for her husband's reaction. *I hope Benny understands why I'm in Mexico today. This whole thing is unbelievable. Dear God, please lead us in the right direction.*

* * *

Dave checked his messages as he left the gym. The best one was from his agent. "The call-back's still on. Don't miss this one." *Don't worry,* Dave thought excitedly. There was a text from Brett with Jake's phone number.

"Sweet," Dave said out loud. *Things are starting to head in the right direction for me!* Dave stored Jake's number, then gave him a call. He was delighted when Jake actually answered.

"Hey, dude, Dave Nixon here. Brett gave me your number. Saw you at the party in the Hills the other night."

"It's cool. What's up?"

"Couple of things. I need a good gym. I usually go to L.A. Fitness, but was thinking maybe I should add to my workout, you know?"

"Yeah, sure. Legends on La Brea would probably be good for you. Tough stuff could about kill a guy like you, though," Jake laughed. "But you'll like it. I go there sometimes."

"Thanks. Great party the other night, don't ya think? You MMA guys can get down. The German Bulldog looked like he was having a good time."

"Yeah, we like to have fun. Bulldog's legendary."

"Hey, do you know Amanda Tate? She's, like, twenty-one and hot. Long dark hair and lives to party."

"I might know her. Name sounds familiar. I've probably seen her around anyway. Why? What's up?"

"She's actually my niece. My older sister's kid. The girl's missing, and by that I mean no one's seen or heard from her for several days. My sister's pretty worried."

"Oh. Well, I haven't seen her lately, but if I do, I'll let you know. Maybe she's with some dude, you know? "

"Yeah, could be. Kinda keep an eye out, and mention it to the Bulldog, too, if you don't mind."

"Haven't seen Bulldog since the party. He's probably copped some shit and is on a binge. He likes to do that sometimes. Just melts away for a few days. He'll slide back in, always does."

"Okay, thanks. See ya soon."

"Later, dude."

* * *

Craig, on the other hand, was disturbed about Amanda's disappearance and the possibility that he, or possibly his bar, could be connected in some way.

Why did I have to mention the bit about her showing up with Justin? Shit. Dave might follow up on that somehow. It'd be okay, but only if Amanda's found safe. Then the rumors and stories would be great for business.

Craig sighed. *God, I'm a greedy mother.*

CHAPTER 33
INTERNATIONAL DRUG SMUGGLING

A
manda saw the station wagon pull around the corner. Then she heard Hector's voice.

"Time to move."

Her heart was pounding so loudly that Amanda was sure she wouldn't be able to hear anything else. She started up the van and pulled behind the jeep Hector was driving.

"*Bueno,*" he said. "*Vamanos, amigos.* Let's go."

The white wagon followed Amanda as the drug-smuggling convoy drove down the street, turned the corner, and headed for the border. It took about twenty-five minutes of driving through Tijuana to get to the area where the cars, trucks, and other vehicles were lined up, waiting their turn to cross into the United States. During that time, Amanda tried to keep her mind from wandering. She fought thinking about her parents, about Daniel, about her friends, about how stupid she'd been to get so caught up in drugs.

When this is all over, I'll kick everything, she thought. *But first, I have to get through this job and go back to their prison. I need some drugs right now. This is hell.* Amanda could feel the sweat trickling down her back. Her head throbbed and her stomach hurt. She squeezed the steering wheel. *When they finally set me free and I can go home, that's when I'll quit. Cold turkey. Yeah, that's what I'll do.* As the caravan approached the lineup area, Hector said, "Get in the third lane from the left. *Comprende?* Understand?"

"Yes, I understand," Amanda answered in a shaky voice as she positioned the van behind the last vehicle in the third lane. "Don't act scared. Don't act like anything. Remember, we're watching you and we have guys on the other side. It's in your best interest to do this right. Oh, and I bet your family wouldn't want you to fuck up, either." Hector made a guttural sound that sounded like a laugh.

Amanda was so scared, she almost wet her pants. It didn't help that she had to pee. Amanda didn't know whether to laugh or cry. Laugh, because her nerves were on edge and she had to pee, or cry, because she was scared shitless and the mention of her family hit her like a punch in the stomach. *If I cause them harm . . .* Amanda tensed up. She forced herself to focus on the matter at hand—getting across the border without any problems.

The lines weren't as long as she'd seen them at other times, and they were moving along at a steady pace. A couple of border guards with their dogs were walking in between the cars and trucks. They'd randomly stop and ask drivers to open their trunks or back doors.

Amanda felt fresh beads of sweat break out on her forehead as she watched the guards. Her stomach was in knots. *Hope they don't stop here.*

Her line moved, and Amanda got closer to the gate. She clenched her teeth, trying to steady her nerves, but sweat was rolling down her body and seeping through her clothing.

Keep calm, keep calm, Amanda reminded herself. *Just need to get through this.*

The border guards with the dogs didn't stop at Amanda's vehicle. They didn't even look at it as they passed through to another line.

Up next, Amanda smiled at the guard as she rolled to a stop.

Grinning, he asked for her driver's license. "Why were you in Mexico?"

Maintaining eye contact with the guard, Amanda answered, "Oh, you know, just looking for souvenirs for my grandmother who's visiting. She's too old to come with me."

"That's nice." The guard was taken in by Amanda's pretty face. "Go ahead."

Amanda smiled. "Thank you," she said and drove on through, not looking back.

As she maneuvered into the lane on the road, Amanda realized she'd been holding her breath. She let it out slowly through her mouth, hissing like a balloon deflating. Suddenly exhilarated, Amanda wanted to scream. *I made it!*

She heard Hector's voice on the phone. "Drive to the Jack-in-the-Box parking lot."

"I am."

Once she reached the fast-food restaurant, Amanda drove to the back, as she'd been directed. She pulled into a vacant space. Almost immediately, four men swarmed the van. One opened the door. "Get out," he said.

Grabbing her pocketbook, she slid out of the van. Amanda recognized one of the men. He had helped move her from the shack to the apartment. She remembered thinking he'd been gentle when he carried her battered body. *Maybe he's not such a bad guy—for one of them.*

The man, named Omar, looked at Amanda. He remembered, too.

Amanda didn't recognize Emilio, nor did she realize he'd also been at the shack. Because he'd done a good job helping dispose of Juan's body, Emilio had been given this new assignment. He was young, eager, and hungry for work.

Both Carlos and Javier had seen something in Emilio they liked. Maybe it was his coldness. Emilio rarely showed emotion. He had been robbed of his emotions at a very young age. Emilio was only three years old when he'd seen his father, a government official, shot at close range, and his mother and sister raped. His sister was stabbed when she fought and tried to resist. She died, fighting. Emilio remembered seeing blood spurt out everywhere. And the screams. He would never forget the screams. Some of them had come from him. His mother yelled and cried and screamed at Emilio to run away. But the tot had been frozen with fear. Shots had exploded loudly near him, and he saw his mother crumble to the floor. Emilio still had been unable to move.

A darkness washed over Emilio then that had remained with him ever since. The killers had decided to take little Emilio with them. They would raise him to be one of them. Traumatized, Emilio didn't speak for over a year after the gruesome murders, but the young boy had watched and learned much from his new environment.

As he grew older, Emilio planned to make something of himself. His family's torturous deaths would not be in vain. He kept those thoughts to himself, however. There were no friends in this business, and he knew it. No one could be trusted. The cartel's leaders were cutthroat. A man had to have eyes all around his head. Emilio eventually became a soldier in the very drug cartel that had mercilessly killed his family. Growing up within the cartel, Emilio had seen and heard many things. He had been witness to torture, and hadn't flinched. Something inside Emilio had died that day, along with his family.

Javier and Carlos liked the hardness about Emilio. They could see he wasn't an emotional weakling. Emilio was keenly aware the cartel thought his life was mapped out, but he was patient. He had plans.

Now, Emilio and the more experienced man, Omar, the driver, got into the van. Omar had done this type of driving many times and felt confident. He knew exactly where to go and what to do. Emilio was still in training, so to speak, learning firsthand the many aspects of the drug smuggling trade.

We'll see how the kid does, thought Omar, glancing at the man who would accompany him on the drive. The van and its contents were in their hands now, until the next stop.

Diego, the third man, was older, in his forties. A Mexican American, he had connections in off-loading the drugs. He'd been dealing with contraband in some fashion since he was a teenager. Although he was born in the United States, Diego had lived as a young boy and teenager in Mexico. He knew both sides of the border quite well. Diego had gone to high school in Chula Vista and liked to brag that the actor, Mario Lopez, had graduated from his same school.

Diego was a not-too-distant cousin of the Morales boys, and they trusted him. Content with his position, he saw it as having little risk, especially compared to what he had done in previous years. He had earned this "cushy" spot after having already done his time, in more ways than one.

Diego was to follow the van in his truck. The green pickup was old and dented, so it attracted little attention. He was just another Mexican American, driving his truck down the road. Nothing unusual about that.

With no time wasted, the men started their vehicles. Diego called Gary over to the truck. He slipped him a small bag containing a new top for Amanda. Gary took the bag to Amanda. "Take your shirt off," he demanded.

"Right here?"

"What do you think? Hurry up."

With no time for embarrassment, Amanda quickly removed the shirt Maria had given her and gave it to Gary. She hurriedly slipped the new top over her head. Gary put the old one in the bag and tossed it to Diego. The men then pulled out of the lot and steered their vehicles toward the agreed-upon destination in the States.

So far, so good, thought Amanda as she watched the men drive away.

"Pull your hair back," Gary ordered. A man of little patience, Gary didn't like having to wait for anything, including waiting for this latest mule to get ready. He wanted to get back to Mexico. He actually felt safer there, away from the American justice system. And he was more than ready to get high.

Amanda took the elastic band out of her jeans pocket and pulled her hair into a low ponytail. She put her sunglasses back on and looked at Gary. He nodded.

Suddenly very tired and hungry, Amanda felt like someone had let all the air out of her body. She was completely drained. The nervous energy she had experienced while driving the loaded van across the border was gone, as were the effects of the amphetamines. In need of a fix, Amanda wasn't sure which feeling was the strongest—exhaustion, hunger, or the jones for drugs. And she still had to pee.

Gary said, "Pretend you're my girlfriend. Let me do

any talking, and don't look anyone in the eye. Don't even think about trying to tip off anyone at the border. There'll be hell to pay if you do. But you know that, don't you?"

"I'll be cool," Amanda whispered. "I just need some food, or water, or something. I can barely swallow." She paused. "I need to get high really bad. I'm hurting a lot. And I have to pee, too."

"You're a fucking pain in the ass, if you ask me," Gary spat.

Amanda winced.

He added, "Don't worry. We'll get you something to drink and eat as soon as we get to Tijuana. You can hit the john then, too." He looked at his charge. "After that, you'll be able to get so wasted, you'll think you died and went to heaven."

Gary smirked. *Same goes for me.*

The duo walked through the parking lot to the street. Gary took Amanda's hand as they turned south.

Amanda reflected upon what had just happened. She had been a mule and driven drugs across an international border on orders from a Mexican drug cartel. She wished this was a bad dream and she could wake up. *Maybe it will be over soon.*

"What'd you think about being a smuggler?" Gary asked. "You up for doing it again?"

Amanda blanched. She had been certain the cartel was going to release her after this job. It hadn't occurred to her they would want her to do more.

"I . . . don't know what I think," Amanda squeaked out through her parched throat. *What if I had gotten busted,* she thought. *Would the American police believe I'd been kidnapped? Would they believe I didn't want to do this?*

Amanda wouldn't allow herself to think any more about

it. She was going back into Mexico with a virtual stranger, and there didn't appear to be any way she could get away from him, or her situation. *At least, not yet.*

CHAPTER 34
ICE AND EBER

Ice had completed the first half of his task, transporting the *pollos* from Mexico into the United States. He had gotten eighteen men across, and soon would be smuggling the remaining ten. The project had not been easy. It had taken weeks to plan the operation, and there had been glitches along the way. Two chickens had gotten into a fight with each other, with one stabbing the other in the neck. A major fight then erupted among the rest of the illegals. Ice and his men had had to fire their weapons to stop it. Two of the fighters were hit by stray bullets and had to be pulled out. One died. The stabbing victim also succumbed to his wounds. Two deaths, one severe shooting injury, and the operation hadn't even commenced. Ice sighed audibly at the memory. It was a high-stakes job, and he knew it.

Good thing the entire incident had happened in Mexico, he thought, *where it's easier to get rid of bodies—both dead ones and those still breathing.*

All in all, Ice felt underappreciated. If he had gotten caught by the border patrol agents on the American side, the judge would've thrown the book at him. That is, if he had made it to the court system. The agents were armed and known to use deadly force if they had to. They often thought they had to. It was a rough business, all the way around.

Ice had received his pay for the completed portion of the job from Javier. Eber had provided the drugs. The rest of his pay would come when he delivered the other ten. He'd be getting more drugs then, too.

Eber had control of the highest-quality drugs for the MFO. He worked for two bosses. Sometimes he'd be with Javier, and other times he'd be with Carlos. No one else would've been able to pull that off, but Eber was half-brother to both the cousins, and only they knew it.

Carlos's father, Roberto Morales, liked to fuck beautiful women. He didn't care who they belonged to. He fucked Solana, his wife, too, of course, but he just couldn't keep his dick under control, especially when she was pregnant. He thought it was bad luck to sleep with her when she was carrying his child. All women were open game to him. He liked to screw other guys' wives on the sly because he felt that he had put something over on them. There were many rumors about Roberto Morales, and everyone waited for the day when a jealous husband or boyfriend would do him in.

Eber was the product of a tryst between Javier's mother, Maritza, and Roberto. Maritza knew when Eber was born that he was Roberto's son. She had kept the information to herself, until Javier's father, Miguel, was killed in an ambush when baby Eber was two. Maritza knew full well that Miguel would've killed her, had he found out. Miguel could fuck around, but it was death to her if she did. Most of the men in the cartel felt the same way, and there were some dead wives to prove it. No man had a libido that matched Roberto's, though. He was in a class of Lotharios by himself.

Sometimes when Ice walked the streets of Tijuana at night, memories of his family in Indiana would slip into his head. When he actually let himself think about it, Ice missed them. He wondered how his brother and sister were doing. They both had kids he hadn't seen in years. His mother had died of cancer several years ago, and his father had never been able to get over the tragedy. *Dad's fucked up in his own way,* thought Ice. *Still, it would be nice to see them all again.* He wondered if they ever thought about him.

The Cranes had been a close family when Ice was growing up in Bloomington. His dad, a professor at Indiana University, had taught mathematics. His brother had been a track star and gone on to be a dentist. Ice had been a problem for his parents, even as a kid. Maybe it was the middle-child syndrome, but whatever, he always felt like he had gotten the short shrift. Beth, his sister, was the baby and had done all the right stuff. After she got her degree, she became a guidance counselor at the high school they had attended. Ice's secret goal was to get back to Indiana and see his family. He was so hooked on drugs, however, he knew it probably would never happen. And getting away from the Morales family would be darn near impossible. Still, Ice liked to think about it. When he wasn't too wasted to think.

CHAPTER 35
THE MEXICAN SYSTEM

"I think we'll drive into Mexico today, instead of parking on the U.S. side," Steve said. "We can leave the truck near McDonald's."

"Whatever you want," said Diane.

"It's hot and sunny already," noted Pam. "Glad I brought my visor."

Diane was wearing a large-brimmed hat and white linen pants and top. "I always cover up to avoid having the sun fry my skin," said Diane. "I had a skin cancer removed from my back when I was twenty-eight and learned my lesson."

Diane looked beautiful in white, with her shoulder-length dark hair and medium skin tone. Amanda favored her mother in looks, but, like many other girls her age, refused to listen about the benefits of sunscreen. *Just one of many things Amanda turns a deaf ear to,* Diane thought.

Tourists were walking the streets of Tijuana, looking for a bargain. Locals were out, too. The area was bustling with activity. Steve led the way toward the *farmacia* where they had initially begun their search for Amanda.

"Let's go down this street and tack up some posters. Everyone goes by here at some point," he said.

They held up posters as they walked and asked passersby, "Has anyone seen this girl?"

No one had.

Pam had finished tacking up her first two posters when she heard her cell phone ring. The sound took her by surprise. She wasn't expecting her cell to have service in Mexico.

"Hi, baby, what are you up to?"

It was Benny. Pam had to confess that she was in Mexico and prepared herself for Benny's unhappy response. Instead, he said, "I knew you'd end up going there. Just be careful."

"I will," Pam promised. "We're putting up posters of Amanda all over the place, in case anyone has seen her. Diane had them made at work. We're going to go to the police station soon to find out more about Amanda's car."

As if on cue, Bert said, "Let's go on over to the police station. We need to get the information about the car. Might lead us to Amanda's whereabouts."

"Look, Benny, I have to go. I'll call later," Pam said. She flipped her cell phone shut and joined the others as they walked back to the car.

"Let's go to the *Oficina de Transito Municipal*. It's the main police station on the corner of Eighth and Avenida Constitucion. I know the way," said Bert. He added that it would be better if only he and Steve did the talking once they got there. "Remember, everything's done differently here. The slower pace alone can drive you nuts. Just a heads up."

Pam and Diane nodded. Steve followed Bert's directions, and in fifteen minutes they were parked in front of the police station. The quartet walked into the crowded police station. Chairs were arranged in rows, where people were waiting to be called.

"You guys can sit here. I'll stand in line to get a number," said Bert.

"I'll wait in line with you," Steve said, as Pam and Diane found a seat.

There was no air conditioning, and the air was still and stifling. After almost an hour, their ticket number was called.

"Finally," hissed Diane. "I'm about to die in this heat."

Pam said nothing, but couldn't help thinking there had to be a better way than this.

Steve and Bert approached the desk. Bert explained in Spanish about the call from the insurance company concerning Steve's stolen Mustang. The officer behind the counter listened with a bored expression. When Bert was finished talking, the officer directed them to the *Oficina de Magistrado Municipal* on *Avenida Independencia* and *Paseo Centenario* to pay the towing fee. Bert translated for Steve. Steve grabbed his head like he was trying to stop it from exploding. He was immensely frustrated from all the waiting in the oppressively hot station, only to be told they had to go somewhere else.

"Can't you tell him the insurance company told us to come here to pay the fee? Give me a break!" Steve was unable to hide his exasperation.

"Let's just go, Steve," Bert said. "It isn't worth it. You can't win here."

Pam walked up to the guys and held up a poster while whispering a suggestion to Bert. He turned back to the *hombre* behind the desk.

"*Por favor,* this family is trying hard to find their daughter. Could you give some of your patrol officers copies of this poster?"

The officer looked at the poster. "*Un momento,*" he said, then went into an office behind his desk. A few minutes later he came out with another man. They spoke with Bert in Spanish. By this time, Diane had joined them at the desk. The superior officer nodded and held out his hand. Pam and Diane gave him about twenty-five posters, which he told Bert in Spanish would be distributed to patrol officers.

"*Muchas gracias,senor,*" said Bert. The others nodded their appreciation.

"*Buena suerte*," the officer replied and went back to his office.

Bert turned to the others and said, "He wished us good luck. At least it wasn't a total waste."

"Thanks for talking to the officers," said Steve. "It's good a lot of cops can see the poster with Amanda's face and know she's missing."

They walked outside and found a convenience store, where they bought bottles of water.

"I can't stand it," Diane moaned. "Every minute Amanda is missing is precious time lost!"

"We're doing all we can, Diane," Bert said. "We need to remain calm. I know it's hard. I told you this would be a slow process. We're actually making some progress, though. Let's just go to the judge now, pay the fee, and then head over to the impound lot."

Pam took pictures from the car on the way to the municipal judge's office. She was glad she wasn't the one behind the wheel, as all the drivers moved rather slowly, ignored basic rules of the road, honked their horns, and cut each other off. People on foot crossed the road whenever and wherever they wanted. *Policia* were everywhere, but they didn't help the flow of traffic. Cops on bicycles were grouped on one corner, talking. Cruisers were on the roads, but no one seemed to pay any attention to the *policia.*

"I can't believe there aren't tons accidents with the way the people drive here," said Pam. "This would drive me nuts on an ongoing basis."

Diane fanned herself with her hat. Steve liked to keep the windows open instead of using the air conditioner.

"Because we're in and out of the car so much, it's better to keep the air conditioning off so we won't get sore throats. I learned this the hard way in the construction business. I'll turn it back on when we're back on the highway."

As they approached their destination, Steve began to search for somewhere to park, finally finding a space two and a half blocks from the municipal judge's office. By the time they got to the office, the hot, tired group was desperate for some refreshing cool air. To their chagrin, the building didn't have air conditioning. They soon found themselves in another large, stifling waiting room. A few floor fans hummed loudly, but the old fans didn't do anything but push the hot air around. Diane and Pam went to the ladies room, while the guys got in yet another line.

Once in the restroom, Diane started crying. "This is just too much for me. I just can't handle it anymore."

Pam gave her sister-in-law a hug. "I wish I could wave a magic wand and bring Amanda here right now. We're all praying, Diane. I think we'll find her."

Diane hiccupped and mumbled, "Thanks."

Diane then took a paper towel, wet it, and blotted her face. She wiped off her tears and refreshed what little makeup she had on. Pam threw some water on her face, too. It felt good. By the time they rejoined the men, Steve and Bert were ready to leave. They had paid the fine and gotten directions to the impound lot.

CHAPTER 36
IMPOUND LOT

It was as if an electrical charge had hit the four as they walked down the block to the truck. They were renewed and hopeful.

"You won't believe what the authorities told me in there," Bert said. "Turns out they believe the car was stolen from the people who stole it."

"You're kidding," said Steve. "Why do they think that?"

"The car was found stripped in an area that's seldom frequented by tourists, for one thing. After questioning some neighborhood kids, the police determined the car was taken when the Mexican who had driven it left it parked and went into a bar."

"Unbelievable! Do they have any idea who the guy was? Did the children give a description of the man? Can they be questioned?"

"No. That's just the word on the street. Nobody recognizes anybody, you know? And forget about asking the kids anything. That'll never happen," Bert said with a shrug.

Steve scowled. "I could really come to hate Mexico."

"But I did get directions to the impound lot," said Bert. "It doesn't sound far, but it's kind of hard to tell."

Steve followed Bert's directions, which took them to the west end of town, up a hill, and onto a very narrow road.

Small, ramshackle houses and shacks lined the winding road. The dilapidated buildings were so close together, they looked as if they were on top of each other. With patched roofs, broken windows (some with plastic taped over them), missing doors, and beat-up furniture in the yards, the poor families lived in squalor. Small children with dirty faces, torn clothing, and no shoes watched them drive past. Mangy-looking dogs barked as women hung clothes out their windows, and young men stood languidly in doorframes, eyeing everyone suspiciously.

At the top of the hill, the road curved. The asphalt was in pieces and there were deep ruts, causing driving to be more difficult as well as kicking up clouds of dust.

Diane coughed. "It's so dusty, I can barely breathe."

"Not much farther now," said Bert.

At the end of the road was the impound lot. Broken-down trucks and cars, demolished vehicles, car parts, tires, and general debris littered the area. Two pit bulls and a mean-looking greyhound mix were on watch. The canines barked and growled ferociously as the truck approached.

"Girls, stay in the truck," said Steve as they pulled into the lot and parked. "Bert and I will take care of this."

"No problem," answered Pam as she watched one of the dogs jump up and bark like mad outside her window. "Be careful, guys. Those dogs look vicious."

A man opened the door of the small, rundown building that served as the office and yelled at the dogs. They didn't stop barking or growling, but the dogs did allow Steve and Bert to carefully make their way over to where the man was standing. The three then went inside, while Pam and Diane locked themselves in the truck.

"I hope we learn something here that'll help us find

Amanda," said Diane, sadly. "My heart hurts so much."

"I know," said Pam. "I pray all the time. God will help us find her."

"I keep saying I feel like I'm having a nightmare, and I can't wake up. But it's true." Diane's face clearly showed the strain she was under.

The women didn't have to wait long. The guard dogs started their barking frenzy again as the door to the shack opened. The proprietor called to the dogs, while Steve and Bert stepped through the debris to the truck and got in.

"Well?" Pam asked anxiously.

"That shithead didn't give a shit about anything," Steve said through clenched teeth. "The car had already been stripped clean by the time it was towed here, which apparently was why it had been towed to this particular lot in the first place. The guy got the VIN and called the insurance company. They've already picked it up." He slammed his fist against the dash.

"You mean the car is *gone?*" asked Diane incredulously. "Why didn't someone tell us that? Didn't the insurance company tell us to come out here?"

"Don't have any answers, Diane. That's just how it works here. Or doesn't work. Or fuck, how should I know?" Steve was at the end of his rope. He, too, had hoped they would learn something about Amanda's whereabouts from the situation with the car.

"Automobiles get stolen all the time in Mexico," Bert said. "The odds of getting any real information off the stripped Mustang as to Amanda's location or situation were slim at best anyway." Noting their crestfallen faces, Bert added, "It was important for us to come out here and try, though. We'll just keep on. I have spoken with a couple of my contacts. The word about Amanda is being spread here in Tijuana. I imagine it won't be long before Amanda, or whoever she's with, hears that people are looking for her." Bert appeared confident.

"I don't know if that's a good thing or a bad thing." Pam was instantly sorry she'd expressed her thought out loud, because Diane immediately burst into tears. "I'm sorry," said Pam. "I'm sure it's a good thing. If Amanda is being held against her will, her captors will let her go so they won't have to deal with the authorities, you know?"

Diane blew her nose and nodded.

The four drove back down the toothpick thin winding road, keeping their eyes peeled, although none of them was sure what exactly they were looking for. As the truck headed back into town, Steve stopped periodically so the girls could jump out and tack up posters on whatever pole or post they could find.

"Anyone hungry?" Steve asked as they entered into the city area. As his passengers answered with a chorus of "Yesses," Steve parked outside the McDonalds in Tijuana.

"I don't feel too confident about eating the food in Mexico. Does the government have codes governing restaurants or anything?" Pam asked.

Steve laughed off her fears. "Diane, Amanda and I have eaten in Tijuana, Rosarita, and other towns in Mexico plenty of times, and we've lived to tell about it. The food's fine."

While still skeptical, Pam was starving, and hunger can drive a person. She joined the others in ordering fries and a shake to "hold them over." The boost to the blood sugar helped everyone, and they returned to the truck for the drive back home.

"The lines to get into the States are so long, and I'm tired." Diane wailed. "They move so slowly."

Nothing moves fast in Mexico, thought Steve.

Pam watched as the *policia* with their drug-sniffing dogs walked between the vehicles doing random searches. The dogs didn't openly indicate they were on to anything, but occasionally a guard would ask someone to open a trunk or van door.

"Do the police ask to search a trunk or search a vehicle, even if the dogs don't bark?" asked Pam.

"It appears to be random searching," answered Bert. "But I've heard rumors the drug cartels have been able to get their people inside the customs agencies. We know the cartels have infiltrated the *policia* to some extent. I don't know if it's true or not about the customs agencies, but you know the old saying, 'where there's smoke, there's fire.'"

"You'd think the government would be doing more, but I've read tons of stuff indicating the Mexican drug cartels are so rich, powerful, and feared, that it's all the honest people in the Mexican government can do just to stay alive," said Pam. "I read an article online that said the Arellano-Felix Organization, known as the AFO or the Tijuana Cartel, is very ruthless and brags that it 'takes no prisoners.' The article went on to say that the cartels pay out around a million dollars a week in bribes to Mexican officials, Mexican police, and Mexican army officers."

"It's true," agreed Bert. "The cartels have their own well-armed and trained paramilitary security forces, too. They even have ties to street and prison gangs on the U.S. side."

"It's amazing how all this goes on around us. And scary, too," said Pam with a shudder.

"Stop talking about the drug cartels!" cried Diane. "What if Amanda has been kidnapped, and they are the ones who have her? We don't know where Amanda is or who she's with. Anything could be happening to her. Those drug cartel people are savages." And with that, the hiccups came along with the tears.

Diane was voicing everyone's fears. Silence ensued for the next several minutes.

Finally, Steve said, "We're next in line. Everyone get your IDs out. Driver's license is sufficient, Pam, in case you didn't know."

"Got it, thanks," said Pam.

The truck rolled to a stop at the customs booth. The agent reached out his hand. "Give me your IDs." He looked them over. "How long were you in Mexico?"

Steve answered, "Just for the day. We came to Tijuana to shop and eat."

"Did you bring anything back with you?" the agent asked.

"Not this time," answered Steve.

The agent nodded as he handed Steve the IDs. "Go on through."

"That's what they want to hear, Americans spending money in their country," said Steve to no one in particular.

They were soon on the highway, not stopping until they reached Bert's exit.

"Should we plan on picking you up same time, same place tomorrow?"

"Sounds good. I'll make some calls tonight. Call me if you hear anything. We're making progress, Steve."

Steve nodded. "I'd love to have something good to report."

Bert said his good-byes and hopped out of the truck.

Exhaustion can wash over a person like a tidal wave, and both Pam and Diane felt it.

"My body's still on East Coast time," said Pam, with

a yawn. Since she now had the backseat to herself, she made a pillow out of her purse and lay down. It wasn't long before Pam nodded off, drifting into a restless slumber.

Diane rested her head on Steve's shoulder. He liked the familiar feeling. The quiet allowed him to mull over the day's events. He didn't feel closer to finding Amanda, regardless of what Bert said. *Please, God, help us bring our daughter home.*

CHAPTER 37
THE CONDO

"We're here, Pam," Steve said as they pulled up in front of the condo.

"Sorry, I fell asleep. Guess I've got jet lag."

"No worries. I appreciate so much that you came out here," Steve replied. He picked up Pam's suitcase and led the way into the foyer.

"Is this the first time you've seen the condo, Pam? I can't remember," said Diane as she pushed the button on the private elevator to their ninth-floor condo.

"No. I was here when you guys bought the place last June. This will be my first time since you've moved in, though. It's beautiful."

The condo had two bedrooms, two baths, a living room, dining room, study area, and a modern kitchen with black granite countertops, silver appliances, and an eat-in area. Gold fixtures adorned the master bedroom and bath.

"I love the view of Balboa Park," said Diane, pointing it out to Pam. "Almost everything we need is within walking distance, too. This condo is perfect for us."

Steve and Diane also owned a cottage-style, two-bedroom house in Point Loma, where they'd lived for years. They considered putting the house on the market, but Steve worked out of the house a lot and didn't want to give it up.

"I thought we were going to use this condo as an investment," Steve told his sister. "We were going to rent it out and let the condo pay for itself. But Diane likes living here, so I don't know now."

"I do like living here. We can rent out the house instead," said Diane.

"That wasn't the plan," said Steve a bit testily.

The couple hadn't come to an agreement about the situation, and had been arguing about it for months. Now Steve spent most of his time at the house, even sleeping there, and Diane stayed at the condo. Pam couldn't tell where Steve and Diane's relationship was headed. Amanda's disappearance was the kind of tragic circumstance that could either bring them closer together, or be the catalyst that propelled them into a more permanent separation.

"We thought it'd be more comfortable for all of us to stay at the condo while you're here, Pam," Diane said. "There's more room. You know how small the house is."

"Thanks, I appreciate your thoughtfulness. This place is gorgeous!" said Pam.

Steve ordered a pizza while Diane showed Pam to her bedroom so she could unpack, take a hot shower, and put on some lounging clothes.

I feel numb, like this isn't really happening, Pam thought while the water rushed over her body.

When the pizza arrived, the trio sat around the kitchen table, chatting, eating, and drinking San Pellegrino.

"What's the plan for tomorrow?" asked Pam as she took a sip of the sparkling water.

"You remember my business partner, Geraldo? I'm

going to give him some of the posters written in English to take to the San Diego Police Department. The sergeant said they'd pass them out to the other precincts. You never know; Amanda could be back here. Or someone may have seen her driving, or in a car, or . . . something. I think she's in Mexico, but I'll do anything and everything to find her." Steve cracked his neck.

The phone rang. It was Steve's friend, Mike, calling to say he would be joining them on their search the next day.

"Thanks, Mike, I really appreciate it. Be here by 7:30 so we can hit the road before there's much traffic. See you tomorrow."

"I'm glad he's coming," said Diane.

"Yeah, he's . . . a good friend," Steve said, choking up.

After cleaning up what little mess there was from their dinner, Pam was ready to call it a night.

"We all need a good night's sleep so we can be ready for an early start in the morning," said Steve. "It's going to be a big day." *At least, I hope so.*

Pam went into the bedroom, quietly closed the door, and called Benny.

"Hi, baby," her husband said, answering right away. "How's everything going?"

"It's a mess, Benny," she said wearily. "Amanda's drug problem might have something to do with her disappearance. But we don't know why, or even how, she got to Tijuana. Did someone make her drive there? Did she go to Mexico on her own, or what?"

"I'm sure the situation's very difficult and frightening for everyone, especially with so many unanswered questions," said Benny.

"Mexico's so different from the States," Pam told him.

"Everything's slower than hot tar. It can drive you nuts, trying to deal with the way the Mexicans do things. And the police stations are a joke."

"Having done business there years ago, I know what you mean. Bert called to give me an update. Doesn't look good at the moment, does it?"

"We don't have any leads, if that's what you're saying. But we're not going to give up. Steve and Diane are both stronger than I think I'd be. I'm going to try and contact *America's Most Wanted* tomorrow."

"Are you referring to the television program?"

"Yes. Maybe they can help. The show is known for assisting law enforcement in finding all types of fugitives. Amanda could have been kidnapped, for example, and they might know if she's a 'type' that a known kidnapper prefers."

"Good idea. Keep me posted on everything. I'll call you tomorrow."

After saying good night to Benny, Pam gratefully slid into her comfy bed and said her prayers. Glad to have the mantra of her prayers occupy her mind, Pam didn't want to think of where Amanda could be, or what might be happening to her. It was just too upsetting.

Diane was in bed when Steve came out of the bathroom. He got in and leaned over to give Diane a kiss.

"If we don't find Amanda soon," Diane whispered, "I think I'll lose my mind."

Steve put his head on the pillow and responded determinedly, "We'll find her. I won't stop until we do."

He drifted off to sleep to the sound of Diane's muffled cries.

CHAPTER 38
A BREAKTHROUGH

T he next morning, Steve was showered, shaved, and ready to go by six o'clock. He was in the kitchen, with both coffee and tea made, when Pam walked in.

"I feel like something might break today," Pam said, in an effort to be encouraging.

"Hope you're right," he answered grimly. "Amanda's been missing eight days today."

"What would you think about my contacting *America's Most Wanted*?"

"The TV show? Yeah, sure, it's a good idea. Anything is a good idea at this point." Steve's face looked pinched, and his voice was tight. The effects of the strain, coupled with not having slept well in several nights, were clearly taking their toll.

"May I use your computer?"

"Of course. It's around that corner." Steve pointed Pam in the right direction.

Pam went to the office area, logged in to the show's website, and found information on how to submit a case. After reading the criteria, Pam called out to Steve, "Hey, I think I'll need to ask you a few questions so I can complete the form for *America's Most Wanted*."

Steve and Diane, who was now up and sipping her tea,

came into the office.

"First, do you have a missing persons report filed with the police? Because it says I'll need the name and contact information of the law enforcement personnel assigned to the case."

Steve told Pam about how the San Diego Police Department said they couldn't be of any help because Mexico wasn't in their jurisdiction. "I went ahead and filled out a missing persons report anyway, so there'd be a record of Amanda's disappearance, but no officer was actually assigned to the case," said Steve.

"At least something's on file with the police, then."

"I do have my copy of the missing person's report I filed in Mexico," Steve said. "Do you think that'll help?"

"I don't know. I'll write up everything, explaining the situation. The worst they can do is say they can't help us. If that turns out to be the case, then maybe they'll have some suggestions or contacts for us. I think it's worth it to try." Pam began typing out the information:

America's Most Wanted - Missing Persons - September 17, 2004

We are writing to you out of desperation. Our daughter, Amanda Tate, 24, has been missing since September 9, 2004. Included here are all the facts from that date until now, with the hope you will be able to help us.

After having had treatment for a medical condition four years ago, Amanda became addicted to Vicodin. Wanting to end her dependency, Amanda went to several rehab facilities over the past twenty-four months. Unfortunately, breaking her addiction has proven to be very difficult for her to do.

On Thursday, September 9, Amanda came to me, her father, yet again, asking for help. At this time, we didn't realize our daughter had been using drugs again, as she was no longer living at home. I took Amanda to Kaiser Chemical Dependency Clinic in San Diego for admission to an in-house rehabilitation clinic. Advised there were no beds available for that night at the clinic, the doctor who evaluated her prescribed some drugs to help Amanda get through the night. The receptionist told us to check back the next day.

Pam continued typing, stopping to ask questions of both Steve and Diane along the way. At one point, Diane went into a rampage, screaming at both Steve and Pam.

"It's both your fault Amanda's missing! There must be some weird gene in your family that makes you all want to do drugs. She didn't inherit this problem from me!" Diane yelled.

Pam stared at her sister-in-law in stunned silence, but Steve pounced on Diane's words with a few of his own. "Listen, Miss Who Thinks She's Perfect, stop right now. Pam's trying to help us, and you're going crazy. It doesn't help anyone for you to be pointing a finger. But if you're so inclined, then be sure it's pointing your way, too." Steve stormed out of the room, leaving a shocked Pam sitting there. Diane followed him, shouting, "Screw you both!"

Pam's head dropped into her hands. Taking deep breaths with her eyes closed, Pam willed the air of tension to dissipate. She stood up and stretched, leaned down and touched her toes, reached toward the ceiling, and bent from side to side. Feeling the tightness loosen, Pam reflected on all that was going on. It was almost beyond comprehension.

I have to give Diane a break here, she thought. *I can barely stand what's going through my mind, and Amanda isn't even my daughter.*

She did the series of stretches one more time, before sitting down to finish writing the information for *America's Most Wanted.*

Soon, Steve returned. "I'm sorry about all this. We're under so much pressure, you know? Don't let what Diane said get to you. She's just upset."

Pam got up and hugged her brother. "It's okay. My heart hurts for both of you."

"Yeah, well. Why don't you finish writing that later, and let's just go. Mike's called, and he's downstairs in the lobby. I'm glad he's going to go with us today. We have to meet Geraldo at the house first. He's going to take some of the posters in English to the San Diego cops."

"No prob. I'll just save this info to the computer."

Diane was standing by the door. The three took the elevator down to the foyer, where they joined Mike. They purchased muffins and drinks from the coffee shop next door and then piled into the truck for the drive to the house in Point Loma.

Geraldo was waiting in the driveway when they pulled up. "I'll put the posters up around San Diego on my way to the police station," Geraldo promised after greeting everyone. "Good luck today. Everybody's praying for you."

"Thanks, man," said Steve.

Steve's next stop was the ATM. "I need to get some cash before we pick up Bert," he explained. "I'm going through money like there's no tomorrow, but I won't care at all if it gets Amanda back."

They arrived at the pickup point at 9:00 a.m. and Bert was already there, talking on his cell phone. He ended the call when he saw the truck pull in.

"I heard the *policia* are on the lookout for Amanda now," said Bert. "The department head passed the posters out to some of the patrol officers. They are aware of the situation."

"That's awesome," said Steve, with more excitement in his voice than he'd had in a long time. He looked at Diane, but she was staring out the window. "Something's going to break for us today, honey, I just know it."

"I hope so." Diane's voice was barely above a whisper.

The plan was to park on the U.S. side of the border, taking advantage of Bert's pass. It was easy to walk over, and they'd avoid the long wait when driving back across.

"The San Ysidro border crossing is the busiest one in the world," Pam said. "I read that somewhere."

"I don't doubt it," said Bert.

The drive south on the 5 was easy. There wasn't a lot of traffic at that time of day, so they just zipped along. When they reached the last exit, Steve turned and went to the government parking lot. Bert showed his credentials, and they were let in. The group parked and disembarked.

"There's a stack of posters for each of us. I have tape and thumbtacks in my backpack," said Diane.

The three men and two women walked to the border. They passed through the first revolving gate, and continued down the walkway that housed a tourist information booth, money changers, and a travel agency. A few Mexican officials were in the walkway scrutinizing the people entering their country, but they seldom requested IDs or even asked anyone anything. Steve went through the second turnstile followed by Diane, Pam, and the two men.

"McDonald's is located at the north end of Plaza Viva Tijuana. Let's meet there if we get separated today," said Steve as they walked toward the familiar landmark. Immediately, they noticed the posters they had put up the day before.

"It's surreal to see posters of a missing person when it's your own daughter's face looking back at you," Steve observed. "I just hope we get some action from these darn things."

"Let's go down this street today," Diane said.

As they walked, they showed the posters to tourists and shoppers as they passed by, asking, "Have you seen this girl?" or "Our daughter is missing. Please, can you help us find her?" and "Does anyone know this girl?"

No one seemed to have seen Amanda or to know anything.

"I can't believe no one's even seen her," said Diane.

"Since there are five of us, we can fan out," Bert suggested. "But we have to keep each other in sight. No need losing anyone in the crowds. I particularly mean Diane and Pam."

Steve and Mike nodded. The men weren't worried for themselves, being confident they could handle about any situation.

Suddenly, a big, burly, scruffy young man stopped Diane and said, "I've seen that girl."

He was weaving a little, and Diane wondered if he might be drunk or high, but she stopped short when he commented on the poster.

"Steve, Steve, come quick!"

Steve turned and ran to Diane. "What's going on?"

"I know her," the young man said. "That's Mindy."

Steve and Pam had an aunt who sometimes called Mandy "Mindy." Maybe this guy was making the same mistake.

"Close enough," said Steve. "Where've you seen her?" He held his breath.

"Well, dude, I hate to say it, but . . ." The man stopped speaking as he struggled to stay upright. "I've done drugs with her before."

"Holy shit!" Steve screamed. "This guy knows Amanda!"

The others came running and spoke all at once, the questions coming fast and furious.

"Where is she?"

"When was the last time you saw her?"

"Where'd you see her?"

"Do you know where she is now?"

The young man took an unsteady step back. "Hold on, dude. It's been a while. Like a few months or something."

"This guy's fucked up," Mike whispered to Bert. "What do you say? American? Late twenties?"

Bert nodded.

It was apparent to all the young man was messed up. His eyes darted around wildly, and he kept scratching his arms. The movement drew attention to his biceps. Pitted from acne, the tattoos he had were still discernible. One arm was inked with a vicious-looking bulldog, on the other were stars and lightning bolts. He was very pale, and his hair clearly hadn't seen shampoo in several days.

"Are you hungry?" asked Steve.

"Yeah, guess I am."

"Let's go to McDonald's, get something to eat, and talk about this."

Steve's heart was pounding double-time. He was sure this guy knew something, and he was bound and determined to find out what it was.

They walked to the McDonald's, where Steve placed an

order for all of them. He then introduced himself, adding, "My wife, Diane, and I are Amanda's parents. She's the girl on the poster. Sometimes she's called Mandy, which is why when you said, 'Mindy,' we got excited." The cashier handed the food to Steve, and he passed it out. "Our daughter's been missing for eight days. We're worried sick about her," he said, looking at the scruffy young man.

"Yeah, that sucks, dude," the young man said as he stuffed food in his mouth.

"The others here are my sister, Pam, and my buddies, Mike and Bert," Steve added.

The young man nodded, wolfing down his food as if he hadn't had anything to eat in a long time. Finally wiping his mouth, he said, "Everyone knows me as the German Bulldog." At that, he straightened up, puffing out his chest. "I'm an ultimate fighting champion."

His firm build and enormous biceps gave possible credence to his words.

Diane eyed him suspiciously. "What are you doing here, then? Being a champion and all, how did you get mixed up in drugs?"

Bulldog shrugged. "I just kind of fell into it, man. Started with my shots, you know? Then the other stuff began looking pretty good, and before you know it, I'm chasing the dragon."

Pam looked at him incredulously. "Where are you from?"

"La Jolla. My dad's a lawyer. He and my mom still live there, but I mostly hang out in West Hollywood. I fight all over Southern Cal. It's all good, you know? I'm going to quit drugs in about a month." He took a big gulp of his drink.

"What? I don't believe that. Why don't you just quit

right now?" Pam asked, astonished.

"I could, I'm just not ready," he said, irritated.

Steve shook his head almost imperceptivity at Pam to quiet her. He didn't want to anger the first person who had responded to their posters.

"So how do you know Amanda?" Steve asked.

With Steve's question opening the door, the others jumped in again, peppering Bulldog with questions.

"Do you know where she might be now?"

"How many times have you seen her?"

"Can you take us to where she is?"

Bulldog started fidgeting in his seat and seemed agitated.

Steve knew the signs. *He's coming down off a high and needs drugs. I can't let this guy go,* Steve thought.

"Why don't you and I go for a little walk," Steve suggested, putting his arm on Bulldog's shoulder. "The rest of you can hang out here."

Steve took Bulldog outside, and after the two got out of earshot, Bert said, "Let's hope this guy can give us something."

"Well, he's the first real lead we've had," said Diane, with a glimmer of hope. "Finding the car didn't do much, so I don't count that."

Steve walked down the block with Bulldog. "Look, man," Steve said, anxious and hopeful at the same time. "I could use your help. You probably know more than you think you do. Will you help me find Mandy? There'll be cash in it for you. You know, like a reward."

Bulldog wasn't as wobbly as he had been prior to eating. He couldn't seem to stop scratching, though. "Sure, dude. I hate it that she's missing. Your daughter could be somewhere just smoking or something. But it's not that safe around here for a chick by herself. I've seen all kinds of shit go down in TJ. Know what I mean?"

Inside McDonald's, Bert and Mike were antsy.

"We're going to go about six blocks in, and pepper the area with posters," Bert told the women. "We'll meet you guys back here at 5:00. What do you think?"

Pam and Diane looked at each other. "Let's put it up to Steve. Something might be happening with this ultimate fighter guy," Pam said. "I'll go ask him what he thinks."

"Good, because just sitting here is driving me nuts," said Mike.

Pam and Diane went outside and found Steve. Pam pulled him aside. "Bert and Mike want to go further into Tijuana, put up posters, and ask around and stuff," she said. "They said they'd meet us here at 5:00. What do you think? They're getting antsy and want to do something."

Steve glanced at his watch. "Tell them to wait just a few more minutes." He turned to Bulldog. "So, what do you think? Want to help?"

"Yeah. I got some time right now." Bulldog grinned at his own words. He had all the time in the world.

Steve told Pam to get the other guys. He turned back to Bulldog in time to hear him say to Diane, "My real name's Greg. No one calls me that, but you can if you want, I guess. Whatever."

"Okay. I like Greg better than Bulldog. Where should we go first?"

"I've seen your girl a few times in an area not far from here, just over a few streets and down one. We should head that way," said Bulldog, pointing south.

With the group together again, they walked a couple of blocks and turned where Bulldog indicated. The area was still commercial, only very rundown.

"It was around here," Bulldog said. "The *farmacias* are pretty friendly, if you know what I mean."

When no one responded to his comment, Bulldog added, "You can buy anything you want. And you can just go in the back room and do the drugs. They'll cut the shit up right there and you can snort it or whatever. Makes it easy." He glanced uneasily at Steve. "I mean, you probably know that already, right?"

Steve nodded.

Unbelievable, Pam thought. *People must have a tough time trying to kick their habits around here.*

"We can stop by this one *farmacia* where I'm certain I've done shit with her before. You two can walk in with me," Bulldog said, gesturing to Steve and Pam, "but the others need to wait outside. If the pharmacist suspects something isn't cool, he won't tell me shit."

Mike, Bert, and Diane walked down the block, looking in windows as if they were shopping. Bulldog turned and led the way into the *farmacia*, with Steve and Pam following

Nonchalantly, Bulldog asked, "Hey, man, you seen that chick, Mindy, or Mandy, or whatever? You know, the hot Americana with the long, dark hair?"

The pharmacist shrugged. "*No entiendo.*"

Pam sighed, "He doesn't seem to understand." She held up a poster, but he shook his head no.

"Let's go," said Bulldog.

When they got outside, Bulldog was clearly annoyed. "The guy just didn't want to give up anything. He speaks English good enough. I've been in that place a shit load of times.

He must've been freaked by you guys. And the fucking poster."

They walked the few stores down to where Bert, Mike, and Diane were waiting and relayed what had happened.

"Where to now?" asked Pam.

"Let's hop a cab, man," said Bulldog. "There's an area where lots of people go to get high. She might be there."

Mike pulled Steve aside and said, "I don't trust this guy."

"It's not an ideal situation, I know. But I absolutely do not want to let go of the only person who says he's seen Amanda."

They hailed a cab. Squeezing six people into a cab wasn't easy, especially when four of them were big guys, but they did it. Bulldog gave the driver an address, and off they went.

Pressed against Bulldog's large frame, Pam got the full force of an odor of someone who hadn't bathed in a while but needed to. She didn't like Bulldog very much so far.

I wonder if he's full of shit. But then, he did say "Mindy" when he saw the poster. Hope he's not just playing us, or it'll be devastating, Pam thought.

The cabbie dropped them off in the middle of Tijuana, where there weren't many tourists. The area was old, tired, and dirty.

Bulldog said, "This here is one of my favorite restaurants for burgers. Anyone hungry?"

Bert and Mike looked at each other, mouths agape.

Diane, too, looked incredulous. "But you just ate . . ."

Steve held up his hand, silencing her. "Sure, let's get something," he said.

They went inside the open-air diner and crammed into two booths. They were the only non-locals in the place.

Guess it didn't matter he had just eaten at McDonald's, thought Pam.

"Get a burger, Pam," said Bulldog. "They're the best in town."

Pam was skeptical. "No, thanks. I'm kind of afraid to eat meat here. It could be dog or some kind of mystery meat. I don't want to get sick. Does Mexico even have any regulations?"

Without warning, Bulldog suddenly jumped up and shouted, "Who do you think you are, talking like that? Are you saying I don't know my shit?" He leaned over the booth, glaring at Pam like he was going to lunge at her.

Steve and Mike shot out of their seats and grabbed Bulldog.

"Calm down, man," said Steve. "She didn't mean anything personal."

Mike had a firm grip on Bulldog's arm and shoulder and said, "Take it easy."

Steve scowled at his sister. "Pam, please," he hissed. "Just find something to eat and don't start anything, okay?"

"Fine. I'll have a salad."

"Me, too," said Diane. "This place is a dive," she whispered to Pam.

"Sure is," Pam whispered back.

Bulldog talked about the drug scene in Tijuana. "Lots of Americans come here to cop. It's so easy, man. You can do the shit here, or carry it back."

"Aren't you afraid to cross the border with drugs?" asked Pam.

"I'm talkin' about taking back just enough for personal stash. You put the shit in a baggie, surround it in more plastic, put it in something to disguise the smell, hide it in your car and book it back. I do it all the time. Nobody messes with me in my Escalade," he boasted.

"You're a pretty humble guy, aren't you?" Pam said snidely. She couldn't help herself. Bulldog irritated the hell out of her.

"Pam! Stop the shit." Steve snapped, getting angry. He was worried that someone would upset Bulldog enough to make him leave.

The orders came and the girls gingerly picked at their salads, while the guys ate their food without a care. Bulldog again ate as if he hadn't seen a morsel in days.

Appearing to ignore Pam's comment, Bulldog said, "There's a hotel a few blocks from here where there's always girls getting high." He popped the last bite in his mouth.

"What are we waiting for? Let's go!" Steve was so ready to find Amanda that he could barely contain himself.

Bulldog made a face. "I gotta tell you, man, it's not a nice place. The girls go there to do drugs and are probably trading sex for them. That's what the hotel's known for."

The blood drained from Diane's and Pam's faces. Although they both had harbored such thoughts in the recesses of their minds at one point or another during the time Amanda had been missing, hearing it said aloud was another thing altogether. They sullenly pushed their plates away.

"I'm not making any moral judgments," said Steve. "I just want to find my daughter and get her out of here. I'm ready to go there right now."

"Okay, I'll take you. I'm done eating anyhow," Bulldog said and then chugged the last of his drink.

Steve stood up. He motioned to Mike and Bert but then

said, "You girls stay here. It's not the kind of place for you."

"I don't want to stay here, just Diane and me," said Pam. "What happens if you guys leave, and we aren't here when you get back? I don't like this area; plus, I promised Benny I'd be prudent."

"I'll take the girls back to the border area," Bert piped up. "You know, by McDonald's. You can meet us there. We'll just hang out and wait. We've all got our cell phones."

"Great idea! Thanks, Bert," exclaimed Steve. He was certain they were going to find Amanda at that hotel. And Pam was right; this was no area for her and Diane to be hanging out.

"Are you ladies up to walking? It's only about seven blocks or so. I know the way," said Bert. "You'll be able to see more of Tijuana as we walk, too."

"Walking's fine with me," answered Pam.

"Me, too," said Diane. "I think walking will be good for our nerves. I don't want to think of Amanda being in a place like that hotel." She started crying.

"It's okay, Diane," Pam said, embracing her. "Once we get Amanda back, we can work through all the other stuff."

Steve paid the tab, and they walked out. Once outside, Steve hugged Diane and Pam. "Wish us luck. Say a prayer we find Amanda."

"We will," Diane said, sniffling.

"Be safe," said Pam. She looked directly at Bulldog, who appeared spaced out. Pam immediately said a silent prayer.

The guys took off in one direction and the girls in another.

Bert and the girls hadn't walked very far when Pam cocked her head to one side and said, "I hear music."

About two blocks ahead was a small parade with musicians, singers, and food vendors. Children were playing, and people were selling their wares on tables lined up outside. The atmosphere was festive.

This should lift the mood, thought Bert.

A makeshift stage was set up in the middle of the street, and the trio stopped to watch. Men in brightly colored costumes sang and danced on the stage.

"I love this music," said Pam. She began moving with the rhythm.

Bert noticed some men watching her, so he whispered, "Don't dance, Pam. The guys here like it too much."

Bert took the women's arms and led them away through the throngs of people who were enjoying the festival. Walking down a side street, they looked at stores and passed by a Catholic church.

"I want to go into this church and light a candle," said Pam. "We can say a prayer for Amanda."

"Sorry, no more stopping. I won't feel good until we're near the border," said Bert. "I'm not taking chances while you both are in my care."

"The German Bulldog must come here often. He seems to know a lot about the drug underworld in Tijuana," said Diane.

"Yes, and he knows the places druggies go to get high. Looks like he's seen better days, too," said Pam. She was wary. "The guy gives me the creeps. He's just too slick. I think it's risky to place much trust in him."

Diane nodded in agreement. "I know what you mean. Steve told me he had promised Bulldog a cash reward to help us get to Amanda. He could just be leading us on a wild goose chase, or worse, into some kind of trap." She shuddered at the thought. "Bulldog's real name is Greg, by the way."

"I don't like the Bulldog, either," said Bert, "but since he's all we have right now, he's worth a shot."

"Of course you're right," said Pam. "Just about anything is worth a shot right now."

Diane slowed her steps as she was hit once again by the enormity of the situation. "Amanda's been missing eight days now," she said somberly. "She has no car and no phone. Each moment is precious. I don't know what's at that hotel, but I just pray the guys will be successful in finding her."

The knot in the pit of Diane's stomach had grown into a boulder.

CHAPTER 39
SELF-ABSORBED UNCLES

"Let's grab some lunch at the Ivy," said Craig on the phone to his brother. "Does 1:30 work for you?"

"Sounds good," Dave agreed. *The Ivy. Great spot to see and be seen.*

Craig arrived a half hour early to peruse the trendy art galleries along Melrose. *I need some artwork for my place,* he thought as he pulled into a parking space. The galleries offered new and out-of-the-ordinary items that Craig liked to purchase for the restaurant. He'd write them off as a business expense, hang them up for a while, and then take them home.

Dave had been in show business for several years and had become a minor celebrity in the area. Ever the attention-seeker, he had a limo drop him off in front of the Ivy.

My luck's changing, and I'm rolling with it. Dave grinned. Getting the call back, deciding to hook up with the super-hot ultimate fighters, and getting his rocks off at the party were all mood enhancers.

Paparazzi always hung around Robertson on the lookout for someone famous to photograph. The shutterbugs hoped for a big star, or the "It" person of the moment, but they'd shoot almost any celeb. Even a "D-lister" could be involved in a newsworthy situation, and, if so, they'd have a photo handy.

The paparazzi were just doing their job.

When Dave emerged from the limo, several paparazzi's flashbulbs went off in his face. Brandishing an ultra-bright smile, he waved them off, as if he was too cool to talk. Craig walked up at the same time, so the brothers were photographed together. Craig enjoyed the attention. It was good advertising for the Windjammer.

"So nice to see you both again," said the lovely hostess as she led the brothers to the much-requested outside corner table.

"Thanks, gorgeous," said Dave, flashing his megawatt smile. "Have someone bring Perrier."

"Of course."

The handsome duo attracted a lot of attention as they sat leisurely sipping their sparkling water with lime. Neither wanted to hit the booze yet.

"Are you gentlemen ready to order?" asked the waiter when he sensed the right moment to approach.

"I'll have the grilled veggie salad," said Dave.

"The lobster pasta works for me." Craig handed the waiter their menus.

Both men saw people they knew at the restaurant. They left their table to do obligatory chatting while waiting for their entrees. See and be seen. Once their food was delivered, the brothers returned to the table to dine and gossip.

"Hear anything new from Diane or Steve about Mandy?" asked Craig as he wiped his mouth. He was speaking to Dave, but his eyes were darting around, watching for who might come in.

"No, I haven't heard from them. I feel bad not calling, but . . ." Dave shrugged. "I did put the word out that Mandy hasn't been seen by anybody for a few days, and to let me know if she's spotted somewhere. One of the ultimate fighters, Jake, told me the German Bulldog goes on binges where he's gone for days at a time. So it happens, you know? How about you?"

"Same here as far as not calling Diane. I figure we'll hear something soon, and Mandy'll be okay. I remember our party girl taking off for Vegas before. It does seem strange, though, no one knowing anything. It'd suck if something happened to her."

"Sure would. So how's the pasta? I'm watching my carbs. Got a major call-back coming up." Dave sat a little taller.

"You feeling like king shit, are you?" Craig said, but he was smiling. "Food's great. Hope you get the job. We'll have a party at the bar."

They continued in this same vein for the duration of their lunch. Both brothers exuded an arrogance that said they felt pretty good about themselves—and had little real concern for Amanda.

CHAPTER 40
GOOD NEWS AND BAD NEWS

A manda and Gary walked across the border, hand in hand. They looked just like any other young couple.

It seems weird no one can tell I'm an international drug smuggler now, Amanda thought. *I feel like what I've done is etched on my face for all to see. I almost wish it was; then maybe someone would try to help me.* She shuddered involuntarily and a small moan escaped her lips. *What's going to happen to me now?*

Hector sat in the white station wagon, waiting patiently for Gary and Amanda. Gary knew exactly where the car would be, and he led Amanda to it.

"Get in," Gary instructed Amanda as he opened the front door.

Amanda slid across the front seat next to Hector, leaving room for Gary. She was sandwiched between the two.

"*Bueno,*" Hector said. "It was easy, no?"

Amanda nodded, not sure what the correct answer was. "I have to pee real bad." She squirmed in her seat.

"Gary, take her to McDonald's and wait outside the door." Hector squeezed Amanda's leg. "Don't try anything you'd be sorry for, *chica,*" he said, his voice hard.

"Thank you. I won't." She had hoped he'd say to get

some food from McDonald's, too, but he didn't, and Amanda was afraid to ask.

Gary and Amanda got out of the car and walked across the street to McDonald's. Something fluttering on a pole across the street caught Hector's eye as he watched them walk. He jumped out of the car and ran across the road to get a closer look. Hector's face flushed and he breathed heavily with barely controlled rage when he saw what was tacked to the pole—a poster with a girl's face printed on it. The girl who had just run drugs for them across the border.

"*Mierda!* Fuck!" He tore the poster off the pole. After staring at Amanda's printed face, he folded the poster and put it inside his shirt. Then he saw another poster on a nearby pole. He took that one, too. Angrily, Hector marched across the street and got back into his car. Plans would have to be changed now.

It's all right, he thought. *There's an alternate plan. For everything.*

Hector made a quick call. "We're going to La Coahuila," he said, and hung up.

Gary and Amanda returned to the car. Amanda's mind was on food and drugs and not necessarily in that order. Gary was looking forward to his fix, too. *Heaven in an inhale.*

Gary was on the lam. He had skipped to Mexico in the early 1990s. One of the men Gary dealt drugs with on a regular basis had gotten lax and sold to an undercover cop, so he needed to relocate. *Dumb shit,* thought Gary. *Then the asshole rolled over, naming me.*

Dealers had a saying, "There are no friends in drugs." Seemingly true, the guy who had turned on Gary had been one of his best friends since grade school.

Since then, Gary had been perpetually on the run,

without any contact with his family or friends. He had slipped out of Ohio a day before he was to be served with a warrant for his arrest.

Eli really fucked me over. The dumb shit. Whenever Gary let his mind drift back to that time, he became very agitated and needed drugs to calm down. Heroin had become his drug of choice. It helped him forget. Forget he took off without saying good-bye. Forget his single mom who had done her best to raise him and his baby sister. Forget his sister. Forget Cheryl, his girl-friend of three years.

The past few years had hardened Gary. Now, it was all about business and getting high. He hadn't let anyone get close to him emotionally since he'd left Columbus. Drug smuggling was his life, and there was nothing he could do about it.

I'm sure as hell not going to return to Ohio and turn myself in. What would that gain me? A quick hello to Mom and my spoiled sister? Gary thought bitterly. *And Cheryl. She's probably long gone by now. And then there'd be years in the can. Nope. Not worth it. I'll stay in the business I know and get fucked up as often as I can.* Which was pretty much every day.

Hector was imagining his next conversation with Carlos. He would have to give him the good and bad news. The good news being the successful first drive across the border by the new, pretty mule. The van had been loaded down, too. Carlos would like that a lot. He'd want to use this girl several times until it was time for a transfer. The bad news being that the transfer would have to be sooner rather than later.

Good thing the girl didn't notice the poster. It'd be a shame if she'd gotten false hope of being rescued. Won't be long before it'll be near' impossible to find her anyway. Can't take the chance of having her talk.

Hector sighed. He hated the idea of relaying the news to Carlos, as the boss had a tendency to shoot the messenger. Literally.

Amanda's head was pounding, pounding, pounding. *I need to get high and go home. Maybe these guys will be so happy with me because nothing went wrong that they'll give me my car, like they said. Driving wouldn't be a problem for me, high or not. And I'll tell them I won't blab about them, either. I don't want anyone to know what's happened. It's all too ugly. Plus, I'd be scared for the rest of my life they'd come after me and my family if I talked, anyway. I couldn't live like that. No, I won't tell. I'll explain all that to these guys, too, as soon as they let me have my car.* Thoughts zoomed through Amanda's head like race cars at Daytona. Made her whole body shake.

"Where are we going?" Amanda asked as she scratched viciously at her arms and legs. Rivers of sweat ran down her body, and she doubled over with intense stomach cramps. She closed her eyes and envisioned her blood as hot tar burning its way slowly through her veins. Soon the pain would be stronger than the hunger.

Hector didn't answer her. His angry expression confused Amanda. *Hadn't everything gone well?* She turned and looked at Gary. He was in his own place, too, but felt her look.

"What?"

"Where . . . are we . . . going?" Amanda's voice was barely more than a whisper.

"To get high, baby."

Even as he spoke the words, however, Gary saw they weren't driving in the direction of the house. He glanced at Hector for an explanation, but got none. Hector kept his focus straight ahead.

Soon they were in an area known as *Zona Norte*, the North Zone, a red-light district in Tijuana where prostitution was legal. Independent sex workers, required to get permits and have monthly health checkups, worked with government consent. The brothels had state regulated health and cleanliness standards. A number of legal prostitutes worked outdoors on the *callejones*, or alleys, and were referred to as *paraditas,* standing girls. They'd often take their johns into one of the cheap, seedy hotels in *Zona Norte.*

Illegal prostitutes, those working without permits, also hung around street corners and alleyways. Their prices were cheap, but their health conditions were questionable.

Gary had often frequented *Zona Norte* when he had first come to Tijuana. Not many tourists went to that area, just guys looking for trouble. Or to get laid. Or both. Gary still liked going there for his sex and drugs.

Street musicians and *los poblanos,* portable restaurants, could also be found in *Zona Norte*. The main tourist section of Tijuana revolved around *Avenida Revolucion,* the leading commercial strip where most tourists went to shop, eat, and bargain. *Avenida Revolucion* was known as a fairly safe area. Other than getting ripped off by paying too much or being the victim of a pickpocket, tourists generally enjoyed themselves on *Avenida Revolucion.*

Zona Norte, on the other hand, was rife with crime. The nastiest area of *Zona Norte* was *Callejon Coahuila*, an alleyway north of *Calle Coahuila*. The tiny, torn-up street boasted cheap hotels and bars. Narrow, uneven sidewalks were crowded with undesirables. Junkies shot up on the street, often puking in public view. Thieves roamed the area in search of victims, and for a cheap price, hookers would do what a customer wanted, right out in the open. Drunks and thugs eager to fight often met with deadly outcomes. Knives were common—and lethal—weapons. *Policia* on patrol had grown accustomed to finding a body or two tossed behind the bushes.

Live shows in the bars there left nothing to the imagination. Money could buy almost anything. Sex, drugs, and cheap thrills. Tourists were easy targets in *Zona Norte,* both by predators and by *policia* shakedowns.

There'd been documented reports of Americans barely making it out of the notorious area alive. And, sadly, reports of some not so lucky.

Zona Norte was where Hector took Amanda.

He drove to the intersection of *Calle Coahuila* and *Avenida Ninos Heros*, near the famous Kinkle Bar, branded as a haven for transvestites. A small hotel known only to locals was nearby. Filthy and cheap, the rundown hotel was used mostly by druggies and prostitutes.

Hector parked in an alley. Then he, Gary, and a shaky Amanda walked to the hotel. Even though Amanda had been to Tijuana too many times to count, she'd never been to *Callejon Coahuila*.

This place gives me the creeps, Amanda thought. As badly as she needed drugs, she recognized that this wasn't a safe place to be.

Gary didn't say a word as they walked. Being practically a regular to *Zona Norte*, he saw the area through different eyes.

Hector had decided to drive straight to the seedy hotel after seeing the posters with Amanda's face. He knew no one there would recognize Amanda, or wouldn't care, even if they did. After making their way through the rundown bar in the front of the hotel, Hector and Gary dragged the weak Amanda up the back steps to a dirty, dark, and dingy room with a putrid smell. Inside were three girls and two men. One of the girls was out cold. The other inhabitants were smoking heroin. Thin, ratty twin beds that bowed in the middle, a small beat-up table and chair, and an old, tiny dresser filled the space. A banged-up door, barely on its hinges, led to the bathroom.

After depositing Amanda inside the room, Hector backed out, whispering to Gary, "Go ahead and get fucked up if you want. Just make sure the girl gets wasted. She's to spend tonight here, at least. I'll send someone by later." Hector hated this place and was anxious to leave.

"Yeah, okay," Gary said to Hector as he left and turned to Amanda. "Sit down. It's party time, baby."

Amanda was hungry, tired, itchy, and had cramps. Her ribs ached from the vicious kicks she had endured. With her head swirling, being told to sit down was a relief. She slumped down on one of the beds, as limp as a rag doll, and a jabbing pain near her heart made her gasp. Drugs were being passed. With shaking hands, Amanda gratefully took the tin foil tube with the mind-numbing heroin on it as it was held out to her.

No one here seems to mind that we just showed up and are doing their drugs. Maybe they're used to drifters coming in to get wasted, or maybe they're just too fucked up to be bothered.

Familiar with smoking the drug, Amanda put the tube to her mouth, while the guy on the bed next to her held a flame from a lighter under the foil. As the heroin cooked, a thick smoke formed. Amanda inhaled the smoke deep into her lungs. *Oh, sweet relief.* Even just the feel of the smoke penetrating her lungs made Amanda feel better.

The loadie lit the homemade pipe again. Amanda sucked in more of the powerful smoke. Falling back on the bed, she knew it would be a while before she'd care about leaving this place.

In the meantime, Hector had driven back to the apartment where Enrique and Travis were waiting. They were going to have to implement the next stage earlier than expected.

But it'll be okay, thought Hector. *There are plenty of pretty girls waiting to work for us. They just don't know it yet.* He grinned. *I love this.*

CHAPTER 41
BULLDOG LEADS THE WAY

Bulldog was on a mission.

If I help these guys, I can make some money. And right now my fucking pockets are empty. It never ceases to amaze me how fast I can blow through coin when drugs are involved. The higher I get, the more I spend.

Occasionally, Bulldog would reflect on a drug deal or two and think maybe he'd gotten ripped off. But at the time the deals went down, he'd be too fucked up to notice, or care. In the end, he considered it an occupational hazard. All Bulldog wanted was drugs. He couldn't live without them.

Steve and Mike walked fast, following close behind Bulldog along the narrow, broken sidewalks. They didn't want to lose him. Intermittently, the men had to step onto the street to get around the degenerates who were lying on the ground, some puking. People pushed and shoved and fell into each other.

"We're in the proverbial den of iniquity," said Mike.

"True," Bulldog intoned.

Both Steve and Mike were mindful of their wallets.

This Bulldog guy is too fucking much, Mike thought. *If he's just playing us, he's going to get his ass kicked. I don't care how much of an ultimate fighter he is, I'll take him down.*

Steve prepared himself for the worst. He knew they

could find Amanda in a compromising position. "All I want to do is get Amanda and go," Steve said.

"I'm with you, buddy," Mike said.

Glad Mike's with me, Steve thought. *No one wants to mess with a navy SEAL, even a former one.*

After hoofing it for about three blocks, Bulldog turned down an alley and onto another street. Sleazy hotels with bars in front lit up the street. Half-dressed prostitutes attempted to lure the men inside.

"Te gusta este?" (Do you like this?)

"Ven conmigo." (Come with me.)

The three men ignored their efforts. Bulldog stopped in front of one of the sordid hotels. "This is the place I've been to before. Smoked some shit with chicks from the States here. Follow me."

Steve and Mike took deep breaths and marched in behind Bulldog. They hung back as Bulldog spoke with the man they assumed was the proprietor. Bulldog and the man seemed to know each other. Finally, Bulldog nodded at Steve and Mike to follow him. They walked down a short, dark hall, stopping at a door with the number five on it. The proprietor opened the door to a filthy room that smelled like an outhouse. Seven people were in the room, and they all needed bathing. One was shooting up, two were snorting something off a dilapidated dresser, and three were smoking what Bulldog knew to be heroin.

"Fucking unbelievable," Steve said under his breath.

One girl, who was completely nude, emaciated, and spaced out, just sat hunched over in her catatonic state. Another girl began giving a guy a blow job, oblivious to the other people in the room. Both females appeared to be American. Amanda wasn't one of the girls.

Steve didn't know whether to be relieved or disappointed. He turned to Bulldog. "My daughter's not here."

The men backed out of the room. Mike had his eye on Bulldog. "Are there other rooms here she might be in?" he asked.

Bulldog told them that Tomas, the proprietor, had said these were the only American girls in the hotel right now. "He said he doesn't remember seeing Amanda. But Tomas wouldn't say shit if he had a mouthful, seeing you guys were with me."

"So it's back to square one then," sighed Steve.

Bulldog wasn't about to give up the idea of a cash reward. "I've got a friend, Alfredo, who's a cop here in Tijuana. He's Mexican, you know, grew up right here. Anyway, he gets off work every day at 4:00. I know he'd help us after work. For a fee, of course."

Might as well spread the dinero around; never know when I'll need Alfredo again for myself, thought Bulldog.

"Look. It's 5:00," Steve said. "We've got to get back to where Bert and the girls are waiting. I'm definitely interested in talking to your friend. We need all the help we can get."

"Alfredo's home by now. I'll call him later and arrange for us to meet up with him tomorrow," Bulldog said. "What do you think, man?"

"Absolutely," said Steve. "Where should we meet? At the McDonald's around 3:00? We can scout the area while we wait for him."

"That's fine. You'll like Alfredo. He knows where the druggies like to hang out and what goes on. He'll be able to help a lot. I want to find her now, too. I mean, shit!"

They walked a couple of blocks before they were able to hail a cab. The cabbie sped through town, dropping them off near McDonald's.

Mike spied Bert as he jumped out of the cab. Steve paid the driver, then hung back with Bulldog. "Look," he said pointedly, "have you ever actually seen Amanda at that hotel?"

Bulldog shrugged. "No, but she coulda been there, man. Most chicks end up in *Zona Norte* if they stay in Tijuana very long."

"This place sucks," Steve said dejectedly. "I appreciate your help, though. We'll see you tomorrow. And don't forget, Bulldog, we're counting on you. And I'll bring your money." Steve knew the talk of money would help Bulldog remember.

"Yeah, sure, I'll be there, man. See ya tomorrow." And with that, Bulldog headed back in the direction from which they had come.

Steve joined the others. Pam and Diane were anxious to know what happened. They were full of questions, but Bert just gave Steve a knowing look.

"The entire area was horrible," Steve reported. "The hotel was a dive. Junkies, prostitutes, filth. Lowlifes everywhere. As much as I'm desperate to find Amanda, I'm almost glad she wasn't there."

Steve told the group about Bulldog's police friend, Alfredo, and the plans to meet up with him the next day. "I suggest we leave now and see if there's any news on the home front."

"I'm wiped out," said Diane.

"I think we all are," said Mike.

"I believe each step is getting us closer to Amanda, though," Steve said. "She's here somewhere, and we're going to find her. Meeting Bulldog was a good thing."

Diane didn't share Steve's optimism, saying only, "I

need something to drink. My throat's so dry."

They decided to get ice cream and drinks before heading back.

"Not many options here when you're tired and hungry and want something quick," said Mike as they walked into McDonald's.

"I'm beginning to feel like a regular," Pam deadpanned.

They ate their hot fudge sundaes at an outside table as they scanned the crowd. Steve noticed that a couple of the posters they had put up a day earlier were missing. "Wonder why those posters are gone."

"Kids, probably," Diane said. Then she added with more enthusiasm, a newfound energy driven by sugar, "Or maybe someone who has seen Amanda took them!"

"I say we put up more posters. This is a very popular area, and you never know," said Pam. She was energized, too.

They tacked up a few more posters on each side of the street before heading to the border crossing area to stand in line.

As the five approached the border checkpoint, they were pleasantly surprised to find that the line wasn't too long. Thirty minutes later, the tired group crossed back into the States and climbed into the truck. Once on the road, they made plans for the following day.

"Since we're not meeting Bulldog until three, let's depart for Tijuana around noon. I'm sure everyone has things they need to do in the morning," said Steve.

"Good idea," said Bert.

"As much as I don't like Bulldog, I think we're getting close," Mike said. "And noon's fine."

Diane, however, suddenly started sobbing. "I have no optimism. Amanda's been gone a long time and I'm scared."

The hiccups followed.

Steve put his hand over hers. "I know how you feel, but we can't give up hope. I refuse to give up. Keep praying, and tomorrow something'll give. This cop connection of Bulldog's will help us. I know it."

CHAPTER 42
AMANDA MEETS ICE

A manda had spent the entire night smoking heroin. She had gotten so wasted that she hadn't been aware Gary had left. *Where did he go?* she wondered after several hours had passed, and she finally noticed that Gary wasn't in the hotel room.

Amanda had no idea what time it was, or what day, for that matter. Glancing at the little slit of a window peeking behind the fabric taped to it, she saw that day had turned to night. Amanda edged over to one of the other girls and asked, "Do you know what time it is?"

The girl looked back at her through glassy eyes, "I don't really care. Do you?"

Amanda pulled herself up and hobbled over to the bathroom. The tiny room was dirty and with such a foul odor that Amanda was sure she'd vomit. *Is anyone coming back for me?* Amanda wondered. *I can't believe they've left me here alone like this.* She took a deep breath. *This is my time to escape! I'll just walk out, and find my way to the border. They can keep my stupid car.*

Amanda stumbled out of the bathroom, fully prepared to make her way out of the nasty hotel room—and to her freedom. Looking around, she saw that a new guy, someone she hadn't seen before, had come in while she was in the bathroom. He was a little older, and looked American.

The guy announced he had some "hot ice" (crystal meth), and one girl immediately said, "I'll blow you for some."

"Sure." He unzipped his pants.

Amanda weakly sat back down on the bed. *I'm shaking too much to walk out of here right now. I could use a hit of that to straighten up.*

Amanda looked the other way while the girl went down on the newcomer. No one else in the tiny drug den seemed to be paying any attention to "the deal" taking place in the room.

When the girl was finished, the satisfied man zipped up his pants. He smiled at the girl and said, "That was great. You get first hit." He reached in his pocket and pulled out a small glass pipe and a little baggie containing a white substance. The material looked like tiny particles of ice.

"Just call me 'Ice,' ladies, because that's what we're going to be smoking," he said with a smirk. The man looked directly at Amanda. Amanda's eyes were glazed. She attempted a smile, knowing he had what she wanted and needed.

Ice loaded the pipe and lit it. The girl who had worked for her hit went first. She wiped her mouth, took the pipe, and inhaled the smoke quickly.

"Mother fucker!" she cried out. "This is good shit."

Amanda had never smoked crystal before, but she considered where she was. *My alternative is to smoke heroin until I die . . . or they run out, which would almost be worse. I just need to get the strength to get out of here. This'll pick me up.*

Her trembling hands took the pipe.

CHAPTER 43
BACK TO MEXICO

S teve slept four hours straight that night, the longest continuous amount of shut-eye he'd had since Amanda's disappearance.

Diane had fallen into a deep but erratic sleep, tossing and turning. She slept for six hours but didn't feel rested when she awoke.

Pam had spoken with Benny on the phone for about twenty-five minutes before she retired for the night. Rehashing the conversation in her mind had kept her up for a while. That, added to the apprehension about Amanda's whereabouts, made for a long night, but short sleep, for Pam.

In late morning, the trio congregated in the kitchen. Steve put on a pot of coffee and brewed some tea for Diane.

"Good morning," said Pam. "The bed's super comfortable. Thanks."

"We're just grateful for your help and support." Steve gave his neck a good crack.

"I'm glad you're here, too," Diane said. "I'm scared. Amanda's disappearing like this is worse than a bad dream. You wake up from a dream." Diane's sadness filled the room.

Pam hugged Diane, then Steve. He forced a brief smile for his sister.

After gulping their drinks, the group resolutely left the condo to begin another day of searching for Amanda. They drove directly to Steve's office, each with a chore to do.

Diane went through the mail Steve's business had accumulated the last few days. "Mostly bills here, Steve. Two checks which I'll put in the safe for deposit later. I'll write checks to pay the bills."

"That's fine," said Steve. He looked around at his office and said, "It's hard to concentrate on anything except what's happened to Amanda."

Pam, who had resumed working on the submission to *America's Most Wanted*, was ready to read the rough draft aloud. It was difficult for both Steve and Diane to hear what was going on put into words.

"Listening to what you've written makes everything seem even more real now," said Diane. "I just can't let go of hoping the phone will ring and it'll be my daughter."

"Let's give it one more day before we send in the letter. I'm more confident now than I've been about finding Amanda and bringing her back home."

Diane didn't share Steve's confidence. "Your fake optimism is giving me a headache."

Steve sighed. "I'm not going to let you bring me down today."

"'Down today'?" Diane sniped. "Remember how all this started, Steve?"

Pam felt uncomfortable but kept silent. *It's tough seeing these two bicker so much. I don't know if Steve's and Diane's sour attitudes toward each other are driven by the tension of Amanda's disappearance, or if they're just usually at each other's throats. It's heartbreaking, but being around all the antagonism is tiring, too. I wish Benny could be here. He always provides good insights.*

"The unknown is always the hardest," said Pam, "but we're all doing the best we can under these very trying and nerve-racking circumstances. I give you both credit for holding it together as well as you do."

The doorbell rang, and Mike entered. "Hey, you guys ready? It's almost noon." Mike walked over and gave Steve a pat on the back. "Let's go, bro."

"You're right. It's time we head out," agreed Steve.

They quickly finished with paperwork, put everything away, and locked up as they left.

They rode silently down the highway to Bert's exit. He was waiting when the truck pulled up. They all decided to grab a bite to eat first, and by two o'clock, the five of them were in Tijuana, showing their posters to anyone who would look.

Pam walked next to Diane, who was in a daze, the strain of the past few days clearly etched on her face.

Bert had an idea. "Let's hop a cab to *Avenida Revolucion*. We can pass out Amanda's picture and ask around there about her. Fresh faces, you know? We can easily be back to the McDonald's by 4:00 to meet up with Bulldog."

"I like calling him Greg," Diane said. "That's his real name. He doesn't seem so crazy when I think of him as Greg."

"Whatever turns you on," Steve said tightly.

Diane let that one go.

Sensing the growing tension between the two, Bert said, "Diane, you come with me across the street. We can cover more territory in two groups and still be close."

Steve, Mike, and Pam went into a *farmacia*. One of the clerks asked if she could help them find something. Steve answered, "Yes. Her." He showed the clerk a poster.

The pharmacist blanched when he saw the poster. Quickly recovering, he acted like he was looking for something on the counter. Mike noticed the pharmacist's reaction when he saw the picture of Amanda. Certain the druggist either knew Amanda, or had seen her, he went to the counter and said, "Look buddy, I know you've seen this girl before. When was the last time she was here?"

"No, I don't know her," the man insisted.

"I don't believe you." Mike leaned in closer to the man.

The pharmacist pushed a button below the counter. A gruff-looking bouncer immediately came out from the back room. The guard at the door stood with his arms crossed and a menacing look on his face.

"Do you want to buy? If not, get out," the pharmacist said in a voice devoid of emotion.

Undaunted, Mike answered, "We're looking for my friend's daughter. She's been missing for days. How about a little help here?"

The bouncer got in Mike's face. Two more big guys came out from the back room, and one came in from the front. Now there were five Mexicans ready to rumble. And only Steve and Mike. And Pam. Steve thought that if Pam hadn't been with them, he and Mike would've taken them on, fueled as they were by a burning desire to find Amanda.

Instead, after a long minute, Steve only said, "If you see my daughter, let her know her father's looking for her." The three then turned around and walked out.

"He knows something," said Mike once they were back out on the street. "I saw it in his eyes when you showed the clerk the poster. I wanted to punch him in the face."

"Maybe we should go to the *policia*," offered Pam.

"Who knows which *policia* can be trusted?" Steve said angrily. "Many officers are on the cartel's payroll. They don't care about us. They'd shoot us if ordered to. I think we should bring Bulldog's cop friend, Alfredo, here later. Maybe he can get some answers from these assholes." Steve felt like punching someone, too.

They continued walking down the street, showing the posters. At the corner was a cop in a police car. Steve ran up to him, holding out the poster. "Have you seen my daughter?"

The officer answered, "We're looking." He showed Steve a poster of Amanda on the front seat next to him.

Steve was overcome with joy! "*Gracias! Gracias!*" Steve shouted as he sprinted back to the others. Bert and Diane had joined Pam and Mike by then. Steve breathlessly told everyone about the cop's having the poster in his patrol car. "I know we're getting somewhere!" Steve said, renewed.

"I think something's going to break soon, too," agreed Mike. He hoped it would be good news, knowing his friends would have a tough time handling anything less.

"Let's go to McDonald's and get a drink while we wait for Bulldog," said Bert, wiping the sweat off his brow.

"Sounds good to me," Pam said. "My throat's parched."

They walked past beggars sprawled on the sidewalks, beseeching passersby for money. Some were missing limbs. All looked downtrodden. Dirty-faced little children begged tourists for candy and money. As Pam opened her pocketbook, she said, "There's so much poverty here. The children break my heart."

They arrived at McDonald's about 3:45, ordered drinks, and took them to an outside table to wait for Bulldog. At 4:15, he sauntered up.

"*Hola*," said Bulldog, still looking like he could use a shower. "Alfredo will be here soon." He smelled faintly of alcohol and was sweating profusely.

"You hungry?" Steve asked him.

"Sure am."

Steve got up and the two went inside. Bulldog ordered three cheeseburgers and a large size order of fries. "I needed some food, man. This is great."

Back outside, Bulldog polished everything off just as Alfredo appeared. The off-duty officer was in his mid-thirties, clean cut, and dressed nicely.

Bulldog made the introductions with Steve's help, then pulled Steve off to the side. "I have somewhere I have to go, man. Think you could pay me now? I'll be back tomorrow." Bulldog seemed a little nervous and was scratching his arms.

"Sure. Thanks for turning us on to Alfredo. Want to meet here at the same time tomorrow?"

Bulldog nodded. Steve got out his wallet and peeled off five hundred-dollar bills. He handed them to Bulldog.

"Sweet. See ya later. Oh, and good luck, man." Bulldog gave a wave and then disappeared into the crowd. They never saw him again.

Alfredo asked Steve to describe the situation as he knew it. After getting the gist, Alfredo said, "Let's go back to *La Coahuila* and hang around there for awhile. Things change a lot after dark. We might be able to find something out."

Steve told the girls to return to the condo in San Diego. "Take the train back. We have to do this now, and *La Coahuila* just isn't safe. You need to get out of here. We don't want to have to worry about the both of you, too."

Pam and Diane agreed. *La Coahuila* was no place for

them. They said good-bye and gave the guys a hug.

"Please be careful. Watch each other's backs," said Pam.

The guys promised they'd be vigilant. Mike went with the girls toward the border, where the line had formed to walk back into the United States. It was a very long line.

Alfredo waited until the girls were out of earshot. "I always have my .45 on me when I'm off duty. Wouldn't go to *La Coahuila* without it, that's for sure."

Bert nodded. "I have mine, too. In fact, I just bought a new gun. Real nice. Kahr PM .45, small and lightweight. Right here in my ankle holster. So we're good to go."

The seriousness of the situation was firmly imbedded in Steve's mind, as was the desperation in his heart. A constant pain gnawed at Steve's insides. Pain caused by horrible thoughts that tumbled down the slippery slope of fear, and led to the black hole of death. Amanda's. And then his. It literally made him sick to think about his daughter and where she might be. *Who is she with? Did she go willingly? How the hell did it get to this point?* Steve prayed for a quick resolution. He knew he wouldn't be able to take much more.

"Don't worry about us," Diane said to Mike when they reached the end of the line at the border. "We'll do fine getting home. Just find my baby."

"Be careful on the train," Mike said. Then he jogged back to join the other three.

* * *

Hector, Enrique, and Travis sat at the table mulling over what to say to Carlos, and, more importantly, how to say it. Carlos wouldn't like to hear that there were posters all over Tijuana with the new mule's picture and information on it. Someone was seriously looking for that girl, which could pose a problem. Carlos detested problems.

While this wasn't the first time a search had been conducted for a young American the cartel held captive, not many went to the extreme that this search seemed to have gone. The parents of those who were addicted enough to risk going to Mexico to buy drugs were often used to their offspring's unexplained absences. When the parents and family finally started looking for their children in Mexico, they weren't usually successful in finding them. Many would eventually stop looking, often because of a lack of leads or resources. The small number who was successful in finding their loved ones typically only found their remains. The cartel played for keeps.

Travis had received a communiqué from an *oficial de policia* on the cartel's payroll, tipping him off to the aggressive search for the kidnapped American girl. He read that all *policia* were instructed to carry a poster with her picture on it in their cruisers and be on the lookout for the captive.

"Fuck. This isn't going to go down well with Carlos," said Travis. "He hates when shit like this happens."

"*Mierda!* She's too beautiful and compliant to toss away," Hector pointed out. "We can use her in other ways. We just need to do it fast."

Enrique was pissed off. He had had some plans of his own for the beautiful captive. Unfinished sexual plans. *Maybe I can still get what I want. I'll just stay close to Hector.*

Travis thought for a moment and then said authoritatively, "We'll ship her to Mexico City. She can table-dance or turn tricks. Nobody'll ever find her, there'll be no body to dispose of, and we can continue making money off her. Best-case scenario."

Hector said, "That's a good plan. The idea has to come from Carlos, though."

"I know," Travis agreed.

Nobody told Carlos what to do or even gave him a direct suggestion. It wasn't wise.

Enrique nodded. While he didn't want to give up a promising sexual adventure with the girl, he was more afraid of angering Carlos.

The cartel was very experienced in trafficking for sexual exploitation. Pretty girls were always in demand, but the three didn't want any heads to roll for the aggravation the search for this girl was causing, "any heads" meaning theirs.

CHAPTER 44
DOING DRUGS

Amanda's first time smoking crystal meth almost blew her head off.

"Holy shit!" she cried as the intensity of the drug hit her brain. Instantly, she was awake and raring to go.

Ice smiled. *Mission almost accomplished,* he thought. Ice reached in his pocket and brought out a joint. "This here's some excellent shit," he said as he lit it.

Amanda's heart was racing so fast. *Too fast?* She didn't like the feeling. *A few tokes would help calm me down. I don't want my heart to explode. Could it actually do that?* Her brain was racing, too. *Whew, I need to slow down, so I can be in a place to handle walking out of here. Gotta get my shit together.*

Amanda took the blunt, inhaled the smoke deep into her lungs, and held it in for as long as she could. She wanted to get the most out of it. In an attempt to exhale slowly, Amanda ended up coughing.

"Pussy," said the girl who had given the blow job.

Amanda ignored her. The other people in the room were completely oblivious to Ice, Amanda, and the American girl. They were content to do their own drugs.

When they finished smoking the joint, Ice looked at Amanda. "Come on, babe, let's go," he said, grabbing her hand

and pulling her up.

"Where to?" asked Amanda, although she was actually happy to be leaving the room. High and spaced out, Amanda was ready for something, anything, which might lead to her freedom.

"Out," answered Ice.

"Hey!" said the other girl. "What about me?"

"Fuck you," answered Ice to the stunned girl.

He and Amanda walked out the door and didn't look back.

"So what time is it anyway?" Amanda wanted to know at least that much. She stumbled as they walked down the stairs.

"Who cares, right?"

Amanda glared at him through dilated pupils.

She's hot as shit, Ice thought. *Even fucked up.* "Oh, I guess about 8:00 or something. You happy now?"

They walked down the alley and out to *Calle Coahuila.* All kinds of people were doing all kinds of nasty and forbidden things.

Amanda felt like she was walking through Dante's Inferno. The hell part. *Funny,* she thought, *I didn't study much in school, but I do remember reading Dante's Inferno. Probably because it was so scary and gave me nightmares.*

Since then Amanda hadn't liked scary movies. Now she was living one.

They stopped at an intersection. Ice turned his head away and made a call on his cell phone. Amanda heard him say something about "chickens."

Wonder what that's all about? While she was waiting for Ice to complete his call, a young male walked by Amanda and whispered, "Geraldo's looking for you." He quickly continued on.

Ice turned around just as the guy was taking off. "Did that dude just talk to you?" he asked with a scowl. "What did he say?"

"He said . . . some guy's looking for me," Amanda said, afraid not to answer him. Paranoia was setting in, and Amanda thought someone might be watching them.

"Who? Who's looking for you?"

Trying to act nonchalant, Amanda shrugged. "Named Geraldo, I think he said."

"Do you know anyone with that name?" Ice studied her for signs of deception.

"No," she lied, as she kept walking next to Ice. It was the best acting job of her life. Geraldo was the name of a man who worked with her father. They were looking for her! She knew it. She knew her father would try to find her. Her parents loved her. They wouldn't let her just disappear. *Please, God, let them find me,* she prayed. ***Please! Please!***

They walked more swiftly now, and, because of the recent ingestion of meth, Amanda found it felt good to move. Ice knew he had to report the guy who'd spoken to Amanda. He believed her about not knowing any Geraldo, but maybe the dude was trying to give her a code or something. Or maybe he had her confused with someone else. Chicks went missing in Tijuana all the time.

They walked several more blocks, weaving through the streets until they stopped at an apartment building. Ice glanced around, and seeing nothing suspicious, said, "Here we are."

The old three-story building had no character or style. It resembled a concrete box. Nighttime made the gray, dingy structure look especially foreboding.

"We're going up to the second floor," Ice informed her. The timeworn stairs on the outside of the building were broken, uneven, pocked, and very narrow, making them difficult to navigate. Amanda was afraid she'd trip. Ice stayed behind her as they went up. He didn't want her to try to run away. Not that she'd get far. One girl had tried, and had received a shotgun blast through the back for her efforts. *Real messy*, Ice remembered. He didn't want to have to deal with a mess like that again.

Amanda stopped on the second floor where an old, beat-up door beckoned. Curious, she was able to peek through tiny slits between the wooden slats on the door as Ice came up behind her. She saw people shooting up and throwing up.

Great, Amanda thought. *From one disgusting place to another.* Then she began wondering what drugs might be in there, and if she could get any. *God, I'm fucked up. Is there no way out?*

Ice reached around Amanda and knocked twice on the door. A Mexican opened the door. Amanda was sure she recognized him.

"Venga." The Mexican backed up to let them in. The tiny living room was decorated with a ratty brown sofa, one overstuffed chair with several burn holes, and two wooden chairs. The lone window was boarded up, and the room was smoky. Several putrid odors were going on at once.

Ice nodded his head to the guy who let them in, and, after warning Amanda not to move, the two men went off to another room to talk.

"Okay, I brought her here," Ice said. "Now it's your turn to babysit. Go ahead and let her smoke some shit. Once she's real high, Enrique and Hector want you to bring her back to the house. Don't let her talk to anybody when you leave here. Got it?"

"*Si.* Hector knows I can do it right."

They returned to the living room. Amanda hadn't moved. Ice walked over to her and said, "Listen, baby, I gotta run. Luis here will take care of you. He's got some good shit, so you'll be floating again soon." And with that he opened the door and walked out.

Amanda couldn't believe how she was being passed around and taken to different places to do drugs. *I can't take this,* she thought. *I want to go home.* She felt like crying. Everything on her body hurt, including her heart. *I need to clean up my act. I want to get better. I want to get out of here. Please help me, God. How much longer? I'm so afraid my parents won't be able to find me.*

Luis said to her, "*Venga, chica.* Come on."

He motioned for Amanda to sit on the sofa next to a skinny Mexican. Holding her ribs, she eased herself onto the sofa. Luis took a broken light bulb containing heroin and lit a flame under it. Soon, it was smoking.

Amanda knew the drug would take her to another place. *What's the use? I can't escape,* she thought miserably.

The guy next to Amanda gave her a glass tube. Accepting it, she used the tube to inhale the fumes from the heroin. The familiar smell went deep into her body.

I will stop, she thought, as she drifted off. *Tomorrow.*

Amanda was out of it for about a half an hour when a loud bang woke her up. Luis and the other guy ran outside, returning a few minutes later.

"Apparently, someone tried to rip off a dealer," Luis said matter-of-factly. "The dude ended up on the wrong side of a gun." *Message,* thought Luis, *don't fuck with your dealer.*

Since Amanda was now somewhat awake, Luis decided

it was time to take her to Enrique's. He made a quick call to let Maria know they were coming. Then he turned to Amanda and said, "*Chica,* it's time to go." Luis reached down, took both her wrists, and pulled her up. Amanda was limp. Skinny, dirty, and tired, she hadn't eaten in days. On top of that, Amanda had ingested copious amounts of drugs. A body can only take so much.

Luis didn't care how weak Amanda was. He had to take her to Enrique's, and he was going to do just that. Luis dragged Amanda into the dirty kitchen, filled a grimy glass with water, and gave it to her. Amanda drank the water, but her hands were shaking so much that the last bit spilled on her shirt.

Luis guided Amanda through the apartment, out the door, and down the stairs. That alone was a feat. She could barely walk, and the steps were tricky. Luis said "Fuck" more than once. His car was parked around back. After they got in the beat-up Impala, Luis reached in his pocket and brought out a little baggie with some white powder. It was cocaine. "Take a couple of hits. This stuff'll wake your ass up." Luis dipped a tiny spoon in the baggie, filling it with the white, sparkling powder. "This is good shit," he said proudly. "Flake. The best." He held the spoon out to Amanda, and she leaned into it.

Holding his hand under her nose, she snorted the drug quickly and hard. The fine powder went straight into her head. *Yeow!* It burned like hell, but in a good, familiar way. She sniffed in a couple of times as Luis filled the spoon again.

Experienced users like Amanda knew that the best thing about snorting cocaine was the immediate rush of the first hit. Once she took that hit, Amanda instantly felt energized.

"Yeah, this is great!" she exclaimed after inhaling the powder a second time. Her heart was beating hard and fast.

Luis was pleased that Amanda was more awake. It would make taking her to Enrique's a whole lot easier.

Even though she was now on a cocaine high, Amanda was still mentally, physically, and emotionally exhausted. In moments of clarity, all she could think of was getting back home. *They keep moving me around. How will anyone be able to find me?* "Do you know where my car is?" she suddenly asked Luis.

"What? I don't know what you're talking about," he answered. "You'll have to ask Enrique."

Amanda didn't want to ask Enrique anything. She hated Enrique.

CHAPTER 45
HAS AMANDA BEEN SEEN?

M ike jogged up to Steve, Bert, and Alfredo. "I think the ladies will be okay now. They're in line to walk across the border."

"Listen, Mike," Steve said solemnly, looking directly into his friend's eyes. "We're going to a very dangerous place. We don't know what we'll find. Both Alfredo and Bert are packing. Maybe you should go back to the States, too. You've done more than enough for me and my family already."

"Are you shitting me?" Mike responded. "I have a knife strapped to my leg, man. I can slit a throat faster than you can spit, if I have to. My hands are lethal weapons, and I have brass balls. I'm willing to do what it takes to find our girl."

Steve nodded and turned his head away from Mike's penetrating gaze. He was overwhelmed by the love and support from his friend.

"I'm ready, too," he said, trying not to let his emotions get the best of him. Now wasn't the time.

Alfredo also was ready. "Great. Let's get in the car and head into Tijuana. The real Tijuana. The Tijuana no one likes to think about or acknowledge."

He led them to his compact car and they piled in. Alfredo knew the quickest routes, and it wasn't long before the men were in the *Zona Norte* area. Alfredo drove behind a restaurant and parked. He got out and knocked on the back door while the others waited in the car. A heavyset Mexican with wary eyes cracked open the door. When he saw it was Alfredo, a big smile appeared.

"*Hola! Que pasa, amigo?*"

"I need to eat a quick meal with my friends here. We have some business to attend to," replied Alfredo.

"Certainly." The man opened the door wider.

Alfredo called out to the guys, and they entered the restaurant through the back door. Since Alfredo didn't want anyone to see them eating, the owner, Miguel, set them up with a small table in the kitchen. He had one of his staff bring the men something to eat. The food was great, and the men ate quickly. Steve asked Alfredo how much to pay Miguel.

"You don't have to give him anything," answered Alfredo. "He's my friend, and we do things for each other."

Steve didn't feel comfortable not paying anything, so he left a twenty-dollar bill on the table as he got up.

Alfredo told Miguel he was going to be leaving his car there for a while. The portly Mexican nodded and said, "*No hay problema*," as he led the men out through the kitchen.

Miguel slowly opened the back door and peered out. Seeing nothing out of the ordinary, he stepped back to allow Alfredo and the others to leave.

"*Hasta luego*," he said.

"Yes, see you later," Alfredo responded. "Thanks." He turned to the others. "Now we won't be hungry, and my car will be safe enough here. We can walk where we need to go."

"Thanks a lot for thinking of dinner. I didn't realize how hungry I was," said Steve.

"Same here," said Mike.

Bert nodded, and then suggested they get some of the posters out of the car to take with them. With posters in hand, they walked out of the alley toward *Calle Coahuila*. It was dusk, and already the mood and energy of the area was changing.

"Some only come at night," noticed Steve.

"They shouldn't come out at all," suggested Mike.

"We need to stick together here," said Alfredo. "Let's walk in pairs. A lot of shit goes on."

Bert nodded to Alfredo. "Since only you and I speak Spanish, I think Steve should walk with you and Mike with me."

"Good idea," said Steve.

Alfredo saw one of the many bars known to have prostitutes in the back room. He knew that young American girls who were drug addicts often worked in those seedy places to get money to support their habits.

"Let's go in here," he said to Steve, then added to Bert and Mike, "You guys stay outside and watch our backs. This place is a real hell hole. Sometimes people go in and never come out."

Bert and Mike hung outside near the door, keeping an eye on everyone and everything.

The bar was dark and smoky inside. Two girls wearing only G-strings were gyrating on a makeshift stage. Other than the dancers, there were only men in the bar. They stood around, drinking, smoking, and leering. A big man with dark, cold eyes approached them and asked, "*Que quieren?*"

Alfredo motioned to Steve to hold up a poster. "He wants to know what we want."

Steve showed the man the photo of Amanda. "I'm looking for a girl named Amanda."

"*Si*, we have Amanda here," said the man with a sneer. He was sure these guys just wanted what all the other men want, and any young thing can provide that.

Steve gasped when the man told him a girl named Amanda was there. Heart pounding, he prepared himself for what he might see.

"Follow me," said the man in a low voice.

Alfredo and Steve followed him into a back room, where he told them to wait. Soon, he returned with three young women who were probably teenagers. They looked American.

"Pick one." The big man wiped his brow. It was hot and stuffy, and he needed a drink.

Steve shook his head. "No, I want Amanda."

When Alfredo translated what Steve said, the man laughed. "*Cualquiero puede ser* Amanda."

Alfredo and the man then had an exchange in Spanish. Alfredo turned to Steve and said, "Let's go. She's not here."

"What did he say?"

"He said that anyone could be Amanda. The guy just wanted to pimp one of his girls. He didn't care about anything else."

They walked back through the dark bar and out the door, stepping over a man who was puking on the sidewalk. Two prostitutes sashayed by. One had on a very short skirt with nothing on under it. The other was wearing tiny shorts, fishnet hose, high heels, and a bra. The men didn't even look at them.

"Amanda's not there," Steve said to the other guys, sounding a bit relieved.

They crossed the street and went to another of the area's seedy hotels. This time, Bert and Mike went in, while Steve and Alfredo stood guard outside. Steve showed the poster to two men who walked past, but they were too wasted to stop and just ignored him.

The men took turns going into bars and seedy hotels for the next couple of hours with no luck. Steve was exasperated, but wouldn't stop.

Mike and Bert went into yet another hotel with a bar.

Next to the hotel was a dirt walkway leading to an old building in the back. Alfredo thought he heard something coming from that area, so he and Steve went to check it out. The men came across a prostitute earning her money with a john, right there on the ground. Both the man and his hired woman reeked of alcohol.

"This place is disgusting. Hell on earth," Steve said.

"Yes," agreed Alfredo. "It's *La Coahuila*, known as 'the worst of the worst.'"

They had turned to go back to the front of the hotel when a young man brushed past them. He looked American and also reeked of alcohol. Obviously drunk and maybe more, he looked right at them through bloodshot eyes.

Steve held up a poster and said, "Hey! Have you seen this girl?"

To their amazement, the guy answered, "Yeah."

Steve grabbed the man's arm. "Where? When?"

"She was around here . . . maybe last night or the night before. I . . . don't know for sure. It's hard to remember days, you know?"

"Here?" Steve shouted. "You mean right here? What time was it? Can you remember that? It's really important, man. This girl's my daughter, and she's been missing for over a week." He was so eager that the words just flew out of his mouth.

Struggling to stand still, the American looked sympathetically at Steve. "I'd say it was around 8:00 at night."

"Was she alone or with someone?"

"I think . . . she was . . . with some Mexican dude." The man was slurring his words.

"Do you have any idea where they could be now or where there were going? Or anything?" Steve asked, knowing how crazy he sounded. *But this fucked-up dude has actually seen Amanda. And recently!*

"No, man, all I know is . . . I just know I saw her around here." *No need to say I did drugs with her and others in a hotel,* he told himself. *Don't want to get too involved. I already did my good deed, saying that much.*

Steve held out a twenty-dollar bill and said, "Keep your eye out, will you? If you see her, let her know that her dad's looking for her."

The guy grabbed the money. "Yeah, sure," he said and abruptly walked away, his mind elsewhere. *Now I can score some shit.*

Alfredo said, "That money was a gift, you know."

Steve nodded knowingly, but he was riding high. "I've given out lots of 'gifts' in these past few days. But I'll do anything to find my daughter."

Mike and Bert had come out of the hotel and witnessed the exchange taking place between Steve and the young American. They had hung back until it was over; now they wanted to find out what had transpired.

"You won't believe this. That kid has seen Amanda! She was around here with some Mexican dude, about 8:00 at night." Steve was practically jumping up and down.

"That's a solid lead!" exclaimed Mike. "What do you

guys think we should do? Alfredo?"

Alfredo answered, "It's pretty late now, and I need to be getting home. You guys go home, too, and get some sleep. Let's plan on being in *La Coahuila* tomorrow night around 8:00. That's when the kid saw her. Maybe she'll be out again around the same time."

Bert looked at his watch. It was just past midnight. "Good idea. We can meet at the same place tomorrow. But I think we should start out earlier than 8:00."

They walked back to the restaurant where Alfredo's car was parked.

"Why don't we just meet tomorrow at 6:00 in front of McDonald's? That should give us plenty of time to come back here and scope out the area," said Steve.

"I'm going to talk to my friends on the force and some of my underground contacts about Amanda, too," said Alfredo. "Having this picture to show will help. People remember faces."

The men got in the car and Alfredo drove to the border. The guys hopped out, thanking him. Steve gave Alfredo the promised five hundred in cash.

"I'll double that next time if we're able to find Amanda and get her back safely," said Steve.

"Fair enough." The off-duty police officer waved and drove away.

The San Ysidro border was open twenty-four hours a day, seven days a week. The wee hours of the morning were usually the best times for a quick entry into the United States, and this night was no exception. The trio went into the building where the custom agents were, showed their IDs, and were let through.

* * *

Diane and Pam had made themselves grilled cheese and tomato sandwiches for dinner. They talked about life and how things had gotten to where they were. They prayed together, too. The evening helped calm the women and did wonders for their overall relationship.

Diane still said the problem was with Steve, but Pam wouldn't hear of it. She noted there was plenty of blame to go around, if you wanted to look at it that way.

"Things happen in life. The people who are there for you when you need them are what it's all about," said Pam.

The women cleaned up the kitchen after dinner and went to the living room to curl up in front of the TV. They only saw the first ten minutes of *The Amazing Race* before drifting off to sleep. The ringing of the phone startled them.

Diane answered, "Hello."

It was Steve. "Hey, babe, we're on our way back. We met a kid who's seen Amanda! We're going back to the same area tomorrow. I'll fill you in when I see you."

Diane's mouth dropped open and she started to cry. This time, though, she had tears of joy. And for the first time in many days, she also had hope.

CHAPTER 46
PLAN B

Hector sat across from Carlos and watched him smoke one of his legendary cigars. Carlos was pleased with the smooth drop-off of the van across the border. But he was very unhappy that there were posters with information of their new mule posted all over Tijuana. Some of the other girls they had abducted hadn't worked out too well for one reason or another. None of them was around to tell her story, though.

Carlos chewed on the cigar; then spit. "I don't wait for things to happen. I make things happen."

Carlos put his head back, looked up at the ceiling for a long minute, and then back at Hector. With his eyes locked on Hector's, Carlos picked up the phone and dialed. He spoke in Spanish, telling the party on the other line he had a new girl he'd be sending down. "You'll be pleased with this one," he said. "Very beautiful. She'll bring in lots of money. She's already moved a load for us. I'm sure her other talents are good, too." Carlos laughed. "Maybe the girl stays in Mexico, or maybe you send her someplace else, no? If the price is right, of course. We can talk. She'll arrive Monday. My man'll call." Carlos hung up and smiled.

Hector nodded, waiting for orders.

There was a knock on the door. Carlos said, "*Abierto.*"

Ice walked in. "I met with Javier. The deal for the rest of the *pollos* is a go for Monday."

"Monday will be a busy day," noted Carlos. "Okay, go."

Ice left to get a good buzz on before his next big job. *Think I'll go to La Coahuila. It's easy to get wasted there.*

Carlos toyed with his cigar. "Tell the girl that on Monday she's going to do another job for us. I want her ready to go, no? Go see Eber and get some good shit for tonight. Let her smoke all she wants. She needs to stay very high. Take her to the roof. No one will see her there."

Hector asked, "Who are you going to have drive her to Mexico City? Or will she fly?"

"Drive. I think Omar and Emilio. She's seen them already and will feel comfortable. Omar's a good driver, and Emilio can be trusted in these situations. Normally, I wouldn't drive only one whore, but she needs to be moved without delay. I'll show those bastards they cannot come to my area with a few fucking posters and find their girl."

Carlos bit down hard on his cigar and spit. He slammed his fist on the desk and swore.

Carlos had a short fuse and he was beginning to boil. When he got hot, everyone knew to give him space. He had been known to take out his anger on whoever was handy. One poor gofer was in the wrong place at the wrong time. Carlos had made an example out of him.

The man's headless torso was found in the street in broad daylight. Not a pretty sight for passersby. The action had gotten everyone's attention.

Carlos motioned for Hector to pour him a drink. "She can ride in the back of the van. If she passes out, it'll be easier for everyone. Less risk of her being recognized, no?"

Hector nodded.

"This girl can be useful to us for a long time. Use the pills."

Carlos downed the tequila with one swig, then puffed on his cigar.

"Yes, sir."

The tequila/cigar combination quieted Carlos. He dismissed Hector with a wave of his hand.

It's too bad the girl has to be sent south, Carlos thought. *She's done a good job, but now her face is everywhere. It's best to get her out of Tijuana and use her somewhere else.*

Carlos blew a thick smoke ring and happily watched it dissipate.

Hector called Enrique and told him of his conversation with Carlos. "The talk was good," he said. "We're still going to use the pretty American, but for other things."

Enrique knew exactly what Hector meant.

Keep her high until it's time for her to go south," Hector told him. "Tell her she's going to be a mule for us again, so she'll be ready to move when the time comes. We'll give her the pills, put her in the back of the van, and she can sleep through the trip. Fewer problems for us. Fill Travis in."

"Got it. I'll make sure the girl doesn't go anywhere," Enrique responded. *I might even have some fun in the process.*

* * *

Luis and Amanda finally arrived at Enrique's. Travis was there, and he let them in. Once Amanda was inside, Travis told Luis he could go.

Luis smiled. He was done with his turn at babysitting.

There was a whore back at a bar who needed his attention. And he was ripe.

Enrique and a prostitute in their hire were going at it in the bedroom. She was good at turning tricks and brought in decent money. She had worked for them as a mule, too, soon after they had kidnapped her.

The girl had made three trips across the border with drugs in a period of two months. The cartel had felt it was enough for her. With her bright red hair and milk-white skin, *la chica Americana* could get recognized if they used her too much for carrying. Carlos felt she was much better as a prostitute, anyway. She seemed to like it, too, but it was hard to tell. They kept her pretty fucked up most of the time. The girl's name was Colleen. She was from Wisconsin.

Apparently no one's spending time looking for her ass, thought Travis when he heard the banging of the bed against the wall. Travis led Amanda to the sofa. "You can hang out here."

Maria appeared with a Coke and a partially eaten bag of chips. It was Amanda's first meal in a while. She ate and drank halfheartedly. The cocaine had killed Amanda's appetite, and she was wiped out. She also felt very spaced out. Surprisingly, the meager provisions helped clear Amanda's head a little.

Once I get out of here, she thought, *I'll never complain about food again.*

CHAPTER 47
READY FOR ACTION

P am and Diane were in the kitchen, cleaning up after a quick breakfast.

"I think today'll be a big day," Pam said encouragingly. "It's unbelievably great luck that the guys ran into someone who had just seen Amanda in Tijuana."

"What good does it do us if we don't have her back?" Diane sighed. "I can't take it anymore. I'm going back to bed." She took her tea and left the kitchen.

It means Amanda was alive, Pam thought. *And she still might be.*

Steve came into the kitchen with Mike, who had arrived earlier, and said they were leaving to pick up Bert and then head into Tijuana.

"We're supposed to meet Bulldog at 4:00 and Alfredo at 6:00," said Steve. "We can also go to another couple of *farmacias* with Bulldog, and possibly get some answers. The pharmacists might talk if Bulldog goes in alone. Bert could go in, too, by himself. He'd be able to understand if the clerks spoke to each other in Spanish."

"Good idea," said Mike.

"I'll say a prayer everything works out, and we get Amanda back today," said Pam.

Steve went into the bedroom to say good-bye to Diane. He kissed her forehead and said, "Just try to get some rest. I'll call you later."

Steve and Mike said good-bye to Pam and left. A strong energy seemed to whiz around inside the truck. Steve and Mike wanted something to break so badly that their bodies were shooting out vibes.

"You're a good friend, Mike," Steve said, reflecting yet again about the enormity of the situation.

"I hope we get to kick some ass," Mike answered. He didn't bother telling Steve he was now packing a gun, too.

When they arrived at the designated spot at the strip mall, Bert was waiting. He hopped in the truck, saying, "The word on the street in Tijuana is someone's looking for an American girl. Amanda's posters are getting attention, my friend. It's even hit the underground."

"Hot damn!" Steve cried excitedly.

Bert shook his head. "That can be both good and bad, depending on where Amanda is, what she's doing, and with whom. Now that it's known someone is looking for her, things might happen. Puts us in a precarious position, too. If Amanda is hanging out with bad people, willingly or not, the motherfuckers aren't going to want us or anybody else snooping around."

"I don't care what anybody else wants," Steve said fiercely. "I want my daughter back. And I'm prepared to do whatever it takes. End of story."

"Amado, Geraldo's cousin, has told me the bits and pieces he hears around. There's definitely been chatter about a search going on for Amanda," added Bert.

The gravity of the situation wasn't lost on Steve or Mike.

Where in the Sam Hell is Amanda? Mike wondered. Although he thought of a few places, none were good.

The truck practically drove itself to the border; the trip had become so familiar. As they had on several occasions in the past few days, the men walked from one country to the other, scanning the area. They saw people walking, talking, sitting, selling. Nothing seemed out of the ordinary.

They waited anxiously to meet Bulldog again near the same McDonald's. And they waited. And waited. When it got to be an hour past the appointed time, a frustrated Steve said, "Shit. I don't think Bulldog is going to show up. He was so fucking happy to get cash yesterday. I bet he used it for drugs. We're probably not going to see him today."

"You could be right," said Mike. "At least he got us to Alfredo."

"Let's get something to eat. Could be a long night," said Bert.

CHAPTER 48
EXECUTING THE PLAN

Enrique and the redhead finally came out of the bedroom. Looking rough, the girl was wearing a tank top and short shorts. Her hair was a mess, and she needed a bath. Amanda didn't want to look at either of them. She leaned back into the sofa and closed her eyes. *I'm in hell.*

Travis was in the kitchen with Maria when Enrique sauntered in to get a drink. "Go get our special guest fucked up," he said to Travis. "She'll be like putty then. We don't want her to start thinking. Tell her she's doing a job for us tomorrow, so tonight she might as well relax and get wasted."

"Yeah, okay."

"She is going somewhere tomorrow," added Enrique with an evil sound in his voice, "only it won't be to the United States."

Travis didn't respond.

"Take the bitch to the shack on the roof. Pablo and a few guys are there now, testing some smack. Eber got a new batch. Says it's some pure shit. I'm sure you'll find it to your liking, too," Enrique sneered.

It was no secret that Enrique and Travis barely tolerated each other. Enrique harbored deep resentment against Travis. He felt that because Travis was an American, he shouldn't be allowed to move up in the ranks or have as much responsibility as he did. *How can he be trusted? The gringo isn't one of us,* Enrique often thought.

Travis was aware of how Enrique felt and didn't care. He knew one day, they'd have it out. Both men carried concealed weapons at all times. A fight between the two would likely be a bloodbath. Odds were, one of them wouldn't make it.

Travis only said, "I'll get her there, but I'm not staying. I've got things to do." He gave Enrique a defiant look.

Maria had listened to everything without saying a word. She would be sorry to see Amanda go, but at least the girl wouldn't be killed. *Not now, anyway,* Maria thought. She knew the outlook for Amanda's future wasn't good, but there was nothing she could do. She was glad she'd sent her young son to his grandmother's for a few days. Maria was tired and didn't want to deal with anything. There'd soon be a new girl. *They come and they go. All the more reason not to get close to any one of them.*

Enrique took the cell phone out of his pocket and called Pablo, letting him know what to expect. "Travis and the girl will be there soon. Let 'em in." He flipped the phone shut. *Maybe I'll go up there myself, later. The girl will be so fucked up by then; she'll be willing to do anything. I won't have to force it. Not that it matters.*

The redhead ambled into the kitchen. When Enrique turned to talk to her, Travis walked out. He went to the living room and said to Amanda, "Hey, you, let's go get high. There's some good H calling your name."

Amanda was so lightheaded when she stood up that she almost passed out. She would've fallen back onto the sofa, had Travis not grabbed her arm.

"Shit," he said. "Don't do that."

"Not my fault," she murmured. Nothing was in Amanda's control anymore, not even her own body. She fought to control the dizziness.

Travis picked up Amanda's purse and handed it to her. She linked her arm through the strap and let it hang from her shoulder. Throughout everything that had happened to her, Amanda's captor's continually made sure she had her handbag with her.

"Tomorrow you're going to cross the border again. Like last time. Do it right and you have no worries," Travis said matter-of-factly.

"Again? Already?" Amanda moaned. *No wonder they always want me to keep hold of my bag,* she thought, *so I'll have my license ready to drive for them.*

"Just do what you're told." Travis's voice was cold.

"Will I get my car back after that?" Amanda asked meekly.

Travis didn't answer. He took her hand and led her outside. "Come on. We have to walk a few blocks. You can do that."

Amanda limped along next to Travis, trying not to despair. *Will my parents ever be able to find me?*

They walked two blocks, turned a corner, and went another half block to an old apartment building with dilapidated concrete steps leading to the second floor and the rooftop.

"Go up," Travis commanded.

"Hope I don't fall," Amanda commented. "The cement could do some damage." *I should be worried about the heroin, not the steps,* Amanda thought, wondering if she was going crazy. *Help me!*

As they climbed up the first set of steps, Amanda tripped and practically bounced off the wall. She had no energy, no life within her. Travis gripped her elbow and shoved her to the second set of steps.

On the next level, Amanda stopped for a second to catch her breath. She felt very weak. Travis gave her a push from behind.

"Keep going."

They continued to the rooftop. It was bare, save for a square, windowless shack at the far corner. Travis pulled Amanda across the roof. He stopped at the door of the shack and knocked. Someone yelled out, "*Que?*"

"It's Travis. Open up."

Pablo opened the door a crack, allowing Travis and Amanda to squeeze through. Travis didn't want to stay and chase the dragon. Colleen had said one of her friends, Sheila, was coming over, ready to party. *I'm ready to get high and get some tail, too,* thought Travis.

"Pablo, get her wasted," said Travis. Then he left Amanda in Pablo's charge.

Although Amanda didn't know it, Travis had just left her with a very violent man who hated women. Pablo thought all women needed a good beating every now and then to "keep them down." Women, he often said, needed to be taught their place.

Amanda could see, even in the dimness of the shack, a hatred burning in his eyes. Fear wrapped its ugly fingers around her, circling her like a vine.

Four other rough-looking Mexicans were in the small room. Three were sitting on an old settee, and the most heavyset one was standing near a tiny table flanked by two chairs. Amanda had never seen any of the men before. She trembled with fear. The room was dark and smoky, with a strange, unpleasant smell. Trash littered the floor. And there were guns.

Pablo said something in Spanish. One of the guys moved from the settee to a chair. Pablo pushed Amanda to the settee and sat down next to her. It was a tight fit. Two guys were on her other side. The one on the end was already passed out. His head was back and his eyes were half closed. The big man standing at the table was preparing the heroin for another round. Amanda would be the first to smoke it.

At least my throbbing head can go to another place, she thought. Amanda had become used to the unrelenting companion of physical pain. In her steady diet of the unknown, pain had become the one constant. As long as she felt pain, she was feeling something. If Amanda allowed herself to drink in what was happening, where she was, and with whom, and what she was doing, etc., she knew she'd lose her mind. Amanda was grateful for the opportunity once again to slide into drug land.

The one Pablo called *"mi perro"* was heating up the good stuff. He handed the glass tube to Amanda, and Pablo watched as she breathed it in. *Not her first time,* Pablo noted.

Even though it would take a couple of minutes before Amanda would feel the full effects of the smoke, the mere act of inhaling heroin made Amanda feel better. *Soon, I won't have to think or feel at all.*

The members of the motley group took turns smoking. The heroin was as good as Eber had claimed. Before long, they were all too high to budge. The guy on the end of the settee vomited into a wastebasket, adding to the sordid smell. It was difficult for anyone in the shack to track the passage of time. Amanda and the Mexicans smoked, passed out, roused slightly, and then smoked more whenever *mi perro* could move enough to light the drug, and they could move enough to inhale it.

* * *

Ice went directly to *La Coahuila* and the bar he knew best. A guy could do pretty much what he wanted there and not get hassled. Ice spied two junkie friends.

"It's tequila time," he said. The friends were just as eager to get wasted as Ice was. They quickly downed three shots each and then went into a back room. Ice had brought some crystal meth with him, and before long, they had smoked his entire stash. After a while, the owner, Manuel, came in and said they had to get out—he needed to use the room.

Manuel had a couple of girls who worked directly for him, and the guys knew exactly why he wanted them out. Dark and dingy, the room had seen better days, but it sufficed. Manuel employed teenage girls, mostly runaways, because they brought in extra money to the bar. Male customers drank more when they could flirt with young girls, and the girls turned tricks when Manuel ordered them to. He also kept them supplied with drugs, which helped ensure their loyalty. Manuel's bartender sold drugs under the counter for him, too. Manuel paid the cartel every week so his business wouldn't get fucked with, and he made a decent coin.

Ice's "friends" stayed in the bar while he went out walking. He was twitching, itching, and jerking as he walked. *Fuck, I should've brought more meth.* Then he remembered he didn't have any more. And he wasn't going to be able to get any until the next job with the *pollos* was done. Ice hated his life. But he was stuck.

CHAPTER 49
A RACE AGAINST TIME

Bert saw Alfredo first. It was 6:20 p.m. He went up to the off-duty officer and told him what he had heard from his sources. Alfredo agreed the news was both good and bad.

"If Amanda's with people who don't want any heat, they might kill her. We need to get lucky, and soon!"

Steve and Mike joined the two, and they walked to Alfredo's compact car. Steve got in the front with Alfredo. His skin was tingly from nerves, and his senses were heightened. Enough was enough, already, Steve was ready for action.

"Bulldog didn't show up today," Steve said to Alfredo. "My guess is he spent the money I gave him on getting high."

"I haven't heard from him, either," Alfredo said. "You're probably right about him running into some drugs. He's not a bad guy, but he's got a bad problem."

Returning to the same restaurant they had gone to the night before, they again parked in the back. Alfredo asked if anyone was hungry. No one was. Alfredo knocked on the door to let his friend, Miguel, know he was leaving his car there. Miguel agreed to keep an eye on the auto for them.

It was time to resume the hunt for Amanda. The men carried the posters.

Steve wanted to cry each time he looked at Amanda's

picture. *These things only happen to people you read about, not to my daughter.*

The four men walked down the alley next to the restaurant. Steve and Alfredo went into a little saloon they had passed by the night before. Dark and smoky, there were three guys at the bar talking to a couple of fat girls.

Steve tried to show one of the girls the poster, but she turned her head away. "Please, look. Have you seen this girl?" he implored.

A bouncer appeared out of the shadows. Alfredo spoke to him in Spanish. It was a short conversation. *No is no in any language,* thought Steve.

Alfredo looked at Steve and nodded toward the door. "He hasn't seen her."

"That's what I gathered."

The men walked all over *Zona Norte*, holding up the poster with Amanda's picture. They went into seedy places and saw things they didn't want to see. Things that made even these grown men sick to their stomachs.

No one they spoke to knew anything—at least they wouldn't admit to knowing anything. No one had seen Amanda. Steve couldn't believe it. *Almost like some code of silence on the streets,* he thought, growing even more frustrated.

The four had to step around more than one person who used the alley as a public bathroom. Puking, shitting, hitting up. It was all done out in the open. Several prostitutes approached the men, but they quickly waved them away.

"It's close to 8:00," said Alfredo. "Let's go back to where Amanda supposedly was seen. To keep a lookout, we can walk by twos on either of the street to get there."

Just as the four were about to separate again, an American walked their way. He was twitching and scratching. *Meth user,* Steve figured.

"Have you seen this girl?" Steve asked the twitcher as he got close.

The man nodded erratically. "Yeah. I know where she is."

The men stopped dead in their tracks.

"You mean, right now? You know where she is *right now*?" Steve asked incredulously.

"Yes," the twitcher responded.

While the other three men blocked the man in, Steve hit him with questions. "Where, man? *Tell me!* She's my daughter! I'll give you a thousand dollars cash if you take us to her!"

While Ice did know where Amanda was, he wasn't sure why he had let it out. Now he was in a dilemma. If he told these guys where the girl was, and Carlos or Javier found out, he'd be a dead man. But here was his chance to finally do something right. And he could use the money. The cartel only gave him enough money to get by. *Cheap bastards,* he concluded. *After all the work I've done for them, too. I could use the money to go visit my family. These guys could be my ticket out.*

"Give me the money," Ice demanded, "and I'll tell you where she is."

Steve almost laughed. "You're crazy, man. You tell us where she is and we get her; then you get the money."

"I could be killed!"

Mike stepped up and put his knife on Ice's neck. "And you could be killed if you don't tell us." The tip of the blade was sharp, and it drew blood on Ice's neck. The look in Mike's eyes told Ice he was dead serious.

"Okay, okay. We can work something out." Sweat was

running down Ice's face, and his pupils were dilated. He needed
drugs in a big way. His heart raced, both because he was fucked
up, and because he had felt the blood drip down his neck. "Do
you have a car?"

"Yes. Let's go," said Bert.

They took Ice by the arm and walked swiftly back to
the restaurant parking lot. Mike's grip on Ice was exceptionally
tight. He wanted to convey a subtle message. Ice got it loud and
clear.

"Why don't you start talking right now?" suggested
Alfredo. He let the muzzle of his gun touch Ice's ribs as they
walked.

Ice was about to pee his pants. Scared and twitching, he
knew he was between a rock and a hard place.

"There's an old apartment building with a little shed on
the rooftop. It's three floors up. The stairs are on the outside. In
the far corner of the roof is the shed. She's in there."

The men couldn't believe their ears. Either this guy was
a good storyteller, or they were on their way to getting Amanda.

"Who's with her?" Alfredo asked.

"Some guys who work for the Morales family. They've
been using her to carry drugs across the border."

Steve's body bristled with the anticipation of finding his
daughter. *Please let this guy be telling the truth.*

"How do you know all this?" Mike demanded.

"I know . . . because I work for them, too. That's why I
said they'd kill me if they even thought I'd talk. They'd do the
same to her, too."

Mike let out a slow whistle. "We need a plan. We can't
conduct a mission without a viable plan." Mike's mind reverted
back to his military training. *Decide, detect, deliver and assess.*

The words ran through his brain like an old song. He was on a mission now. A covert rescue operation.

"The cartel knows someone's looking for her. Tomorrow she's going to be transported to southern Mexico. They have a prostitution trade running out of Mexico City. You'd never find her then." Ice was twitching uncontrollably.

Rage burned inside Steve like a wildfire out of control. He felt that he could kill someone with his bare hands. Heart pounding, he took several deep breaths in an effort to stay focused on rescuing Amanda.

"How many people are in the shed with the girl? Is she tied up?" Alfredo asked.

Ice shrugged. "I don't know for sure, but probably four or five. She's not likely tied up, but they're guarding her closely. They keep her pretty fucked up, so it wouldn't be easy for her to go anywhere, even if she did have the chance. It's their MO." Ice scratched his arms with fervor. "They won't be expecting you, that's for sure. The guys with her are getting high, too."

"Do they have weapons?" Bert asked. He, too, wanted to come up with a plan.

"Of course. But I don't know what they do up there besides get wasted."

Ice couldn't seem to stop his tongue, and he was twitching like crazy now. He kept thinking about the cash they were going to give him. *Maybe they'd up the ante if they actually get the girl. I think I'll put the trip back home on hold because I could buy a lot of meth with that money. I could sell some and still have plenty of stash for a while. That's if Carlos or Javier or that bastard Enrique don't discover I ratted them out.* Ice's heart was racing like a runaway train. He couldn't control himself as he peed his pants. "Fuck!"

The guys didn't want to waste time, but they needed a good strategy. They only had three guns, a knife, and one determined, brave, crazed father. They arrived at the car and piled in. Alfredo had the best plan of the bunch.

"Since Mike's a trained SEAL, you should give him your gun, Bert. Someone has to stay in the car with this guy here, and that can be you."

"I brought a gun, so Bert can keep his. He might need it."

There was no way Steve would stay behind; they all knew that. Alfredo figured Bert, with his police training, would be able to keep the twitcher from getting away while the others went on the rescue mission. They might need some of Mike's special skills to get Amanda out.

"I'm fine with guarding this guy." Bert glared at Ice and snarled, "Don't even think of trying to run."

Steve got out his wallet and gave Bert one thousand dollars. "This is for Twitcher, here, once we get Amanda," he said. "If something happens to all of us, but Amanda was there, like he said, make sure he still gets the money."

Bert took the grand. "You guys do what you have to do."

Alfredo explained his plan: They'd creep up the stairs and move silently across the roof to the shed. Mike would kick open the door, and they'd rush the place, with Alfredo leading the way. He'd hold up his badge with one hand and yell, "*Policia!*" In the other hand would be his drawn .45. Steve would grab Amanda. Mike would also have his gun aimed, and his knife within easy reach.

The rescuers were banking on three things: The element of surprise, that the men detaining Amanda wouldn't have their

KIDNAPPED BY THE CARTEL

weapons in their hands and ready to fire, and that everyone in the shed would be too high to react quickly. They also needed to imply that there were more *policia* outside, ready to blow the captors apart if they tried anything funny. Then they'd hightail it across the roof and down the stairs, run the half block or so, hop into the car, and race to the border.

"I hope there's no *policia* in the shack who are on the Morales' payroll," said Alfredo, "because if there are, we're talking a different game. Usually, those guys don't do drugs, and they'd be ready to shoot to kill, if need be. I could know them, too."

"They won't be using cops to guard her," said Ice.

"Good to know," said Alfredo.

The men agreed to the plan.

"Let's go," said Steve.

They followed the directions Ice had given them to the apartment building. When the building was in sight, Alfredo pulled over to park. They were about half a block away. Alfredo parked where there wasn't a street light. He didn't want anyone to look out of one of the apartments and easily see the car.

Steve touched Mike's arm and said, "Look, we don't know what's going to happen up there. I'm willing to give my life, trying to save my daughter. I don't expect you to put yourself in the same situation."

Mike glared at Steve. "We've already covered this. I've been on worse missions for people I never even met. I've known Amanda since she was a baby. Let's roll."

The three got out of the car. Bert pushed Ice to the floor to keep him hidden from view, and the others went out into the unknown.

Silently, Steve said a fervent prayer and crossed himself.

Help us, Lord. The prayer calmed him, and he was ready for whatever would happen next.

The men scanned the apartment building as they approached. Cacti and shrubs grew intermittently along the side of the building, thick enough to provide cover, if need be. No one was walking around outside, which was good. The rescuers scurried to the building undetected. They crept quickly up the broken, narrow, uneven steps, which proved to be a little more challenging than they had expected. After the first flight, there was a door to an apartment. Steve saw through the slats to what looked to be hell on earth. Junkies hitting up, someone vomiting, general filth and nakedness—and that was just in the tiny living room.

This, too, is La Coahuila, Steve thought. *The worst of the worst.*

As the trio continued up the next flight of stairs, they heard a door open and shut, and then two men talking in Spanish. The three froze, backs against the wall. The door opened and shut again. Only one man had gone back in. The other hurried down the steps and came upon the rescue team.

Startled, he said, "What the fuck?" The man turned his head and hollered back upstairs in Spanish, "Someone's out here!"

"Shut up," Mike hissed

Like greased lightning, the Mexican pulled out a switchblade, popped it open, and went for Mike's jugular. Mike was stronger and faster. He seized the man's head and gave a quick twist, snapping his neck. The man slumped to the ground, a bloodless kill, over in seconds.

"No choice," Mike said in a hushed tone.

Not wanting anyone in one of the apartments to come

out and stumble upon the body while they were on the roof, Steve helped Mike pick up the body and heave it over the side. It thumped to the ground between the building and a bush. No one inside the building appeared to have heard anything.

"We've no time to waste," Alfredo said.

They shot up to the next floor and came to another door. This time Steve didn't pause to glance in. If he had, he would've seen Hector sitting on the sofa, smoking heroin while getting a blow job from the skinny blonde. Hector was too high and caught up in his activities to hear the men outside slip past the door.

The men climbed to the rooftop and looked around. It was quiet, no movement anywhere. In the far corner was the shed, just as the twitcher had said.

Steve took a deep breath. *God help us.*

Adrenaline filled the rescuers with the courage and strength they needed to face whatever awaited. With stealth-like movements, they swiftly crossed the roof to the door.

Mike kicked hard with his steel-toed boot and the door banged open. Alfredo rushed in, displaying his badge and brandishing his weapon. *"Policia!* Don't move!"

Everyone inside the smoke-filled shed was wasted, a stroke of luck for the liberators. Through half-shut eyes, Amanda saw the door fly open and a cop with a badge burst in. Although completely terrorized, she was too high to move. Then, unbelievably, Amanda thought she saw her dad.

Steve and Mike saw Amanda at the same time. Mike yelled, "Go! I've got your back!" as Steve ran over and grabbed Amanda's wrists. The men on either side of her had their hands on her arms, but they let go as Steve pulled her up, threw her over his shoulder, and bolted out the door.

Weakly, Amanda cried, "Dad!"

Pablo was buzzed, but he wasn't too high to know they had fucked up. Certain more *policia* were outside, he shouted in a mixture of Spanish and English, "Hey, she's free to go! We weren't holding her."

Alfredo shouted at the men in the shed, "Stay where you are. Don't move until you've counted to one hundred, or you'll get your heads blown off, one by one, as you come out."

Mike picked up two guns he'd seen on the floor by the sofa as he backed out, a Bushmaster .233 and a Glock handgun. *Nothing but the best for the cartel.* He yanked the door shut as he and Alfredo ran after Steve and Amanda. They held onto Steve's shirt from the back so he wouldn't fall down the treacherous stairs while he carried his daughter. Amanda's whole body shook with sobs.

Even as he ran, Steve whispered, "Shh, shh, it's okay. You'll be okay."

Once they reached the bottom of the stairs, the men ran full-out to the car. Steve felt like he had the strength of ten men. Amanda felt light as a feather as he sprinted. As they neared the car, they heard shouting and gunshots. Soon, the cops would come, and all hell would break loose. They had no way of knowing if the cops who showed up would be on the cartel's payroll, so there was no time to lose.

Bert grabbed Ice by the collar and pulled him up from the floor of the car. He thrust the cash into his hand and said, "Get out!" as the men came running, with Amanda now in Steve's arms.

"Fuck no, man! Take me with you. They'll kill me!" cried Ice. The reality of what he'd done had sunk in, and the commotion scared him to death. He knew that the guns aimed at these guys would be aimed at him as well.

"Nope. Wasn't the deal. There's no room anyway. You've got cash. Get a cab!" Bert answered. This was no time for mercy.

As Mike opened the car door, Bert gave Ice a push and Mike pulled him out. Steve threw Amanda in the backseat and got in after her. He pushed her head down, covering his daughter's body with his own. Just as Alfredo and Mike jumped in the front seat, two men came running down the street with handguns drawn and bullets flying.

Alfredo gunned the car in reverse for half a block, then turned and screeched away. Mike was shooting out the window with the cartel's own guns as they roared down the street. They needed a fast getaway because the big guns had been brought out now, too.

Nothing like the sound of a submachine gun to get your attention, Alfredo thought. He kept the headlights off for a few blocks and zigzagged down the street.

Amanda was petrified, her thin body wracked with sobs.

When they were almost in the commercial area of Tijuana, Mike wiped down the captors' guns and tossed them out the window as they flew down the street.

Racing through Tijuana to the border, Steve whispered to Amanda, "You're safe now. You're safe. You just have to keep it together enough to walk across the border. Can you do that, Mandy? We'll hold you up."

Although she was in a fog, Amanda nodded. Could her mind be playing tricks on her? Was she really with her dad and leaving Mexico? She had been messed up on drugs and suffering from abuse, fear, no food, and lack of sleep for countless days. Now, she thought she might be hallucinating. Or dreaming. But it sure seemed real.

Steve got his wallet out again and peeled off another thousand dollars for Alfredo. They pulled up as close to the border walking area as they could.

Alfredo was elated. "We did it! We did it!"

Steve was crying. He gave Alfredo the money and a hug. "As God is my witness, I cannot thank you enough. We never would've found my daughter without you. I'll never forget you, Alfredo."

Alfredo was tearing up also. "Go now," he said. "Hurry up!"

Mike gave Steve a hand with Amanda. They walked up to the customs building and then turned to wave one last time to the *policia* who had risked his life to help them. Alfredo nodded and sped away into the night.

Amanda was between Steve and Mike. They had their arms linked through hers, and her feet barely touched the ground as they walked. Bert led the way like nothing was out of the ordinary.

The border guards didn't even flinch as the group walked up. Bert told the guards that they'd gone into Tijuana for some dinner and partying. Amanda had had too much to drink and got sick. Unnaturally skinny, with filthy hair and body and blank eyes, Amanda looked every bit the refugee she was. Yet, with Bert's credentials, the officials let the group go through without hesitation.

Once they got into the United States, Amanda suddenly let go. Trembling and crying, she also got the dry heaves.

Steve picked her up again and carried her as they walked to the truck. "Will you drive, Mike?"

"Absolutely."

Steve carefully put his daughter in the backseat and

climbed in next to her. A sobbing Amanda gratefully rested her head on her dad's lap.

I can't believe it," Steve whispered. "I just can't believe it. My heart is about to burst after what we just went through! God damn!" He wiped his eyes.

Mike felt like he had just run a marathon. And won. *It's gratifying to know I've been instrumental in Amanda's rescue,* he thought. *Too bad about the broken neck, but it was necessary. Collateral damage.* He started the truck.

Bert knew his company would be extremely pleased with the outcome of this missing person's case. *Amanda was one of the lucky ones. She got out alive.*

As soon as they were on Highway 5, Steve called Diane and Pam. "We have Amanda!" Steve said, his voice choking up.

Everyone in the truck could hear Diane and Pam screaming.

Amanda had been rescued after eleven days of hell. Eleven days of hell for everyone.

Typical Tijuana.

Corner farmacia in Tijuana.

Catholic Church in Tijuana.

Along the road to the impound lot in Tijuana.

Farmacias are everywhere, and so are drugs.

Policia on bikes in Tijuana.

Prostitutes on the street corner in Tijuana.

Rooftop shed similar to the one from which the character of Amanda Tate was rescued in Tijuana.

KAREN DEVEREAUX SCIOSCIA is an author, freelance writer, and corporate executive speech writer. She writes a weekly column for the *Charlotte Observer* in North Carolina, is a Yahoo.com contributor, and has had several articles published in magazines.

Visit her on Facebook at "Author Karen D Scioscia," on Linkedin, or at websites:
www.KarenDScioscia.com or
www.KidnappedbytheCartel.com